SHE TOOK IT RATHER WELL . . .

"Miss, I'm sorry to have to tell you that Mr. Vereker has met with an accident."

Her brows drew together. "Are you breaking it to me gently? You needn't bother. Is he dead, or what?"

The Inspector's manner became a shade sterner. "Yes, miss. He is dead," he answered.

"Good lord!" said the girl. To the Constable's shocked amazement, a twinkle appeared in her eye. "I thought you were trying to run my dog in," she remarked. "Sorry I was a trifle brusque. Is my half-brother really dead? What happened to him? Car smash?"

The Inspector had no longer any compunction in disclosing the truth. "His body was discovered in the stocks at Ashleigh Green at one-fifty this morning. Your half-brother, miss, died as the result of a knife thrust through the back."

"Oh," said Antonia. "Rather beastly."

"Miss Heyer's characters and dialogue are an abiding delight to me . . . I have seldom met people to whom I took so violent a fancy from the word 'go.' "

—Dorothy Sayers

"Diverting."

—Saturday Review

"Very neat and mystifying."

—London Times

"Mark this down as a number one yarn."

—New York Times

Berkley books by Georgette Heyer

DEATH IN THE STOCKS
FOOTSTEPS IN THE DARK
WHY SHOOT A BUTLER?

DEATH IN
THE STOCKS

GEORGETTE HEYER

BERKLEY BOOKS, NEW YORK

This Berkley book contains the complete
text of the original hardcover edition.
It has been completely reset in a typeface
designed for easy reading, and was printed
from new film.

DEATH IN THE STOCKS

A Berkley Book / published by arrangement with
E.P. Dutton

PRINTING HISTORY
Dutton edition / May 1970
Bantam edition / June 1971
Berkley edition / November 1986

All rights reserved.
Copyright 1935 by Georgette Rougier.
Copyright © renewed 1962 by Georgette Rougier.
This book may not be reproduced in whole or in part,
by mimeograph or any other means, without permission.
For information address: E.P. Dutton & Company,
2 Park Avenue, New York, NY 10016.

ISBN: 0-425-09338-7

A BERKLEY BOOK ® TM 757,375
Berkley Books are published by The Berkley Publishing Group,
200 Madison Avenue, New York, New York 10016.
The name "BERKLEY" and the stylized "B" with design
are trademarks belonging to Berkley Publishing Corporation.
PRINTED IN THE UNITED STATES OF AMERICA

CHAPTER 1

IT was past midnight, and the people who lived in the cottages that clustered round the triangular green had long since gone to bed and to sleep. No lamp shone in any window, but a full moon sailed in a sky the colour of sapphires, and lit the village with a pale light, as cold as the sheen on steel. Trees and houses cast grotesque shadows, black as soot; every object in the moonlight stood out sharply defined, but without colour, so that even a prosaic line of petrol pumps looked a little ghostly.

There was a car drawn up at one end of the green, its headlights throwing two golden beams ahead, and its engine throbbing softly. One of its doors stood open. Something moved in the shadow of the great elm tree beside the car; a man stepped into the moonlight, glanced this way and that, as though fearful of seeing someone, and after a moment's hesitation got quickly into the car and began to turn it, jarring his gears a little. He looked once towards the elm tree, at some object dimly discernible in the shadow, and then, having swung the car right round, drove away up the London road. The noise of his engine died slowly in the distance; somewhere at hand a watch-dog barked once, and then was silent.

The shadow of the elm tree was shortening as the moon travelled across the sky: the eerie light seemed to steal under

1

the branches, and presently shone on two feet in patent leather shoes, stuck through the holes of a pair of stocks. The feet remained motionless, and as the moonlight crept nearer the glimmer of a white shirt-front showed.

An hour later a cyclist rounded the bend in the road by the King's Head. Police-Constable Dickenson was returning home from a night patrol. The moonlight now fully illumined the stocks. A gentleman in evening-dress was sitting in them, apparently asleep, for his body had sagged forward, his head lolling on his chest. Police-Constable Dickenson was whistling softly as he rode, but the whistle stopped suddenly, and the front wheel of the bicycle swerved. The stocks were a feature of Ashleigh Green, but the Constable could not remember having seen anyone imprisoned in them before. It gave him quite a turn. Tight as an owl, he thought. Looks like somebody's been having a game with you, my lad.

He got off his bicycle, and pushed it on to the grass and carefully propped it against the elm tree. The figure on the bench did not move. "Now then, sir, wake up!" said the Constable, kind but reproving. "Can't spend the night here, you know!" He laid his hand on one sagging shoulder, and gave it a slight shake. "Come along, sir, you'll be better off at home, you will." There was no response, and he shook the shoulder rather harder, and put one arm round the man to hoist him. There was still no response, but an arm which had lain across its owner's knees was dislodged and hung dangling, the hand brushing limply against the Constable's trousers. The Constable bent, peering into the downcast face, and sought in his pocket for his torch. The light flashed on, and the Constable stepped back rather quickly. The figure on the bench, disturbed by his shaking, toppled over sideways, its feet still held in the stocks. "Gawd!" whispered Police-Constable Dickenson, feeling his mouth to be very dry all at once, "Oh, Gawd!" He did not want to touch the figure again, or even to go nearer, because there was something sticky on his hands, and he had never seen a dead man before.

He stopped, and rubbed his hand on the grass, telling himself he was a proper softy. But he hadn't been expecting it, and his stomach had kind of turned over. Made a chap feel sick for a minute; it was like as if one's innards took a jump into one's chest. Breathing a little jerkily he went up to the figure again, and ran his torch over it, and rather gingerly touched one of the slack hands. It wasn't exactly cold, not clammy, like you read about in books, but just cool. He didn't know but that he wouldn't rather it had been icy. That faint warmth was nasty, somehow.

He pulled himself up. It wasn't his job to get fanciful, but to make up his mind what was the right thing for him to do first. The man was dead, sure enough; it was no use standing over the body; he'd better get on to the Police Station at Hanborough as soon as possible. He pushed his bicycle back on to the road, mounted it again, and rode swiftly along to the other end of the green, to the cottage with the prim muslin curtains and the tidy flower-beds which had County Police painted on a narrow board over the front door.

He let himself in and made his way to the telephone, taking care to tread softly so that his wife, who was asleep upstairs, should not wake and call to him to go up. He'd have to tell her what had happened if she did, and she was expecting her first, and none too well.

He lifted the receiver, wondering whether he'd done the right thing after all, leaving a corpse stuck down in the middle of the village. It didn't seem decent, somehow.

The Station-Sergeant's voice spoke. He was surprised to hear his own voice so steady, because really he felt a bit shaken, and no wonder. He told his story as matter-of-factly as he could, and the Sergeant, not nearly so phlegmatic, said first: *"What?"* and then: "In the stocks?" and lastly: "Look here, are you *sure* he's dead?"

Police-Constable Dickenson was quite sure, and when the Sergeant heard about the blood, and the wound in the back, he stopped making incredulous exclamations, and said briefly: "All right. You cut along and see no one touches the body. The Inspector will be down with the ambulance in a couple of shakes."

"Hold on a minute, Sergeant," said the Constable, anxious to give all the information he could. "It isn't a stranger. I was able to identify him—it's Mr. Vereker."

"Mr. Who?" demanded the Sergeant.

"Vereker. The gentleman from London as bought Riverside

Cottage. You know, Sergeant: comes down weekends.''

"Oh!" said the Sergeant, rather vaguely. "Not a local man.''

"Not properly speaking," agreed the Constable. "But what beats me is how he came to be sitting in them stocks at this hour of night. He's in evening-dress, what's more.''

"Well, you get back and keep your eye on things till the Inspector comes along," said the Sergeant, and hung up the receiver.

Constable Dickenson heard the click of it, and was rather sorry, because now that he had had time to recover from his first amazement he could see several queer things about the murder, and would have liked to have talked them over with the Sergeant. But there was nothing for it but to do as he was told, so he put his receiver back on the hook, and tiptoed out of the house again to where he had left his bicycle propped against the iron railing.

When he got back to the stocks the dead man was lying in the same position. There was no sign that any one had been there since the Constable left, and after looking over the ground for a bit with the aid of his torch, in the hope of discovering some clue, or footprint, the Constable leaned his back against the tree, and tried, while waiting for the Inspector to arrive, to puzzle out the problem for himself.

It was not very long before he heard the sound of a car in the distance, and in a few moments it drew up beside the green, and Inspector Jerrold hopped out nimbly, and turned to give a hand to a stout man in whom the Constable recognised Dr. Hawke, the Police-Surgeon.

"Well?" said the Inspector briskly. "Where is this body, Dickenson? Oh!—ah!" He stepped up to the bench, and ran his torch over the still figure there. "H'm! Not much for you here, Doctor, from the looks of it. Turn those headlights this way, Hill. That's better. Like this when you found him, was he?''

"No, sir, not properly. He was sitting up—well, when I say sitting, he was kind of slouching forward, if you know what I mean. I thought he was asleep. Him being in evening-dress, and his feet in the stocks like that, I never thought but what he'd had a glass too many—so I went up to him and put my hand on his shoulder to give him a bit of a shake, and wake him up. Twice I shook him, and then it struck me there was something queer about him, and I felt the palm of my hand kind of wet and sticky, and I switched my torch on to him and—and then of course I saw he was dead. Me shaking him like that made him fall sideways, like you see.''

The Inspector nodded, his eyes on the Doctor, who was kneeling behind the body. ''Sergeant Hamlyn says you identified him. Who is he? Don't seem to know his face.''

''Well, I daresay you might not, sir. It's Mr. Vereker, of Riverside Cottage.''

''Oh!'' said the Inspector with a little sniff. ''One of these week-end people. Anything out of the way, Doctor?''

''I shall have to do a P.M., of course,'' grumbled the Doctor, getting up rather ponderously from his knees. ''But it looks quite a straight case. Knife wound a little below the left shoulder-blade. Death probably occurred instantaneously.''

The Inspector watched him at work on the body for a moment or two, and presently asked: ''Formed any opinion of the time it was done, sir?''

''Say two to four hours,'' replied the Doctor, and straightened his back. ''That's all for the present, thanks.''

The Inspector turned to Constable Dickenson. ''Know how the body was sitting when you found it?''

''Yes, sir.''

''All right. Put it back as near as you can. Ready with that flashlight, Thompson?''

Constable Dickenson did not care much for the task allotted him, but he went up at once to the body and raised it to the original position, and carefully laid one arm across the stiffening legs. The Inspector watched him in silence, and when he stepped back at last, made a sign to the photographer.

By the time the photographer had finished his work the police ambulance had arrived, and a light was turned on in one of the windows of an adjacent cottage. The Inspector cast a shrewd glance up at the window and said curtly: ''Right. You can take him out now. Careful how you touch that bar! We may get a finger-print.''

The bar of the stocks was raised, the body lifted out, and carried to the ambulance, just as the lighted window was thrown up and a tousled head poked out. A ghoulishly expectant voice called out: "What's the matter? Has there been an accident? Anybody hurt?"

"Just a bit of an accident, Mrs. Duke," replied Constable Dickenson. "Nothing for you to worry about."

The head was withdrawn, but the voice could be heard adjuring one Horace to get up quick, because the police were outside with the ambulance and all.

"What I know of this village, we'll have a whole pack of busybodies here inside of ten minutes," said the Inspector, with a grim little smile. "All right, you men: mortuary. Now then, Dickenson, let's hear what you can tell us. When did you discover the body?"

"By my reckoning, sir, it would be about ten minutes to two. It was just on two when I rung up the Station, me having been out on patrol."

"You didn't see anyone here? No car? Didn't hear anything?"

"No, sir, nothing."

"Was the man—what's his name—Vereker, staying at Riverside Cottage?"

"Not to my knowledge he wasn't, sir, but then he didn't, not during the week as a general rule. It being Saturday, I figured it out he must have been on his way down to the cottage. Mrs. Beaton would know whether he was there. She'd have had her orders to go in and make things ready for him."

"Does she live out?"

"Yes, sir. Pennyfarthing Row, a couple of minutes from the cottage. She keeps the place clean, and gets in milk and eggs and such, when he's coming down. He often gets down late on Saturdays, so she was telling me. I have known him to bring his valet down to do for him, but just as often he comes alone." He paused, and corrected himself. "When I say alone, I mean he often don't bring a servant with him."

"What *do* you mean?" inquired the Doctor.

"Well, sir, he sometimes brings friends down with him." He gave a little cough. "Most often females, so I've heard."

"Wife? Sister?" interrupted the Inspector.

"Oh no, sir! Nothing like that," replied the Constable, rather shocked.

"Oh, that kind of female!" said the Inspector. "We'd better go round first thing in the morning to Riverside Cottage, and see if there's anything to be got there. There's nothing here. Ground's too dry for footprints. We'll get along, Doctor, if you're ready. You'll hand in your report tomorrow, Dickenson, see? You can go off to bed now." He moved away towards the car with the Doctor. Constable Dickenson heard him say in his dry way: "Looks to me like a case for the Yard. London man. Nothing to do with us. Nice easy case too—if they can lay their hands on the woman."

"Quite," agreed the Doctor, smothering a yawn. "If he had a woman with him."

CHAPTER 2

INSPECTOR JERROLD made a very early call on the Chief Constable next morning, and found him eating his breakfast. He apologised for disturbing him, but the Colonel merely waved him to a chair, and said: "Not at all. What's your trouble? Anything serious?"

"Pretty serious, sir. Man found stabbed to death at Ashleigh Green at 1:50 this morning."

"Good God! You don't say so! Who is it?"

"Gentleman of the name of Arnold Vereker, sir, of Riverside Cottage."

"God bless my soul!" ejaculated the Colonel, putting down his coffee-cup. "Who did it? Any idea?"

"No, sir, none. No clues at all so far. The body was found by Constable Dickenson—in the stocks."

"In the *what?*"

"Does sound odd, doesn't it, sir? But that's how it was."

"Do you mean he was put in the stocks and then stabbed, or what?"

"It's hard to say, sir. Not much bleeding, you see: nothing on the ground. Might have been stabbed first, though why anyone should take the trouble to put the body in the stocks I can't make out. He was in evening-dress, no hat or overcoat, and the only thing we've got so far that looks like helping us at all is his hands, which were dirty. Smear of motor-oil on one, inference being he'd had to change a tyre, or do some repair on a car. But his car's not there, and not at the garage either. Of course, he may have walked into the village from Riverside Cottage—it's under a mile away—but it seems a funny thing to do at that hour of night. The Doctor doesn't put the hour of the murder earlier than twelve o'clock, or thereabouts. No, it looks like he was motoring down with someone or other for the week-end. What I thought, sir, was that I should go off to Riverside Cottage first thing after seeing you to find out if he was staying there, or expected down last night. Seems to have been a gentleman with irregular sort of habits.''

"Yes, I believe so," said the Colonel. "Didn't know him myself, but one hears things. A City man—mining interests, so I was informed. I don't fancy it's much of a case for us, Inspector. What do you feel about it?''

"Well, sir, pretty much what you do. Of course, we don't know that it wasn't a local affair, but on the face of it it doesn't look like it. I've got a man out at Ashleigh Green making inquiries, but I don't expect to get much. You know what it is out in the country, sir. Folks go to bed early, and if there wasn't any noise made, barring the car—assuming there was a car—no one would be likely to wake up—or take any notice if they were awake. The Doctor's of the opinion death must have been pretty well instantaneous. There's no sign of any struggle. Dickenson tells me this Mr. Vereker was in the habit of bringing friends down from town over the week-end. What we want is his car. That might tell us something. How I look at it, sir, is we'll have to get on to the Yard for information, whatever happens.''

"Quite right. Not our case at all. Still, you should certainly go to this cottage you speak of and see what you can pick up. Does he keep any servants there?''

"No, sir. There's a woman by the name of Beaton who keeps the place tidy, by what I understand, but she lives out. I'll see her, of course, but I don't expect to find anyone at the Cottage. 'Tisn't likely. But I might get a line on it.''

The Inspector was wrong. Half an hour later, when he and

Constable Dickenson got out of the police car at Riverside
Cottage, thre were unmistakable signs that the cottage was occupied.

It was a small house of stuccoed brick and jade green shut-
ters, standing in wooded grounds that ran down to the river.
The position was what house-agents would describe as pic-
turesque and secluded, no other house being visible in summer
from any of its windows.

As the car drew up a dog started barking inside the house,
and the Constable said at once: "That's funny. Mr. Vereker
never had a dog down here to my knowledge."

The Inspector set his finger on the electric bell, remarking as
he did so: "Might be the charwoman's. Who looks after the
garden, and the electric light plant?"

"Young Beaton, sir. He comes in a couple of days a week.
But he wouldn't bring his dog with him, not into the house.
There's someone here all right. I can hear him moving about."

The Inspector pressed the bell again, and was about to press
it a third time when the door was opened to them by a girl with
a head of burnished copper curls, and very large and brilliant
dark eyes. She was wearing a man's dressing-gown of expen-
sive-looking brocade, which was several sizes too large for her,
and was chiefly occupied in keeping back a powerful bull-
terrier who did not seem to view the visitors with much
favour.

"Shut up, you fool!" commanded the girl. *"Heel!——*
What on earth do you want?" This last remark was addressed
in a tone of considerable surprise to the Inspector.

"Inspector Jerrold, miss, from Hanborough," said the Inspector, introducing himself. "If convenient, I should like to
have a word with you."

She looked at him frowningly. "I don't know what you
want to have a word with me about, but you can come in if
you like. Get back, Bill!"

The two men followed her into a square hall, decorated in a
modernist style, with curtains and a carpet of cubist design, a
number of tubular steel chairs, and a squat table of limed oak.
The girl saw Constable Dickenson blink at it and said with a
flickering smile: "You needn't think I did it." The Constable
looked at her rather quickly, involuntarily startled. "You'd

better come into the kitchen. I haven't finished breakfast. The scenery's better, too.'' She strolled ahead of them through the door at the end of the hall into a pleasant kitchen with a tiled floor, a homely-looking dresser, and a breakfast of eggs and coffee and toast spread at one end of the large table. An electric cooker stood at one end of the room, and a small electric brazier had been attached by a long flex to the light fixture, and was switched on for the purpose of drying a linen skirt which was hung over a chair-back in front of it. The Inspector, pausing on the threshold, cast a swift, trained glance round the room. His gaze rested for a moment on the damp skirt, and travelled to the girl. She walked round the table, picking up a slice of half-eaten toast and butter from her plate in a casual way as she passed, and pulled a chair forward. ''Sit down, won't you? I warn you, I shan't make any statement till I've seen my solicitor.'' She looked up as she spoke, and raised her brows. ''Joke,'' she explained.

The Inspector smiled politely. ''Yes, miss, naturally. Might I ask if you are staying here?''

''God, no!''

The Inspector glanced at the brocade dressing-gown, and looked inquiring.

''Quite right, I spent the night here,'' said the girl coolly. ''Anything else you'd like to know?''

''Did you come down with Mr. Vereker, miss?''

''No, I didn't. I haven't seen Mr. Vereker.''

''Indeed, miss? Was he not expecting you?''

A rather hard glint crept into the girl's fine eyes. ''Well, everything was very nicely prepared, but I don't fancy it was on my account. But what the hell it has to do with——'' She broke off, and laughed suddenly. ''Oh, I see! Sorry to disappoint you, but I'm not a burglar—though I did get in through a window. The dressing-gown is merely borrowed till my skirt's dry.''

The Inspector directed his gaze towards the skirt. ''I quite understand, miss. Must have been a bad stain, if I may say so.''

''Blood,'' said the girl, between sips of coffee.

Constable Dickenson gave a slight gasp. ''Blood?'' said the Inspector evenly.

The girl set down her cup, and met his look with a belligerent gleam in her eyes. "Just what do you want with me?" she demanded.

"I'd like to know how you came to get blood on your skirt, miss," said the Inspector.

"Yes? Well, I should like to know what right you have to ask me that—or anything else, for that matter. Get on with it! What is it you're after?"

The Inspector drew out his note-book. "There's no need to take offence, miss. We've had a little upset in these parts last night, and I have to find out one or two details. May I have your name and address, please?"

"Why?" asked the girl.

A shade of severity crept into the Inspector's voice. "You'll pardon me, miss, but you're behaving in a silly way. There's been an accident connected with this house, and it's my duty to get what information I can about it."

"Well, you aren't likely to get much out of me," observed the girl. "Don't know anything. My name's Antonia Vereker. Address, 3 Grayling Street, Chelsea. What the devil's the matter now?"

The Inspector had looked up quickly from his note-book. "A relation of Mr. Arnold Vereker?" he said.

"Half-sister."

The Inspector lowered his gaze to the book again, and carefully wrote down the name and address. "And you say you have not seen Mr. Vereker since you came here?"

"Haven't seen him for months."

"How long have you been here, miss?"

"Since last night. Sevenish."

"Did you come especially to see your brother?"

"Half-brother. Of course I did. But I haven't seen him. He never turned up."

"You were expecting him, then?"

"Look here!" said Antonia strongly. "Do you think I should have motored thirty-five miles to this place if I hadn't expected to see him?"

"No, miss. But you said a minute or two back that Mr. Vereker was not expecting you. I was merely wondering how it was that with him not expecting you, and you not having seen him for months, you were sure enough of finding him here to come all that way.''

"I wasn't sure. But I know his habits. Coming here over the week-end is one of them.''

"I take it you wanted to see him urgently, miss?''

"I wanted to see him, and I still want to see him,'' said Antonia.

"I'm afraid, miss, that won't be *possible*,'' said the Inspector, getting up from his chair.

She stared at him in a smouldering way. "Oh, won't it?'' she said.

"No, miss. I'm sorry to have to tell you that Mr. Vereker has met with an accident.''

Her brows drew together. "Are you breaking it to me gently? You needn't bother. Is he dead, or what?''

The Inspector's manner became a shade sterner. "Yes, miss. He is dead,'' he answered.

"Good lord!'' said the girl. The fierce look left her face; she glanced from one to the other of the two men. To the Constable's shocked amazement, a twinkle appeared in her eye. "I thought you were trying to run my dog in,'' she remarked. "Sorry I was a trifle brusque. He had a bit of a fight last night, and a dam' fool of a woman who owned the other dog swore all sorts of vengeance on him. Is my half-brother really dead? What happened to him? Car smash?''

The Inspector had no longer any compunction in disclosing the truth. "Mr. Vereker was murdered,'' he said bluntly. He noticed with satisfaction that he did seem at last to have startled her a little. She lost some of her colour, and looked as though she did not know what to say. He added after a short pause: "His body was discovered in the stocks at Ashleigh Green at one-fifty this morning.''

"His body was discovered in the *stocks?*'' repeated the girl. "Do you mean somebody put him in the stocks and he died of fright, or exposure, or what?''

"Your half-brother, miss, died as the result of a knife-thrust through the back,'' said the Inspector.

"Oh!'' said Antonia. "Rather beastly.''

"Yes,'' said the Inspector.

She stretched out her hand mechanically towards an open

box of cigarettes and began to tap one of them on her thumb-nail. "Very nasty," she observed. "Who did it?"

"The police have no information on that point at present, miss."

She struck a match, and lit the cigarette. "Well, I didn't, if that's what you want to know. Have you come here to arrest me, or something?"

"Certainly not, miss. All I wish to do is to make a few inquiries. Anything you can tell me that would throw some light on——"

She shook her head. "Sorry, but I can't. We haven't been on speaking terms for months."

"Excuse me, miss, but, if that is so, how do you come to be in Mr. Vereker's house now?"

"Oh, that's easy," she replied. "He wrote me a letter which made me see red, so I came down to have it out with him."

"May I ask if you have that letter, miss?"

"Yes, but I don't propose to show it to you, if that's what you're after. Purely personal."

"I take it the matter was very pressing? Mr. Vereker would have been in London again on Monday?"

"Well, I didn't feel like waiting till Monday," retorted Antonia. "He wasn't in Eaton Place when I rang up, so I took a chance on his being here. He wasn't, but the beds were made up, and there was some milk and butter and eggs and things in the larder, which made it look fairly certain that he was expected, so I waited for him. When he didn't turn up at midnight I went to bed, because it seemed to be a bit late to go home again then."

"I see. And you haven't been out of the house since—I think you said it was about seven o'clock—last night?"

"Yes, of course I've been out of the house since then," she said impatiently. "I took the dog for a run just before I turned in. That's when he had the fight. A mangy-looking retriever set on him about half a mile from here. Blood and fur all over the place. However, there was no real damage done."

The Constable was surveying the bull-terrier, lying watch-fully by the door. "Your dog wasn't hurt, miss?" he ventured.

She looked contemptuous. "Hardly at all. He's a bull-terrier."

"I was only thinking, miss," said the Constable, with a deprecating glance towards the Inspector, "that it was odd your dog wasn't bitten too."

"You don't seem to know much about bull-terriers," said Antonia.

"That'll do, Dickenson," intervened the Inspector. He addressed Antonia again. "I shall have to ask you, miss, if you would come back to the Police Station with me. You'll understand that you being a relative, and in Mr. Vereker's house at the time, the Chief Constable would like to have your statement, and any particulars you can give of the deceased's——"

"But I tell you I don't know anything about it," said Antonia snappishly. "Moreover, if I'm wanted to make statements, and sign things, I'll have a lawyer down to see I don't go and incriminate myself."

The Inspector said in a measured way: "No one wants you to do that, miss. But you must surely realize that the police are bound to want all the information they can get. You can't object to telling the Chief Constable quite simply anything you know about your brother——"

"Don't keep on calling him my brother! Half-brother!"

"I beg pardon, I'm sure. Anything you know about your half-brother, and what you yourself were doing at the time of the murder."

"Well, I've already told you that."

"Yes, miss, and what I want you to do is to tell it again, just in what words you please, at the Station, where it can be taken down in shorthand, and given you to read over, and correct, if you like, and sign. There isn't any harm in that, is there?"

The girl stubbed the end of her cigarette into her saucer. "It seems to me there might be a lot of harm in it," she said with paralysing frankness. "If you're going to investigate my half-brother's murder you're bound to find out quite a lot of happy little details about our family, so I might just as well tell you at the outset that I loathed the sight of Arnold. I didn't happen to murder him, but I haven't got an alibi, and, as far as I can see, things rather point my way. So if it's all the same to you—and equally if it isn't—I shan't say anything at all till I see my solicitor."

"Very well, miss, it's just as you like. And if you'll accompany me to Hanborough you can ring up your solicitor from the Station.''

"Do you mean I've got to hang about in a Police Station all day?'' demanded Antonia. "I'm damned if I will! I've got a luncheon engagement in town at one o'clock.''

"Well, miss,'' said the Inspector placably, "I've no wish to force you into making a statement if you don't want to, but if you'd only see sense and act reasonably I daresay the Chief Constable wouldn't see any need to detain you.''

"Have you got a warrant for my arrest?'' Antonia shot at him.

"No, miss, I have not.''

"Then you can't stop me going back to Town.''

The Inspector showed signs of beginning to lose his temper. "If you go on like this much longer, miss, you'll soon see whether I can take you up to the Police Station or not!''

Antonia lifted an eyebrow, and glanced towards the dog. "Would you like to bet on it?'' she inquired.

"Come along, miss, don't be silly!'' said the Inspector.

"Oh, well!'' said Antonia. "After all, I do want to know who did kill Arnold. I've often said I'd like to, but I never did, somehow. Do you mind if I put on my skirt, or would you like me just as I am?''

The Inspector said he would prefer her to put on her skirt.

"All right. But you'll have to clear out while I do. And while you're waiting one of you might look up Mr. Giles Carrington's number in the telephone book, and get on to him for me, and tell him he's got to come down here at once, because I'm being charged with murder.''

"Nobody's charging you with anything of the sort, miss, I keep on telling you!''

"Well, you will be soon,'' said Antonia, with the utmost cheerfulness.

CHAPTER 3

MRS. BEATON, when interviewed, proved a disappointing witness. Constable Dickenson had warned the Inspector that she was not one to talk, but the Inspector soon formed the opinion that her reticence had its root in a profound ignorance of her employer's affairs. When Arnold Vereker was at the cottage she was never required to do more than cook breakfast, and tidy the house before going home again at twelve o'clock. Mr. Vereker nearly always brought a hamper down with him from Fortnum & Mason's, and sometimes, when he did not come alone she never even set eyes on his guests. She had received a wire from Mr. Vereker on Friday, warning her that he was coming down on Saturday, and might bring a visitor, but who the visitor was, whether man or woman, or at what hour they would arrive, she had not the least idea.

The Chief Constable, adopting a fatherly attitude, failed to make any impression on Antonia Vereker, and there was nothing for it, with regard to her evidence, but to await the arrival of Mr. Giles Carrington. Unfortunately Mr. Giles Carrington had gone to play golf by the time a call had been put through to his residence, and although the servant who answered the telephone promised to ring up the golf club at once no dependence could be placed on the message's reaching him before lunch-time.

Consigning Miss Vereker to the care of the Station-Sergeant, the Inspector and the Chief Constable went into consultation, and were very soon agreed on the advisability of calling in New Scotland Yard at once. The stocks had revealed no finger-prints, and the Doctor's autopsy very little more than his first examination.

The Station-Sergeant, who described himself as a rare one for dogs, got on much better with Antonia than the Inspector had done. He spent half an hour arguing with her on the merits of the Airedale over the Bull-terrier, and would have been pleased to have continued the argument indefinitely had his work not called him away. She was left in a severe apartment with a couple of Sunday papers and her own thoughts, her only visitor being a young and rather shy constable, who brought her a cup of tea at eleven o'clock.

It was past one o'clock when a touring car drew up outside the Police Station, and a tall, loose-limbed man in the mid-thirties walked in, and announced in a pleasant, lazy voice that his name was Carrington.

The Inspector happened to be in the Charge-room at the moment, and he greeted the newcomer with relief not unmixed with dubiety. Mr. Carrington did not look much like a solicitor to him. However, he conducted him to the Chief Constable's office, and duly presented him to Colonel Agnew.

There was another man with the Colonel, a middle-aged man with hair slightly grizzled at the temples, and a square, good-humoured face in which a pair of rather deep-set eyes showed a lurking twinkle behind their gravity. The Colonel, having shaken hands with Giles Carrington, turned to introduce this man.

"This is Superintendent Hannasyde, from New Scotland Yard. He has come down to investigate this case, Mr. Carrington. I have been putting him in possession of the facts as we know them, but we are a little—er—hampered by your client's refusal to make any sort of statement until she has consulted you."

Giles shook hands with the Superintendent. "You must forgive me: I haven't the least idea what your case is," he said frankly. "The message that reached me—on the third tee —was that my cousin, Miss Vereker, wanted me to come down at once to Hanborough Police Station. Has she been getting herself into trouble?''

"Your cousin!" said the Colonel. "I understood——"

"Oh, I am her solicitor as well," smiled Giles Carrington. "Now what is it all about?"

"I'm afraid it's rather a serious business," replied the Colonel. "Miss Vereker's determined refusal to assist the police by giving any evidence—— But I trust that you will be able to convince her that her present attitude is merely prejudicial to her own interests. Miss Vereker's half-brother, Mr. Carrington, was discovered in the village stocks at Ashleigh Green in the early hours of this morning, dead."

"Good heavens!" said Giles Carrington, mildly shocked. "When you say dead, what precisely do you mean?"

"Murdered," said the Colonel bluntly. "A knife-thrust in the back."

There was a moment's silence. "Poor chap!" said Giles, in precisely the same way as he might have said "Dear me!" or "What a pity!" "And do I understand that you have arrested Miss Vereker, or what?"

"No, no, no!" said the Colonel, a look of annoyance coming into his face. "That is merely the ridiculous notion Miss Vereker seems to have got into her head! Miss Vereker, on her own admission, spent the night at her half-brother's house, Riverside Cottage, and all that she was wanted to do was to tell us just why she was there, and what she was doing at the time of the murder. Since she is a close relative of the murdered man, it did not seem unreasonable to expect her to give us what information she can about Mr. Vereker's habits and friends; but beyond informing Inspector Jerrold that she loathed her half-brother, hadn't set eyes on him for months, and had come down to Riverside Cottage with the intention of 'having something out with him,' she refuses to say a word."

A half-laughing, half-rueful look crept into Giles Carrington's eyes. "I think I'd better see her at once," he said. "I'm afraid you've been having rather a difficult time with her, sir."

'I have," said the Colonel. "And I think you should know, Mr. Carrington, that her attitude has been extremely—equivocal, let us say."

"I'm sure it has," said Giles sympathetically. "She can be very tiresome."

The Superintendent, who had been watching him, said suddenly: "I wonder, Mr. Carrington, whether by any chance you are also Mr. Arnold Vereker's solicitor?"

"I am," replied Giles. "I am also one of his executors."

"Well, then, Colonel," said Hannasyde, with a smile, "we must be grateful to Miss Vereker, mustn't we? You are the very man I want, Mr. Carrington."

"Yes, I've realized that for some time," agreed Giles. "But I think I had better see my cousin first."

"Undoubtedly. And Mr. Carrington!" Giles lifted an eyebrow. The twinkle in the Superintendent's eye became more pronounced. "Do try to convince Miss Vereker that really the police won't arrest her merely because she disliked her half-brother."

"I'll try," said Giles gravely, "but I'm afraid she hasn't much of an opinion of the police. You see, she breeds bull-terriers, and they fight rather."

The Superintendent watched him go out in the wake of Inspector Jerrold, and turned to look at the Colonel. "I like that chap," he said in his decided way. "He's going to help me."

"Well, I hope he may," said the Colonel. "What struck me most forcibly was that he showed almost as little proper feeling at hearing of his cousin's death as the girl did."

"Yes, it struck me too," said Hannasyde. "It looks as though Arnold Vereker was the sort of man who had a good many enemies."

Meanwhile Giles Carrington had been escorted to the room where Antonia awaited him. The Inspector left him at the door, and he went in, closing the door firmly behind him. "Hullo, Tony!" he said in a matter-of-fact voice.

Antonia, who was standing by the window, drumming her fingers on the glass, turned round quickly. She was looking a little pale, and more than a little fierce, but the glowering look faded, and some colour stole into her cheeks when she saw her cousin. "Hullo, Giles!" she returned, with just a suggestion of embarrassment in her manner. "I'm glad you've come. Arnold's been murdered."

"Yes, so I've heard," he answered, pulling a chair up to the table. "Sit down and tell me just what asinine tricks you've been up to."

"You needn't assume I've been asinine just because I happen to be in a mess!" snapped Antonia.

"I don't. I assume it because I know you awfully well, my child. What are you doing here, anyway? I thought you weren't on speaking terms with Arnold."

"I wasn't. But something happened, and I wanted to see him at once, so I came down——"

He interrupted her. "What happened?"

"Well, that's private. Anyway——"

"Cut out the anyway," returned her cousin. "You've called me in to act for you, Tony, and you must take me into your confidence."

She set her elbows on the table and leaned her chin on her clasped hands, frowning. "I can't, altogether. However, I don't mind telling you that my reason for wanting to see Arnold was because he'd started to interfere with my life again, and that made me see red."

"What had he done?"

"Written me a stinking letter about——" She stopped. "About my engagement," she said after a moment.

"I didn't know you were engaged," remarked Giles. "Who is it this time?"

"Don't say who is it this time, as though I'd been engaged dozens of times! I've only been engaged once before."

"Sorry. Who is it?"

"Rudolph Mesurier," said Antonia.

"Do you mean that dark fellow in Arnold's Company?" asked Giles.

"Yes. He's the Chief Accountant."

There was a short pause. "This is quite beside the point," apologized Giles, "but what's the great idea?"

"Why shouldn't I marry Rudolph if I feel like it?"

"I don't know. I was wondering how you came to feel like it, that's all."

She grinned suddenly. "You *are* a noxious cad, Giles. I do think I ought to marry someone or other, because Kenneth will, sooner or later, and I don't want to be left stranded." A rather forlorn look came into her eyes. "I'm sick of being all alone, and having to look after myself, and, anyway, I like Rudolph a lot.''

"I see. And did Arnold object?"

"Of course he did. I thought he'd be rather pleased at getting rid of his responsibilities as a matter of fact, because he's tried often enough to marry me off. So I wrote and told him about it, because though you say I'm unreasonable I quite realize I can't get married, or anything, without his consent till I'm twenty-five. And instead of sending me his blessing, he wrote the filthiest letter, and said he wouldn't hear of it.''

"Why?"

"No reason at all. Snobbery."

"Now, look here, Tony!" Giles said. "I know Arnold, and I know you. I don't say he was the type of fellow I cultivate, but he wasn't as bad as you and Kenneth thought him. Yes, I know you two had a rotten time with him, but it's always been my firm conviction that you brought a lot of it on yourselves. So don't tell me that he refused to give his consent to your marriage without letting you know why. He was much more likely not to care a damn what you did.''

"Well, he didn't like Rudolph," said Antonia restively. "He wanted me to make a better match."

Giles sighed. "You'd better let me see his letter. Where is it?"

She pointed to the ashtray at the end of the table, a sort of naughty triumph in her eyes.

Giles looked at the black ashes in it, and then rather sternly at his cousin. "Tony, you little fool, what made you do such a damned silly thing?''

"I had to, Giles; really I had to! You know that awful way we all have of blurting out what we happen to be thinking? Well, I went and told those policemen I'd had a letter from Arnold, and they were instantly mustard-keen to see it. And it hadn't anything to do with the murder; it was just private, so I burned it. It's no use asking me what was in it, because I shan't tell you. It just wasn't the sort of letter you want anyone else to see.''

He looked at her frowningly. "You're not making things very easy for me, Tony. I can't help you if you don't trust me.''

She slipped her hand confidingly into one of his. "I know, and I'm awfully sorry, but it's just One of Those Things. We needn't say I've burned the letter. We can chuck the ashes out of the window, and pretend it's lost."

"Go on, and tell me the rest of the story," Giles said. "When did you receive the letter?"

"Yesterday, at tea-time. And I rang up Eaton Place, but Arnold wasn't there, so I naturally supposed he was coming down to Ashleigh Green, with one of his fancy-ladies, and I got the car out, and came after him."

"For the Lord's sake, Tony, leave out the bit about the fancy-lady! No sane policeman will ever believe you would motor down to argue with Arnold when you thought he had a woman with him."

She opened her eyes at him. "But I did!"

"Yes, I know you did. You would. But don't say it. You don't know he had a woman with him, do you?"

"No, but it seemed likely."

"Then leave that out. What happened when you got to the cottage?"

"Nothing. Arnold wasn't there. So I squeezed in through the pantry window, and waited for him. You know how it is when one does that. You keep on saying, 'Well, I'll give him another half-hour,' and time sort of slips by. And anyway I knew he was coming, because the place was prepared. Well, he didn't turn up, and didn't turn up, and I didn't much fancy motoring back again at that hour, so I went to bed."

"Can you prove you didn't go out of the cottage again that night?" Giles said.

"No, because I did: I took Bill for a run somewhere about half-past eleven, and he had a dust-up with a retriever."

"That may be useful. Anyone with the retriever?"

"Yes, a woman like a moulting hen. But it isn't useful, in fact, rather the reverse, because I walked towards the village, as far as the cross-roads and I was coming back when I met the hen-and-retriever outfit. So I might quite easily have stuck a knife into Arnold before that. And perhaps I ought to tell you that I got retriever-blood on this skirt, and had to wash it. Because when the police came I was drying it. So what with that and my being a trifle snarkish with them at first, on account of thinking they'd come about the dog-fight, I daresay I may have set them against me."

"I shouldn't be surprised," said Giles. "One other question: Does Kenneth know you're here?"

"No, as a matter of fact he doesn't. He was out when I got Arnold's letter. But you know what he is: I daresay he hasn't even noticed that I'm not home. If he has, he'll merely suppose I told him I was going away for the night and he forgot."

"I wasn't worrying about that. Did anyone know you were coming here?"

"Well, I didn't say anything to anyone," replied Antonia helpfully. She regarded him with a certain amount of anxiety. "Do you suppose they'll think I did it?"

"I hope not. The fact that you spent the night at the cottage ought to tell in your favour. But you must stop fooling about, Tony. The police want you to account for your movements last night. We must trust that they won't inquire too closely into the letter Arnold wrote you. Otherwise you've nothing to conceal, and you must just tell them the truth, and answer any questions they may put to you."

"How do you know I've nothing to conceal?" inquired Antonia, eyeing him wickedly. "I wouldn't have minded murdering Arnold last night."

"I assume you have nothing to conceal," Giles said a little sharply.

She smiled. "Nice Giles. Do you loathe being dragged into our murky affairs?"

"I can think of things I like better. You'd better come along to the Chief Constable's office, and apologize for being such a nuisance."

"And answer a lot of questions?" she asked doubtfully.

"Yes, answer anything you can, but try not to say a lot of unnecessary things."

She looked rather nervous. "Well, you'd better frown at me if I do. I wish you could make a statement for me."

"So do I, but I can't," said Giles, getting up, and opening the door. "I'll find out if the Chief Constable is disengaged. You stay where you are."

He was gone several minutes, and when he returned it was with the Superintendent and a Constable. Antonia looked at the Constable with deep misgiving. Her cousin smiled reassuringly and said, "This is Superintendent Hannasyde, Tony, from Scotland Yard."

"How—how grim!" said Antonia in a small voice. "It's particularly bitter because I've always thought how much I should hate to be mixed up in a murder case, on account of having everything you say turned round till you find you've said something quite different."

The Superintendent bent to pat Bill. "I won't do that," he promised. "I only want you to tell me just how you came to visit your brother last night, and what you did."

Antonia drew in her breath. "He was *not* my brother," she said. "I'm sick to death of correcting that mistake. He was nothing more than half."

"I'm sorry," said the Superintendent. "You see, I've only just come into this case, so you must forgive me if I haven't quite mastered the details. Will you sit down? Now I understand from Inspector Jerrold that you came to Ashleigh Green yesterday because you wanted to see your half-brother on a private matter. Is that correct?"

"Yes," said Antonia.

"And when you arrived at the cottage what did you do?"

Antonia gave him a concise account of her movements. Once or twice he prompted her with a question, while the Constable, who had seated himself by the door, busily wrote in shorthand. The Superintendent's manner, unlike the Inspector's, was so free from suspicion, and his way of putting his questions so quiet and understanding, that Antonia's wary reserve soon left her. When he asked her if she was on good terms with Arnold Vereker she replied promptly: "No, very bad terms. I know it isn't any use concealing that, because everyone knows it. We both were."

"Both?"

"My brother Kenneth and I. We live together. He's an artist."

"I see. Were you on bad terms with your half-brother for any specific reason, or merely on general grounds?"

She wrinkled up her nose. "Well, not so much one specific reason as two or three. He was our guardian—at least, he'd stopped being Kenneth's guardian, because Kenneth is over twenty-five. I lived with him till a year ago, when I decided I couldn't stick it any longer, and then I cleared out, and joined Kenneth.''

"Did your bro—half-brother object to that?"

"Oh no, not in the least, because we'd just had a flaming row about a disgusting merchant he was trying to push me off on to, and he was extremely glad to be rid of me.''

"And had this quarrel persisted?"

"More or less. Well, no, not really. We merely kept out of each other's way as much as possible. I don't mean that we didn't quarrel when we happened to meet, but it wasn't about the merchant, or having left Eaton Place, but just any old thing.''

The twinkle grew. "Tell me, Miss Vereker, did you come down to Ashleigh Green with the intention of continuing an old quarrel, or starting a new one?"

"Starting a new one. Oh, that isn't fair! You made me say that, and it isn't in the least what I meant. I won't have that written down for me to sign.''

"It shan't be," he assured her. "But you did come down because you were angry with him, didn't you?"

"Did I say that to the Inspector?" Antonia demanded. He nodded. "All right, then, yes.''

"Why were you angry, Miss Vereker?"

"Because he'd had the infernal neck to say I wasn't going to marry the man I'm engaged to.''

"Who is that?" inquired the Superintendent.

"I don't see what that's got to do with it.''

Giles Carrington interposed: "Is your engagement a secret, Tony?"

"No, but——"

"Then don't be silly.''

She flushed, and looked down at her hands. "His name is Mesurier," she said. "He works in my half-brother's firm.''

"And your half-brother objected to the engagement?"

"Yes, because he was a ghastly snob.''

"So he wrote a letter to you, forbidding the engagement?"

"Yes—— That is—— Yes.''

The Superintendent waited a moment. "You don't seem very sure about that, Miss Vereker.''

"Yes, I am. He did write."

"And I think you've destroyed his letter, haven't you?" said Hannasyde quietly.

Her eyes flew to his face: then she burst out laughing: "That's clever of you. How did you guess?"

"Why did you do that, Miss Vereker?"

"Well, principally because it was the sort of letter that would make anyone want to commit murder, and I thought it would be safer," replied Antonia ingenuously.

The Superintendent looked at her thoughtfully for a moment, and then got up. "I think it was a pity you destroyed it," he said. "But we won't go into that now."

"Are you going to arrest me?" Antonia asked.

He smiled. "Not immediately. Mr. Carrington, if I could have a few moments' conversation with you?"

"Can I go home?" said Antonia hopefully.

"Certainly, but I want you to sign your statement first, please. The Constable will have it ready for you in a moment or two."

"Where's your car, Tony?" asked Giles. "At the cottage? Well, wait for me here, and I'll take you out to collect it, and give you some lunch."

"Well, thank God for that," said Antonia. "I've just discovered I've got exactly two and fivepence ha'penny on me, and I want some petrol."

"How like you, Tony!" said Giles, and followed the Superintendent out of the room.

CHAPTER 4

THE Chief Constable had gone to lunch, and his office was empty. Hannasyde closed the door and said: "I shall want to go through the dead man's papers, Mr. Carrington. Can you meet me at his house to-morrow morning?"

Giles nodded. "Certainly."

"And the Will . . . ?"

"In my keeping."

"I shall have to ask you to let me see it."

Giles said, with a flickering smile: "It would be a waste of your time and my energy to protest, wouldn't it?"

"Thanks," said Hannasyde, his own lips curving a little. "It would, of course." He took out his notebook and opened it. "I understand that the dead man was chairman and managing director of the Shan Hills Mine? Is that correct?"

"Quite correct."

"Unmarried?"

Giles sat down on the edge of the table. "Yes."

"Can you tell me of what his immediate family consists?"

"His half-brother and half-sister, that's all." Giles took out a cigarette and tapped it on his case. "Arnold Vereker was the eldest son of Geoffrey Vereker by his first wife, my father's sister, Maud. He was forty last December. There was one other son by that marriage, Roger, who would be thirty-eight if he were alive now—which, thank heaven, he's not. He was not precisely an ornament to the family. There was a certain amount of relief felt when he cleared out years ago. He went to South America, and I believe got himself mixed up in some revolution or other. Anyway, he's been dead about seven years now. Kenneth Vereker and his sister Antonia are the offspring of a second marriage. Their mother died shortly after Antonia's birth. My uncle died a month or two before Roger, leaving both Kenneth and Antonia under Arnold's guardianship."

"Thank you, Mr. Carrington: I hoped you would be able to help me. Can you tell me what sort of man Arnold Vereker was?"

"A man with a genius for making enemies," replied Giles promptly. "He was one of those natural bullies who can yet make themselves very pleasant when they choose. Queer chap, with a streak of appalling vulgarity. Yet at the bottom there was something quite likeable about him. Chief hobbies, women and social climbing."

"I think I know the type. From what I can make out he had a bit of a bad reputation down here."

"I shouldn't be surprised. Arnold would never go week-ending to an hotel for fear of being seen. He always wanted to stand well in the eyes of the world. Hence Riverside Cottage. Is it known, by the way, whether he had one of his fancies with him last night?"

"Very little is known, Mr. Carrington. We have not yet traced his car. That may conceivably tell a tale. Whoever it was murdered your cousin presumably drove away in the car."

"Neat," approved Giles.

The Superintendent smiled faintly. "You share Miss Vereker's dislike of the man?"

"More or less. And I have one of those cast-iron alibis which I understand render one instantly suspect. I was playing bridge in my father's house on Wimbledon Common."

The Superintendent nodded. "One more question, Mr. Carrington. Can you tell me anything about this man"—he consulted his notebook—"Mesurier?"

"Beyond the fact that he is the Chief Accountant in my

cousin's firm, nothing, I'm afraid. I am barely acquainted with him.''

"I see. I don't think I need keep you any longer now. You'll be wanting to take Miss Vereker away. Shall we say ten o'clock in Eaton Place to-morrow?''

"Yes, certainly. You'd better have my card, by the way. I should be very grateful if you would let me know what happens.''

He held out his hand, the Superintendent grasped it for a moment, and opened the door for him to pass out.

Antonia was engaged in powdering her face when Giles rejoined her.

"Hullo!'' she said. "I thought you'd deserted me. What did he want?''

"One or two particulars. I'm Arnold's executor, you know. Come along and I'll give you some lunch.''

Miss Vereker was hungry, and not even the intelligence that she might have to be present at the inquest interfered with her appetite. She ate a hearty meal, and by three o'clock was once more at Riverside Cottage, backing her car out of the garage. "Are you coming back to Town, too?'' she inquired.

"Yes, as soon as I've found out the date of the inquest. I'll look in to-night to have a word with Kenneth. Mind the rose-bush!''

"I've been driving this car for over a year,'' said Antonia, affronted.

"It looks like it,'' he agreed, his eyes on a battered mud-guard.

Antonia slammed the gear-lever into first and started with a jerk. Her cousin watched her drive off, narrowly escaping a collision with the gate-post, and then got into his own car again, and drove back to Hanborough.

Rather more than an hour later Antonia let herself into the studio that she shared with her brother, and found him in an overall, a cup of tea in one hand and a novel in the other. He was a handsome young man, with untidy dark hair and his sister's brilliant eyes. He raised them from his book as she came in, said "Hullo!'' in a disinterested voice and went on reading.

Antonia pulled off her hat and threw it vaguely in the direction of a chair. It fell on the floor, but beyond saying damn she did no more about it. "Stop reading: I've got some news," she announced.

"Shut up," replied her brother. "I'm all thrilled with this murder story. Shan't be long. Have some tea or something."

Antonia, respecting this mood of absorption, sat down and poured herself out some tea in the slop-basin. Kenneth Vereker finished reading the last chapter of his novel, and threw it aside. "Lousy," he remarked. "By the way, Murgatroyd has been yapping at me all day to know where you've been. Did you happen to tell me? Damned if I could remember. Where *have* you been?"

"Down at Ashleigh Green. Arnold's been murdered."

"Arnold's been what?"

"Murdered."

Kenneth looked at her with lifted brows. "Joke?"

"No, actually murdered. Popped off."

"Great jumping Jehoshaphat!" he exclaimed. "Who did it?"

"They don't know. I believe they rather think I did. Someone shoved a knife into him, and stuck him in the stocks at Ashleigh Green. I went down to see him, and spent the night there."

"What the devil for?"

"Oh, he wrote me a stinker about Rudolph, so I thought I might as well go and have it out with him. But that's not the point. The point is, he's dead."

Kenneth looked at her in silence for a moment. Then he carefully set down his cup, and poured himself out some more tea. "Too breath-taking. Don't know that I altogether believe it. Oh, Murgatroyd, Tony says Arnold's been done-in."

A stout woman in a black frock and a voluminous apron had come into the studio with a clean cup and saucer. She said severely: "That's as may be, and if it's true you couldn't say but what it's a judgment. But there's no call for anyone to drink their tea out of the slop-bowl that I know of. For shame, Miss Tony! And where was you last night, I should like to know? Answer me that!"

"Down at Arnold's cottage. I forgot to tell you. What a

mind you've got, Murgatroyd! Where did you think I was?''

"That's neither here nor there. What's all this nonsense about Mr. Arnold?''

"Murdered,'' said Antonia selecting a sandwich from the dish. "What's in this?''

"Stinking fish,'' replied her brother. "Go on about Arnold. Was he murdered in the cottage?''

"There's anchovy in them sandwiches, and I'll thank you, Master Kenneth, not to use such language!''

"Shut up, we want to hear about Arnold. Do get on, Tony!''

"I've told you already he was in the village stocks. I don't know any more.''

"And quite enough too!'' said Murgatroyd austerely. "I never heard of such a thing, putting corpses into stocks! Whatever next!''

"Not in the best of good taste,'' conceded Kenneth. "Did you discover him, Tony?''

"No, the police did. And then they came to the cottage and took me off to the Police Station to make a statement. So I sent for Giles, because I thought it safest.''

"And I hope,'' said Murgatroyd, picking up Antonia's hat, "that Mr. Giles gave you a piece of his mind, which I'll be bound he did. Getting yourself mixed up in nasty murder cases! Fancy anyone up and murdering Mr. Arnold! I don't know what the world's coming to, I'm sure. Not but what there's many as could be spared less. If you've finished with that tray I'll take it into the kitchen, Miss Tony.''

Antonia finished what was left in the slop-bowl and put it down.

"All right. There'll be an inquest, Ken. Giles says I shall probably have to show up. He's coming here to-night to see you.''

Her brother stared at her. "See me? What for?''

"I didn't ask.''

"Well, I don't mind him coming if he wants to, but why on earth——''

He broke off, and suddenly swung his legs down from the arm of the chair in which he was lounging. "Ha! I have it!''

"Have what?''

"I'm the heir," said Kenneth.

"So you are!" said Antonia slowly. "I never thought of that!"

"No, nor did I, but under Father's Will I must be. Two hundred and fifty thousand pounds! I must get on to Violet and tell her!"

He jumped up, but was checked by his sister. "Rot! How do you know?"

"Because I made it my business to find out when Arnold wouldn't advance me a mere five hundred. Murgatroyd, Murgatroyd! I'm rich! Do you hear? I'm rich!"

Murgatroyd, who had come back into the room to fold up the tea-cloth, replied: "Yes, I hear, and if you take my advice, Master Kenneth, you'll keep a still tongue in your head. The idea of shouting out, 'I'm rich!' when your half-brother met his end like he has!"

"Who cares how he met his end as long as he did meet it? What's Violet's number?"

"Don't you talk like that, Master Kenneth! How would you like to have a knife stuck in you? Nasty, underhand way of killing anyone, that's what I call it."

"I don't see it at all," objected Kenneth. "It's no worse than shooting a person, and far more sensible. Shooting's noisy, for one thing, and, for another, you leave a bullet in your man, and it gets traced to you. Whereas a knife doesn't leave anything behind, and is easy to get rid of."

"I don't know how you can stand there and say such things!" exclaimed Murgatroyd indignantly. "Downright indecent, that's what it is! Nor no amount of fine talking will make me say other than what I do say, and stand by! It's a dirty, mean trick to knife people!"

Kenneth waved his hands at her in one of his excitable gestures. "It isn't any dirtier or meaner than any other way! You make me sick with that kind of mawkish twaddle! What *is* Violet's number?"

"You needn't get so cross about it," said Antonia. "Personally I rather agree with Murgatroyd."

"People who start a sentence with personally (and they're always women) ought to be thrown to the lions. It's a repulsive habit."

"I probably must have caught it from Violet," said Antonia musingly.

"Shut up about Violet! Does she really say it?"

"Often."

"I'll tell her about it. What—for the fiftieth time—is her number?"

"Nothing four nine six, or something. You'd better look it up. Did either of you take the dogs for a walk this morning?"

"Take the dogs for a walk? No, of course I didn't," said Kenneth, flicking over the leaves of the telephone directory. "Hell, someone'll have to do this for me! There are pages of Williams! Blast the wench, why must she have a name like that?"

"There's no call for you to swear," said Murgatroyd. "You want to look for the initial. No, Miss Tony, you know very well that one thing I won't do is take those murdering dogs of yours out. You get rid of them and have a nice little fox-terrier, and we'll see."

"Oh, well, I'd better take them now, I suppose," replied Antonia, and put on her hat again and strolled out.

The flat, which was over a garage, had a small yard attached to it, reached by an iron stair leading out of the kitchen. The garage, which Antonia rented, had a door giving on to the yard, and had been converted into a roomy kennel. Three bull-terrier bitches occupied it, and greeted their mistress in the boisterous manner of their kind. She put them all on leashes, called Bill to heel, and started out for a walk, sped on her way by Murgatroyd, who came to the top of the iron stairs to say that if she happened to be passing a dairy she might bring in another half-dozen eggs. "Ten to one we'll have that Miss Williams here to supper," Murgatroyd said gloomily. "Enough to make your poor Mother turn in her grave! Her and her poster-sketches! And what's to stop her and Master Kenneth getting married now Mr. Arnold's no more?"

"Nothing," replied Antonia, resisting the efforts of one of the bitches to entangle her legs with the leash.

"That's what I say," agreed Murgatroyd. "There's always something to take the gilt off the ginger-bread."

Antonia left her to her cogitations, and set off in the direction of the Embankment. When she returned it was an hour later, and she had forgotten the eggs. Having given her dogs their evening meal, she ran up the steps to the kitchen, where she found Murgatroyd making pastry. A fair girl, with shrewd grey eyes and a rather square chin, was sitting with her elbows on the table, watching Murgatroyd. She smiled when she saw Antonia. "Hullo!" she said. "Just looked in for a minute."

"I haven't got the eggs," announced Antonia.

"It's all right: I got them," said the other girl. "I hear your half-brother's been murdered. I don't condole, do I?"

"No. Is the blushing Violet here?"

"Yes," said Leslie Rivers in a very steady voice. "So I thought I wouldn't stay."

"You can't anyway: there isn't enough to eat. Seen Kenneth?"

"Yes," said Leslie Rivers again. "He's with Violet. I suppose it's useless for me to say anything, but if Kenneth isn't careful he'll land himself in the jug. I should think the police are bound to think he murdered your half-brother."

"No, they won't. They think I did. Kenneth wasn't there."

"He hasn't got an alibi," stated Leslie in her matter-of-fact way. "He doesn't seem to see how with him inheriting all that money, and being in debt, and loathing Arnold, things are bound to point his way."

"I bet he didn't do it, all the same," replied Antonia.

"The point is you may find it hard to prove he didn't."

"I wonder if he could have?" Antonia said thoughtfully.

Murgatroyd let the rolling-pin fall with a clatter. "I never did in all my born days! Whatever will you say next, Miss Tony? Your own brother too, as wouldn't hurt a fly!"

"If you had a fly-swotting competition, he'd win it," Antonia replied sensibly. "I'm not saying he did kill Arnold: I only wondered. I wouldn't put it above him, would you, Leslie?"

"I don't know. He's a weird creature. Yes, of course I would. What rot you are talking, Tony! I'm going."

Five minutes later Antonia wandered into the studio and nodded curtly to the girl in the big arm-chair. "Hullo! come to celebrate?"

Miss Williams raised a pair of velvety brown eyes to Antonia's face, and put up a well-manicured hand to smooth her sleek black hair. "Tony darling, I don't think you ought to talk like that," she said. "Personally, I feel——"

"Good God, you were right!" exclaimed Kenneth. "My adored one, where did you pick up that bestial habit? Don't say personally, I implore you!"

A faint tinge of colour stole into the creamy cheeks. "Well, really, Kenneth!" said Miss Williams.

"For God's sake don't hurt her feelings!" begged Antonia. "I'm damned if I'll have any nauseating reconciliations over supper. And while we happen to be on this subject, who the devil asked you how you think I should talk, Violet?"

The brown eyes narrowed a little. "I suppose I can have my opinions, can't I?" said Miss Williams silkily.

"You look lovely when you're angry," said Kenneth suddenly. "Go on, Tony: say something more."

Miss Williams' beautiful lips parted and showed small very white teeth. "I think you're perfectly horrid, both of you, and I utterly refuse to quarrel with you. Poor little me! What chance have I got with two people at me at once? How awful for you to have actually been at Mr. Vereker's house when it happened, Tony! It must have been ghastly for you. I simply can't bear to think of it. Let's talk of something else!"

"Why can't you bear to think of it?" asked Kenneth, not so much captious as interested. "Do you object to blood?"

She gave a shudder. "Don't, Kenneth, *please!* Really, I can't stand it!"

"Just as you like, my treasure, though why you should turn queasy at the thought of Arnold's being stabbed I can't imagine. You never even knew him."

"Oh no, I shouldn't know him if I saw him," said Violet. "It isn't *that.* I just don't like talking about gruesome things."

"She's being womanly," explained Antonia. Her eye alighted on a couple of gold-necked bottles. "Where the hell did they spring from?"

"I boned 'em off Frank Crewe," replied Kenneth. "We've got to celebrate this."

"*Kenneth!*"

"That's all right," soothed Antonia. "He meant his accession to wealth."

"But you can't drink champagne when Mr. Vereker's been murdered! It isn't decent."

"I can drink champagne at any time," replied Antonia. "What have you done to your nails?"

Violet extended her hands. "Silver lacquer. Do you like it?"

"No," said Antonia. "Kenneth, if you're the heir you'll have to make me an allowance, because I want a new car."

"All right, anything you say," agreed Kenneth.

"There are sure to be Death Duties," Violet said practically. "It's absolutely wicked the amount one has to pay. Still, there's the house as well. That'll be yours, won't it, Kenneth?"

"Do you mean that barrack in Eaton Place?" demanded Kenneth. "You don't imagine I'm going to live in a barn like that, do you?"

"Why ever not?" Violet sat up, staring at him. "It's an awfully good address."

"Who cares about an awfully good address? If you'd ever been inside it you wouldn't expect me to live there. It's got Turkey carpets, and a lot of Empire furniture, and pink silk panels in the drawing-room, and a glass lustre, and marble-topped tables with gilt legs."

"We could always get rid of anything we didn't like, but I must say I like nice things, I mean things that are good."

"Turkey stair carpeting and gilt mirrors?" said Kenneth incredulously.

"I don't see why not."

"Darling, your taste is quite damnable."

"I can't see that there's any need for you to be rude because I like things you don't like. I think Turkey carpets are sort of warm and—and expensive looking."

Antonia was measuring out the ingredients for cocktails, but she lowered the bottle of gin she was holding, and directed one of her clear looks at Violet. "You don't care whether a thing's good to look at or not as long as it reeks of money," she remarked.

Violet got up, quickly yet gracefully. "Well, what if I do like luxury?" she said, her low voice sharpening a little. "If you'd been born with a taste for nice things, and never had a penny to spend which you hadn't worked and slaved for, you'd feel the same!'' One of her long, capable hands disdainfully brushed the skirt of her frock. "Even my clothes I make myself! And I want—I want Paris models, and nice furs, and my hair done every week at Eugène's, and—oh, all the nice things that make life worth living!''

"Well, don't make a song about it,'' recommended Antonia, quite unmoved. "You'll be able to have all that if Kenneth really does inherit.''

"Of course I inherit,'' said Kenneth impatiently. "Hustle along with the drinks, Tony!''

Antonia suddenly put down the gin bottle. "Can't. You do it. I've suddenly remembered I was supposed to meet Rudolph for lunch this morning. I must ring him up.'' She took the telephone receiver off the rest, and began to dial. "Did he ring me up, do you know?''

"Dunno. Don't think so. How much gin have you put in?''

"Lashings . . . Hullo, is that Mr. Mesurier's flat? Oh, is it you, Rudolph? I say, I'm frightfully sorry about lunch. Did you wait ages? But it wasn't my fault. It truly wasn't.''

At the other end of the telephone there was a tiny pause. Then a man's voice, light in texture, rather nasal, rather metallic, in the matter of modern voices, replied hesitatingly: "Is it you, Tony? I didn't quite catch—the line's not very clear. What did you say?''

"Lunch!'' enunciated Antonia distinctly.

"Lunch? Oh, my God! I clean forgot! I'm devastatingly sorry! Can't think how I could——''

"Weren't you there?'' demanded Antonia.

There was another pause. "Tony dear, the line's really awful. Can't make out a word you say.''

"Put a sock in it, Rudolph. Did you forget about lunch?''

"My dear, will you ever forgive me?'' besought the voice.

"Oh yes,'' replied Antonia. "I forgot too. That's what I rang up about. I was down at Arnold's place at Ashleigh Green, and——''

"Ashleigh Green!''

"Yes, why the horror?''

"I'm not horrified, but what on earth made you go down there?''

"I can't tell you over the telephone. You'd better come round. And bring something to eat; there's practically nothing here."

"But, Tony, wait! I can't make out what took you to Ashleigh Green. Has anything happened? I mean——"

"Yes, Arnold's been killed."

Again the pause. "Killed?" repeated the voice. "Good God! You don't mean murdered, do you?"

"Of course I do. Bring some cold meat, or something, and come to supper. There'll be champagne."

"Cham—— Oh, all right! I mean, thanks very much: I'll be round," said Rudolph Mesurier.

"By all of which," remarked Kenneth, shaking the cocktails professionally, "I gather that the boy-friend is on his way. Will he be bonhomous, Tony?"

"Oh, rather!" promised Antonia blithely. "He can't stand Arnold at any price."

CHAPTER 5

THERE was no sitting-room in the Verekers' flat other than the big studio. Supper was laid on a black oak table at one end, after one dog-whip, two tubes of paint, *The Observer* (folded open at Torquemada's cross-word), *Chambers's Dictionary*, *The Times Atlas*, a volume of Shakespeare, and the *Oxford Book of Verse* had all been removed from it. While Murgatroyd stumped in and out of the studio with glasses and plates, Kenneth took a last look at the half-completed cross-word, and announced, as was his invariable custom, that he was damned if he would ever try to do another. Rudolph Mesurier, who had arrived with a veal and ham pie, and half a loaf of bread, said he knew a man who filled the whole thing in about twenty minutes; and Violet, carefully powdering her face before a Venetian mirror, said that she expected one had to have the Torquemada-*mind* to be able to do his cross-words.

"Where did them bottles come from?" demanded Murgatroyd, transfixed by the sight of their opulent gold necks.

"Left over from Frank Crewe's party last week," explained Kenneth.

Murgatroyd sniffed loudly, and set down a dish with unnecessary violence. "The idea!" she said. "Anyone'd think it was the funeral party already."

Constraint descended on the two visitors. Violet folded her lovely mouth primly, and cleared her throat; Rudolph Mesurier fingered his tie and said awkwardly: "Frightful thing about Mr. Vereker. I mean—it doesn't seem possible, somehow."

Violet turned gratefully and favoured him with her slow, enchanting smile. "No, it doesn't, does it? I didn't know him, but it makes me feel quite sick to think of it. Of course I don't think Ken and Tony realize it yet—not absolutely."

"Oh, don't they, my sweet?" said Kenneth derisively.

"Kenneth, whatever you felt about poor Mr. Vereker when he was alive, I do think you might at least pretend to be sorry now he's dead."

"It's no use," said Antonia, spearing olives out of a tall bottle. "You'd better take us as you find us, Violet. You'll never teach Kenneth not to say exactly what he happens to think."

"Well, I don't think it's a good plan," replied Violet rather coldly.

"That's only because he said that green hat of yours looked like a hen in a fit. Besides, it isn't a plan: it's a disease. Olive, Rudolph?"

"Thanks." He moved over to the far end of the studio, where she was seated, perched on a corner of the dining-table. As he took the olive off the end of the meat-skewer she had elected to use for her task, he raised his eyes to her face, and said in a low voice: "How did it happen? Why were you there? That's what I can't make out."

She gave him back look for look. "On account of us. I wrote and told him we were going to get married, thinking he'd be pleased, and probably send us a handsome gift."

"Yes, I know. I wish you'd consulted me first. I'd no idea——"

"Why?" interrupted Antonia. "Gone off the scheme?"

"No, no! Good God, no! I'm utterly mad about you, darling, but it wasn't the moment. I mean, you know I'm hard up just now, and a fellow like Vereker would be bound to leap to the conclusion that I was after your money."

"I haven't got any money. You can't call five hundred a year money. Moreover, several things aren't paying any dividend this year, so I'm practically a pauper."

"Yes, but he had money. Anyway, I wish you hadn't, because as a matter of fact it's landed me into a bit of a mess. Well, not actually, I suppose, but it's bound to come out that we had a slight quarrel on the very day he was murdered."

Antonia looked up, and then across the room towards the other two. They seemed to be absorbed in argument. She said bluntly: "How do you know which day he was murdered?"

His eyes, deep blue, and fringed with black lashes, held all at once a startled look. "I—you told me, didn't you?"

"No," said Antonia.

He gave an uncertain laugh. "Yes, you did, over the telephone. You've forgotten. But you see the position, don't you? Of course, it doesn't really matter, but the police are bound to think it a bit fishy, and one doesn't want to be mixed up in anything—I mean, in my position one has to be somewhat circumspect."

"You needn't worry," said Antonia. "It's me they think fishy. I was there."

"Tony, I simply don't understand. Why were you there? What in the world can have *taken* you there? You haven't been on speaking terms with Vereker for months, and then you dash off to Riverside Cottage for the week-end—it doesn't seem to me to make sense!"

"Yes, it does. Arnold wrote me a stinking letter from the office on Saturday morning, and I got it that day. I went down to tackle him about it."

"Ah, you darling!" Mesurier said, laying his hand in hers, and pressing it. "You needn't tell me. He wrote something libellous about me. I can just imagine it! But you shouldn't have done it, my sweet. I can look after myself."

"Yes, I daresay you can," answered Antonia, "but I wasn't going to have Arnold spreading lies about you all the same."

"Darling! What did he tell you?"

"He didn't tell me anything specific, because I never saw him. He wrote a few pages of drivel, all about how I should very soon know the sort of blackguard I meant to marry, and how you were a skunk, and a thief, and various other things like that.''

"Gosh, he was a swine!" Mesurier exclaimed, flushing. "He realized, of course, that in another year he couldn't prevent our marriage, so he tried to blacken me to you. Have you got that letter?"

"No, I burned it. I thought it would be safer."

He looked at her intently. "You mean in case the police got hold of it? You aren't keeping anything back, are you, darling? If Vereker made any definite accusation I wish you'd tell me."

"He didn't." Antonia got off the table as Murgatroyd came into the studio, and glanced towards her brother. "If you've finished quarrelling, supper's ready." She thought it over, and added conscientiously: "And if you haven't, it still is."

Kenneth came towards the table. "I've made her cross again, haven't I, my lovely? Where's the oil and vinegar?"

"I'm not cross," Violet said in a sad voice. "Only rather hurt."

"My adored!" he said contritely, but with a gleam of his impish smile.

"Yes, that's all very well," said Violet, taking her place at the table, "but I sometimes think you only care about my good looks."

He flashed his brilliant, half-laughing, half-earnest glance at her. "I worship your good looks," he said.

"Thank you," replied Violet dryly.

"She isn't really so good-looking," observed Antonia, wrestling with the joints of a cold fowl. "Her eyes are set a bit too far apart, for one thing, and I don't know if you've noticed, but one side of her face isn't as good as the other."

"But look at that lovely line of the jaw!" Kenneth said, dropping the wooden salad spoon, and tracing the line in the air with his thumb.

"When you've *quite* finished, both of you!" Violet protested. She looked provocatively at Mesurier, seated opposite to her, and said: "Aren't they awful? Don't you think we're frightfully brave to marry them?"

He responded in kind, and they kept up an interchange of light badinage throughout the meal. Attempts to draw the other two into the conversation were not very successful. Kenneth had a glowering look on his face, which Violet could always conjure up by flirting with another man; and Antonia, when appealed to by Violet to assure Mesurier that she didn't look marvellous in red, but, on the contrary, positively haggish, replied with such disastrous frankness that the topic broke off like a snapped thread.

"You're an artist, aren't you?" said Rudolph hastily.

"No," said Kenneth.

"Well, I may not be an artist as you highbrows understand it——"

"You aren't. You can't draw."

"Thank you, dear. But I *do* make a living out of it," said Violet sweetly. "As a matter of fact I do poster-designs and commercial work, Mr. Mesurier. I found I had a sort of knack"—Kenneth sank his head in his hands and groaned —"a sort of knack," repeated Violet, "and I suppose my stuff caught on. I've always had a sense of colour, and line and——"

"Oh, darling, do shut up!" begged Kenneth. "You've got about as much sense of colour and line as Tony's bull-terriers."

Violet stiffened. "I don't know if you're trying to annoy me, but——"

"My angel, I wouldn't annoy you for the world, but if only you'd just *be*, and not talk!" begged Kenneth.

"I see. I'm to sit mum while you air your views."

"She can't possibly not talk at all, Kenneth," said Antonia reasonably. "What he means is, Don't talk Art."

"Thank you, I'm quite aware that nobody but Kenneth knows anything about Art."

"Well, if you're aware of it, why the hell do you——"

"Champagne!" said Rudolph, leaping into the breach. "Miss Williams, you will, won't you? Tony?"

"Why is there never any ice in this place?" demanded Kenneth, suddenly diverted.

"Because we bought the oak coffer with the money we meant to spend on a refrigerator," replied Antonia.

This change of topic, coupled with the champagne, saved

the party from breaking up there and then. No further references were made to Art, and by the time the quartette rose from the table, and drifted over to the other end of the room Violet had softened towards Kenneth, who was passionately anxious to make amends; and Rudolph had volunteered to make Turkish coffee if Murgatroyd didn't mind. He and Antonia went off to the kitchen together, and under Murgatroyd's scornful but indulgent eye brewed a decoction which, though it would have puzzled a Turk, was quite drinkable.

It was a warm evening, and all this exertion made Antonia so hot that she announced her intention of having a bath. She withdrew into the bathroom, reappearing in the studio a quarter of an hour later in beach pyjamas, which became her very well, but offended Murgatroyd, who told her she ought to be ashamed of herself, on a Sunday and all. Kenneth, flat on the divan, had taken off his coat, somewhat to Violet's disapproval, and was lying with his hands linked behind his head, and his shirt open at the throat. Violet sat on a floor cushion, looking graceful and cool, and self-possessed; and Rudolph Mesurier, who had compromised with the heat by undoing the buttons of his rather too-waisted coat, leaned against the window blowing smoke rings.

Ten minutes later the door-bell rang, and Antonia said: "That'll be Giles."

"Lord, I'd forgotten he was coming!" said Kenneth.

Violet reached instinctively for her vanity case, but before she had time to do more than peep at her reflection in the tiny mirror, Murgatroyd had ushered in the visitor.

"Here's Mr. Giles!" she announced grimly.

Giles Carrington paused on the threshold, surveying the group in some amusement. "You look like an illustration of high life and low life," he remarked. "Sunbathing, Tony?"

"Come inside, and pour yourself out a drink," said Kenneth. "And don't be shy of telling us the worst: it's all in the family. Am I the heir, or am I not? If I am, we're going to buy a refrigerator. There's no ice in this ruddy place."

Giles paid not the slightest attention to this, but smiled down at Violet. "It's useless to expect either of my cousins to introduce us. My name is Carrington."

"I know; they're hopeless. Mine is Williams. I'm Kenneth's fiancée, you know."

"I didn't, but I congratulate him. Good-evening, Mesurier."

"Oh, how sweet of you!" Violet said, with an arch look up at him.

"That's only his nice Eton manners," said Antonia reassuringly. "When's the Inquest, Giles?"

"On Tuesday. You'll have to attend."

"Blast! Are you going to be there?"

"Yes, of course. I'll take you down." Giles poured himself out some whisky, and splashed soda into it. "Arnold's car has been found," he said casually.

"Where?" asked Antonia.

"In a mews off the Cromwell Road."

"Will that help the police at all, do you suppose?" inquired Violet.

"I hardly think so. Nothing but Arnold's suit-case and hat and a hamper of provisions was found in it, I believe."

"What, no blood?" said Kenneth lazily. "No gory knife? I call that a sell for the police."

"Haven't they discovered any clue at all?" Rudolph asked. "Surely there must be something to show who it was? I mean, finger-prints, or something?"

"I'm afraid I can't tell you that," replied Giles in his cool, pleasant way. "The police haven't taken me quite so far into their confidence."

"Did you see anything more of that lamb-like Superintendent?" said Antonia, clasping her hands round her knees.

"Yes, I gave him a lift back to Town."

Kenneth sat up. "Look here, whose side are you on?"

Giles Carrington looked up quickly. Kenneth grinned. "No, I didn't mean that exactly, but you've got to act for us."

"That is what I'm trying to do," answered Giles.

"Lots of snags in the way," murmured Kenneth, lying down again. "Tony's pitchforked herself bang into the middle of it, and I don't think I can prove an alibi. All the same," he added, tilting his head back to watch the fluttering of a moth against the skylight, "they'll find it pretty hard to fasten the murder on to me. For one thing, I haven't got a knife, and never had a knife; and for another, no one would ever believe I could do a job as neatly as this one, without leaving any trace behind. Also I haven't had any very recent quarrel with——" He jerked himself upright again. "Damn! What a fool I was! I wrote and asked him for some cash, and he refused. I'll lay any odds you like he's kept my letter and a copy of his answer."

"Oh, Kenneth, don't talk such rubbish!" Violet begged. "Of course they don't think you did it!"

"They probably will, but they'll find it devilish hard to prove," said Kenneth. "What do you think, Giles?"

"If you like to call at my office to-morrow at twelve, I'll tell you," replied Giles, finishing his drink.

Violet got up, smoothing her skirt. "Of course you can't talk with Mr. Mesurier and me here," she said. "Anyway, it's time I went home. I've got a long day to-morrow. Kenneth, promise me you'll stop being silly, and tell Mr. Carrington everything. You know perfectly well you didn't do it, and anyone would think you had, from the way you go on."

"Yes, you all three ought to talk it over," agreed Mesurier. "Can I see you home, Miss Williams?"

Violet accepted this offer with one of her demure smiles, and in spite of Kenneth's loud and indignant protests, the pair insisted on taking their leave. Murgatroyd came in to clear away the glasses when they had gone, and interrupted Kenneth, who was cursing his cousin for breaking up the party, by saying: "That's enough from you, Master Kenneth. You listen to what Mr. Giles has to say, and keep a still tongue in your head. And if you want anything I'll be in the kitchen."

She went out, and they heard her go into the kitchen and shut the door. Kenneth sat down again on the divan, and leaned his elbows on his knees. "I'm sick of this murder already," he said. "They'll never find out who did it, so why worry?"

Giles took out his pipe, and began to fill it. "Get this into your head," he said. "If the police don't discover any clue to the identity of the murderer your position's going to be serious."

Kenneth looked up. "Why? I thought Tony was the chief suspect."

"What do you suppose is the first thing the police will look for?" Giles said. "Motive. Tony's motive is merely one of revenge, or spite, or whatever you like to call it. Your motive is a good deal stronger. You're hard up, you tried to get money out of Arnold, and by his death you inherit a large fortune."

"Yes, but I didn't think of that for quite some time after Tony had told me Arnold was dead. Did I, Tony?"

"I doubt whether that would impress a jury," said Giles. "What were you doing last night?"

"I went to look Violet up."

"At what time?"

"Not sure. Half-past eightish. Murgatroyd was out, and Tony seemed to have waltzed off for the night, so I wandered out on my own."

"Did you go to Miss Williams' house?"

"Flat. Yes, but she was out. No one answered the bell, so I drifted along to some cinema or other. No, I don't know which one it was and I don't know what the film was called, because I went in after it had started, and it was so dull I slept through most of it."

"Well, what did you do when you left the cinema?"

"Went for a walk," replied Kenneth.

"Where to?"

"Richmond."

"Why on earth did you do that?" said Giles, patient but despairing.

"Why not?" retorted Kenneth. "It was a fine night, and very warm, and I'd had a nice nap in the cinema. It seemed an obvious thing to do."

"Did it!" said Giles.

"But he does go for walks at night, Giles!" Antonia put in anxiously. "We both do, when it's too hot to go to bed."

Giles sighed. "When did you get home?"

"Oh, somewhere about three or four, I suppose. I didn't notice the time."

"And you can't think of anyone who saw you come in or out of the cinema, or on your way to Richmond, and who would be able to recognize you? Didn't you meet a policeman?"

"No, I don't think so. One or two cars passed, but I don't remember meeting anyone."

"In fact, not one word of this story can you prove," said Giles.

"No," replied Kenneth blandly, "and not one word of it can the police disprove."

CHAPTER 6

GILES'S car drew up outside Arnold Vereker's house in Eaton
Place just as Superintendent Hannasyde ascended the stone
steps. The Superintendent turned, and when he saw Giles get
out of the car, smiled, and said: "Good-morning, Mr. Carrington. You're very punctual."

"It saves trouble, don't you think?" said Giles. "Have you
rung?"

"Not yet," replied Hannasyde, pressing the electric button.

The door was opened almost immediately by a thin butler
who had a sour expression and looked as though he suffered
from dyspepsia. His gaze swept the Superintendent by, and
came to rest on Giles. He gave a slight bow, and opened the
door wider.

" 'Morning, Taylor," Giles said. "Superintendent Hannasyde and I want to go through Mr. Vereker's papers."

"Yes, sir?" The butler eyed Hannasyde for one disapprov-
ing minute. "The library is locked, as the Superintendent left
it yesterday, I understand."

It was plain that the butler had no opinion of policemen
who walked into well-ordered houses, and locked rooms up as
they pleased.

"A bad business about Mr. Vereker," Giles said, handing
him his hat and gloves.

"Extremely distasteful, sir."

"I should like to have a word with you, please," said Hannasyde, taking a key out of his pocket, and fitting it into the lock of a door on the right of the front door.

"Certainly, sir," said Taylor frigidly. "I regret having been out when you called yesterday, but Sunday is my Day."

"Yes, I understand. Come in here, will you? Mr. Carrington, will you take these?" He held out a collection of keys on a ring, which Giles took, while the butler walked over to the window, and drew back the curtains.

The library had the same air of conscious opulence that pervaded every room in Arnold Vereker's house. It had expensive leather chairs, and expensive sets of calf-bound volumes in oak bookshelves. There was a very thick pile carpet, and a very richly carved desk. Everything spoke aloud the unguided taste of a high-class firm of decorators; nothing gave any indication of the owner's personality.

Hannasyde waited until Taylor had arranged the curtains to his satisfaction, and then asked: "How long have you been in Mr. Vereker's employment?"

"I have been here for three years, sir," replied Taylor, in a voice that informed the Superintendent that that was a record.

"Then you are probably acquainted with Mr. Vereker's habits. Was it his custom to spend the week-ends at his country cottage?"

"He occasionally did so, sir."

"And when he did was it usual for him to drive himself down, or did he take his chauffeur?"

"Sometimes the one and sometimes the other, sir."

"Upon Saturday, when he left town, was the chauffeur with him?"

"I believe not, sir. There had been a little unpleasantness."

"What do you mean by that?"

"Between Mr. Vereker and Jackson, the chauffeur, sir. Mr. Vereker gave Jackson his notice on Saturday morning, Jackson having brought the car round five minutes late again. There was a highly unpleasant scene upon the frontsteps. I regret to say that Jackson so far forgot himself as to answer Mr. Vereker back. It was quite a brawl, not what one would expect in a gentleman's house at all. Jackson talked extremely wildly, Mr. Vereker hardly less so. Both being hot-tempered, if I may say so."

"And when Mr. Vereker left the house on Saturday evening, Jackson was not driving the car?"

"No, sir. It was merely brought round to the door—Mr. Vereker having stated that he did not wish to see Jackson's face again."

"I see. At what hour did Mr. Vereker leave this house?"

"He left at ten minutes to eight, sir."

"You seem sure of that. What fixed the time in your memory?"

"Mr. Vereker himself, sir. He remarked on it. I understood him to have a dinner engagement. He was not—ahem—pleased at being detained."

"What detained him?"

The butler drew in his breath, for this was the moment for which he had been waiting. "A visitor, sir."

"Who was this visitor?"

"I could not say, sir. He was not a person I had ever seen before. In fact, I should not describe him as the type of gentleman I have been in the habit of admitting to the house. Very down-at-heel, he was, and most determined to see Mr. Vereker. Upon my informing him that Mr. Vereker was not at home, he set his foot in the door and replied that he should not leave until he had seen him."

"Do you mean that his attitude was threatening?"

The butler considered. "Hardly that, sir. Oh no, not threatening! Very affable, he was, in a silly kind of way. Stood there smiling. I formed the impression that he was under the influence of drink. I was about to summon Matthew—the footman, sir—to assist in putting him outside when Mr. Vereker came down the stairs ready to go out."

"In evening-dress?"

"Precisely, sir. Mr. Vereker called out to know what was the matter. The stranger kept on smiling, in what I could only think a very peculiar way, under the circumstances, and after a moment he said, amiable as you please: 'You'd better be at home to me, old fellow.' Those were his exact words, and the effect of them upon Mr. Vereker was remarkable. Mr. Vereker was a gentleman with a high complexion, but he turned quite pale, and stood there with his hand on the banister, staring.''

"Did he seem to be afraid?''

"I should not like to say that, sir. He looked to me to be very angry and amazed.''

"Do you remember what he said?''

"He did not speak at all, sir, until the stranger said that it would save a lot of unpleasantness if he had a few words with him alone. Then he gave a kind of choke, and told me to let the man in. I did so, of course, and Mr. Vereker led the way into this room, and shut the door.''

"How long were they both here?''

"Until Mr. Vereker left the house, sir, which he did in company with his visitor. It might have been twenty minutes, or half an hour.''

"Have you any idea what took place between them? Was there any quarrel?''

"I should not call it a quarrel, sir. I never heard the stranger's voice raised once, though I could not help but hear Mr. Vereker shouting occasionally. It is my belief that it was money the man wanted, for Mr. Vereker said, 'Not one penny do you get out of me!' several times.''

"Did you hear him say anything else?''

"Not a great deal, sir. The term scoundrel was frequently made use of, and Mr. Vereker said once, very loudly: 'So you think you can frighten me, do you?' But what the other man replied I don't know, him speaking all the time in a soft voice. After a little while Mr. Vereker seemed to calm down, and I was unable to catch what was said. But at ten minutes to eight they both came out of the library, and by the way Mr. Vereker damned me for being in the hall to open the door for him I judged that something had happened to put him in a bad temper. The other man was as amiable as ever, and seemed to be laughing up his sleeve, to my way of thinking. He said Mr. Vereker could give him a lift, and Mr. Vereker threw him a look which quite startled me, accustomed as I was to his moods. I could see he hated the man, and it is my belief that he had a deal of trouble forcing himself to agree to take him in the car with him. But whatever the reason he did actually do so, the stranger making himself very much at home, and Mr.

Vereker with his mouth shut like a trap. That, sir, is the last I ever saw of Mr. Vereker.''

The Superintendent had listened to this story with an unmoved countenance. ''Would you know the man if you were to see him again?''

''I think so, sir. I should, I believe, recognize both his smile, and his voice. His person was not, however, in any way remarkable.''

''Very well. You do not know of anyone else who may have visited Mr. Vereker on Saturday?''

''Mr. Vereker was at his office until lunch-time, sir, and no one called at this house during the afternoon. He went out at four o'clock, and did not return until shortly before seven. Miss Vereker rang up about six, but my orders being to inform anyone who wanted him that he had gone out of town, I did so.''

''Do you know why Mr. Vereker gave that order?''

''It was not unusual, sir. He had been out of temper all day, and when that occurred he never wanted to see or speak to anyone, least of all a—a member of his family.''

''I see. One other question: do you know what Mr. Vereker's plans were for Saturday evening?''

''Oh no, sir! Mr. Vereker was never communicative. I inferred from his attire that he was dining in town before motoring into the country, but where or in what company I fear I have no idea.''

''Thank you. I won't keep you any longer, then.''

The butler bowed, and looked towards Giles. ''I beg your pardon, sir, but in the face of this unexpected occurrence there is a feeling amongst the staff that everything is very unsettled. I do not know whether the staff is to be kept on——?''

''That will be for the heir to decide,'' answered Giles pleasantly. ''Meanwhile, just carry on as you are.''

''If you say so, sir,'' said Taylor, and withdrew.

Hannasyde waited until he had gone before saying: ''What did you make of that, Mr. Carrington?''

''Not very much,'' shrugged Giles. ''I daresay it might be a good thing if you could run the seedy stranger to earth, but it sounds to me as though it were a somewhat inexpert blackmailer at work. Would you like the safe opened first?''

"Yes, please. And a certain amount of animus displayed against the chauffeur. Or merely protective measures?"

"Probably a bit of both," said Giles, opening a very obvious door in the panelling beside the fireplace, and disclosing a steel safe. "Servants are always anxious to protect themselves against any possible accusation—even," he added bitterly, "when it's only one of watering the whisky. Here you are."

The Superintendent moved across the room to his side, and together they went through the contents of the safe. There was nothing in it relevant to the case, only share-certificates, a bank-book, and some private papers. Giles put them back, when the Superintendent had finished with them, and shut the safe again.

"We'll try the desk," he said, going over to it, and sitting down in the swivel-chair.

"Did you bring the Will?" asked Hannasyde.

Giles drew it from his inner pocket, and handed it over. The Superintendent sat down on the other side of the desk, and spread open the crackling sheets, while Giles sought amongst the keys on the ring for one which fitted the drawers of the desk.

The Superintendent read the Will, and at the end laid it carefully down, and said in his measured voice: "I see that the residuary legatees are Kenneth and Antonia Vereker, who share equally all that is left of Arnold Vereker's fortune when the minor legacies have been paid."

"Yes," agreed Giles, glancing through a paper he had taken from one of the drawers. "That is so."

"Both of them, then, benefit very considerably by Arnold Vereker's death."

"I can't tell you, off-hand, how much Arnold's private fortune amounted to. Somewhere in the neighborhood of sixty thousand pounds."

The Superintendent looked at him. "What about his holding in the mine?"

"That," said Giles, laying a sheaf of papers on one of the heaps he had made on the desk, "in default of male issue by Arnold, goes to Kenneth, under the terms of his father's Will. I thought you'd want to see that, so I brought a copy."

"Thanks," said Hannasyde, stretching out his hand for it. "I really am grateful. You're saving me a lot of time, Mr. Carrington."

"Don't mention it," said Giles.

The Superintendent read Geoffrey Vereker's Will, knitting his brows over it.

"This is a most extraordinary document," he remarked. "All that seems to be left to his other children is his private fortune—and even that is divided between the four of them. What's the meaning of it, Mr. Carrington?"

"It isn't quite as extraordinary as it appears," replied Giles. "The Shan Hills Mine was an obsession with my uncle. In his day it wasn't the huge concern it is now. My uncle believed in it, and made a private company to work it. It was to be developed, and it was on no account to pass out of the family. So he left his holding to Arnold, with a reversion to Arnold's eldest son, if any; and failing a son, to Roger and his heirs; or, in the event of Roger's death without legitimate male issue, to Kenneth. The private fortune amounted to thirty-three thousand pounds, and was at that time the more substantial bequest. It was divided equally between the four children. But a few years after my uncle's death, his belief in the potentialities of Shan Hills was justified by the discovery, on one of the leases, of a very rich deposit—a limestone replacement deposit, if you're interested in technicalities. Arnold floated the mine as a public company—and you know pretty well how it stands to-day. Arnold's holding probably represents about a quarter of a million."

"A very nice little packet to inherit," commented Hannasyde dryly.

"Very nice," agreed Giles.

There was a short pause. "Well, we'd better go through the desk," said Hannasyde. "Have you found anything that might have a bearing on the case?"

"Nothing at all," said Giles. He handed a diary across. "I hoped this might reveal his Saturday night engagement, but he's merely crossed off Saturday and Sunday. I haven't come across his cheque-book yet, by the way. Was it on him?"

"Yes, I've got it," Hannasyde said, producing it. "I see he drew a cheque for a hundred pounds to self on Friday. At first glance rather a large sum to carry about with him, but he seems to have been in the habit of doing it.''

"He was. He got rather a kick out of a fat wad in his pocket, I think.''

"Lots do. What surprised me a little, though, was to find that he only had thirty pounds and some loose change on him when his body was discovered. Seventy pounds seems to be a lot to have spent in a couple of days, unless he paid some bills, of course.''

Giles glanced through a pile of receipts. "Nothing here for that date. Might have bought a trinket for his latest fancy.''

"Or the butler's mysterious stranger might have relieved him of it,'' said Hannasyde thoughtfully. "I should like to meet this smiling stranger.'' He picked up a small letter-file, and began methodically to go through its contents. Most of the letters he merely glanced at, and put aside, but one held his attention for some moments. "H'm! I suppose you've seen this?''

Giles looked up. "What is it? Oh, that! Yes, I've seen it. There's some more of that correspondence—oh, you've got it!''

The Superintendent was holding a baldly worded request for five hundred pounds, written in Kenneth's nervous fist. The letter stated with exquisite simplicity that Kenneth was broke, engaged to be married, and must have funds to pay off a few debts. Appended to it was a typewritten sheet, headed Copy, stating with equal simplicity that Arnold had no intention of giving or lending a feckless idiot five hundred pence, let alone pounds. Further search of the file brought to light a second letter from Kenneth, scrawled on a half-sheet of notepaper. It was laconic in the extreme, and expressed an ardent desire on the writer's part to wring his brother's bloody neck.

"Very spirited,'' said the Superintendent non-committally. "I should like to keep these letters, please.''

"Do, by all means,'' said Giles. "Particularly the last one.''

"Kenneth Vereker is, I take it, a client of yours?''

"He is.''

"Well, Mr. Carrington, we won't hedge. You're no fool, and you can see as clearly as I do that his movements on Saturday night will have to be accounted for. But I'm no fool either, and we shall get along a good deal better if I tell you here and now that these letters don't make me want to go after a warrant for this young man's arrest at once. A man who makes up his mind to kill someone isn't very likely to write and tell his victim that he'd like to do it.''

Privately Giles placed no such confidence in his cousin's level-headedness, but he only nodded, and said: "Just so.''

The Superintendent folded the three letters and tucked them into his pocket-book. His eyes twinkled a little. "But if he's anything like his sister—well, that alters things,'' he said. "Now let's take a look at this memorandum.''

He picked it up as he spoke and opened it. Giles began to replace the papers in the drawers. "Hullo!'' said Hannasyde suddenly. "What do you make of this, Mr. Carrington?''

Giles took the book, and found it open at a page of figures. In the first column were pencilled various dates; against these were set names, apparently of different firms; in the third column were certain sums of money, each with a note of interrogation beside it, and a counter-sum, heavily underlined. At the bottom, each line of figures had been totalled, and the difference, which amounted to three hundred and fifty pounds, not only underlined, but wholly encircled by a thick black pencil-mark.

"John Dawlish Ltd.,'' said Giles slowly, reading one of the names aloud. "Aren't those the people who make drills? These look to me like Company accounts.''

"They look to me as though someone has been monkeying with the accounts, and Arnold Vereker found it out,'' said Hannasyde. "I think we'll step round to the Shan Hills office, if you don't mind, Mr. Carrington.''

"Not at all,'' replied Giles, "but I don't quite see why you should want me to——''

He was interrupted by the butler, who at the moment opened the door, and stood holding it. "I beg your pardon, sir, but Mr. Carrington would like to speak to you on the telephone,'' said Taylor.

Giles looked up, surprised: "Mr. Carrington wants to speak to me?''

"Yes, sir. Shall I switch the call through to this room, or

would you prefer to speak from the hall?''

"No, switch it through, will you?'' Giles lifted the receiver of the desk telephone, and glanced towards Hannasyde. "Do you mind?—It's my father, though what he wants, I can't imagine. By the way, it is he who is the legal adviser to Arnold's Company. Arnold transferred his private affairs to me, partly because we were more of an age, and partly because he and my father couldn't hit it off, but the business remained in—— Hullo, sir! 'Morning. Yes, Giles speaking.''

The Superintendent opened his note-book, and began tactfully to read through the entries. He could hear a staccato quacking noise, which he rightly inferred to be the voice of Mr. Carrington, Senior. It sounded irascible, he thought.

Giles's side of the conversation was mild and soothing. He said: "So sorry, sir. Didn't I tell you I should come straight to Eaton Place? . . . well, never mind: what's happened? . . . something to do with *what?*'' The lazy look faded; he listened intently to the quacking noise, which went on for quite some time. Then he said: "All right, sir, I'll bring him round as soon as we've finished here.'' The voice quacked again, and the Superintendent was almost certain that he heard the words, "flat-footed policemen.'' However, Giles merely said: "In about twenty minutes, then. Good-bye,'' and laid down the receiver. He raised his eyes to the Superintendent's face, and said: "My father wants to see you, Superintendent. He tells me he found a letter from Arnold Vereker waiting for him at the office this morning, which he thinks you ought to see.''

CHAPTER 7

THE offices of Carrington, Radclyffe & Carrington were on the first floor of a house at the bottom of Adam Street, facing down the length of Adelphi Terrace. The head of the firm occupied a large, untidy room overlooking the river through a gap in the adjacent buildings. When Giles ushered Hannasyde into this apartment on Monday morning, the head of the firm was seated at an enormous desk, completely covered with papers, muttering fiercely at the shortcomings of his fountain pen. The head of the firm was a well-preserved sixty, with grizzled and scanty hair, a ruddy complexion, and the same humorous gleam which lurked in his son's grey eyes. In other respects father and son were not much alike. Giles was tall and lean, and never seemed to be in a hurry; Charles Carrington was short, and of a comfortable habit of body, and lived in a perpetual state of bustle. It was a source of surprise to those not intimately acquainted with him that he should be a lawyer. Those who knew him best were not dismayed by his odd mannerisms, or his inability to find anything. They knew that although he might convey the impression of being a fussy and rather incompetent old gentleman, he had still, at sixty, a remarkably acute intellect.

He looked up when the door opened, and, as soon as he saw

his son held up an ink-stained hand, and barked: "You see! What did I tell you? They always leak. What on earth should put it into your mother's head to give me one of the infernal things, when she knows perfectly well I never could stand them, and never shall—— Look at this! Take the confounded thing away! Throw it out the window!—Give it to the office boy! And you needn't tell your mother I'm not using it!"

"All right, I won't," said Giles, removing the pen. "This is Superintendent Hannasyde from Scotland Yard."

"Oh, is it?" said Mr. Carrington, wiping his fingers with a piece of pink blotting-paper. "Good-morning. Investigating my nephew's murder, aren't you? Well, I wish you joy of it. Ill-conditioned young cub! Don't stand! Don't stand! Take a chair! Giles, push those deeds on to the floor, and let the Superintendent sit down."

He began to hunt amongst the dusty heap of documents on his desk, remarking that in this office you had only to lay a thing down for a minute for it to disappear completely. The Superintendent, surveying the general disorder with an awed gaze, made a sympathetic murmur, and wondered whether there was the least hope of discovering Arnold Vereker's letter in the welter on the desk.

But Mr. Carrington, having thrown one bundle of papers at his son, with the Delphic utterances: "Section 35 of the Act; they'd better settle it out of court"; and dropped two used envelopes vaguely in the direction of wastepaper basket, pounced upon a sheet of closely written notepaper, and scowled at it, rubbing the tip of his nose with his forefinger. "This is it," he announced. "You'd better have it, Superintendent. May mean nothing: may mean a lot. Here, Giles, you take a look at it! What did the fellow think I could tell him that he didn't know already? Arnold all over! Wasting my time with his rubbishy questions! But I don't like to hear this about Tony: what's the wretched child about to get herself entangled with this young waster? Read it!"

By this time Giles was doing so. When he came to the end, he held it out to Hannasyde, saying: "I think this comes rather pat, don't you?"

The letter was on office paper, but written by hand, and by

a man in a raging temper. *"Dear Uncle,"* it began, and continued abruptly: *"What is the legal position of this firm in the case of systematic tampering with the accounts on the part of an employee? I've caught this damned whipper-snapper Mesurier out, and I want to prosecute, but wish to know how I stand before taking definite action. I have had him up, and he has the insolence to expect me to condone it because, if you please, he is paying back what he calls the 'loan' in his own good time! Does this prejudice my case, or not? Major portion of the sum stolen is still owing. Surely I have a case? Don't reply with any sentimental drivel; the skunk has got himself engaged to that damned little fool, Antonia, and I want him exposed. Kindly give this matter your immediate attention, and advise."*

The Superintendent read this through with his usual deliberation. "Yes, it does come pat," he said. "You're quite right. A bit hard on this chap Mesurier, wasn't he?"

Mr. Carrington, who was once more hunting through the litter on his desk, temporarily abandoned this new search, and swung his chair round so that he faced Hannasyde. "Hard? Infernally vindictive, sir, that's what my nephew Arnold is—was!" He paused, and added with a growl: *"De mortuis nil nisi bonum,"* as a sort of general absolution. "But I never in my life met a fellow with a worse temper, or worse manners, or a worse heart, or a more obstinate, pig-headed——"

"He wasn't as bad as all that, sir," objected Giles.

"Don't interrupt," said Mr. Carrington sternly. He transferred his attention to Hannasyde. "You can keep that letter. You look a sensible man, as far as I can judge. I've no desire to get this Mesurier fellow into trouble, but I've still less desire to see you Yard men barking up what I trust is the wrong tree. I'm not acting for that benighted young nephew of mine— though why I call him my nephew I don't know: he isn't— and thank God for it! but from what I know of him—— Yes, what is it?"

A clerk had tapped at the door, and entered. He said in a low voice: "For Mr. Giles, sir."

"Well?" said Giles, turning his head. "Anything urgent?"

"Mr. Kenneth Vereker has called, sir, and would be glad if

you could spare him a few minutes. He says it is very urgent."

"Tell him I'm engaged at the moment, but if he cares to wait, I'll see him later."

Hannasyde craned forward. "I wonder if you would mind if I saw Mr. Kenneth Vereker?" he asked.

Giles and his father's eyes met for an instant. Charles Carrington said briefly: "Tell Mr. Vereker that Superintendent Hannasyde is here and would like to see him."

"Yes, sir." The clerk went out.

Two minutes later Kenneth walked in, dressed in disreputable grey flannel trousers, a shirt with a soft collar and a flowing tie, and an old tweed coat. A plume of dark hair fell over one eyebrow and the eyes themselves were bright, and inquisitive and alert. "Hullo, Uncle! Hullo, Giles!" he said airily. "Where's the lamb-like policeman! Good Lord, I don't see anything lamb-like about you! Another of Tony's lies! I've come to the conclusion I'd better reserve my defence, by the way. Saw it in the *News of the World* yesterday, and it seemed to me a good idea."

"I wish," said Mr. Carrington testily, "that you would refrain from walking into my office looking like a third-rate artist from Chelsea!"

"Why?" asked Kenneth, interested.

"Because I don't like it!" replied Mr. Carrington, floored. "And nor do I like that effeminate tie!"

"If it comes to that I don't like yours," said Kenneth. "I think it's a ghastly tie, but I shouldn't have said so if you hadn't started on mine, because I believe in the Rights of the Individual. But as a matter of fact it's about my clothes that I'm here, more or less." He turned to Hannasyde and said affably: "You don't mind if I get my business done first, do you?"

"Not at all," answered Hannasyde, on whom, for all his apparently disinterested attitude, not one gesture or inflexion of the voice had been lost. "If you would like to speak to Mr. Carrington alone, I can wait outside."

"Oh lord, no! It isn't private!" Kenneth assured him. "It's only about Arnold's money. I am the heir, aren't I, Giles? Damn it, I must be! He can't have upset Father's Will. Well, can I have some of it advanced to me? I must have some new shirts, for one thing, and I can't get 'em on tick since Arnold said he wouldn't be responsible for my debts, blast him! Also, Maxton's have sent me a stinker to say if I don't settle their account they will have to take steps. And if taking steps means jug, I can't possibly be jugged for at least another fortnight, because I'm working on a picture. So do you mind coughing up some of the needful?''

It was quite impossible to stem this tide of disastrous eloquence. After one quick, warning frown, Giles abandoned the attempt, and heard his client out in silence. Mr. Charles Carrington, his elbows on the arms of his chair, and his fingertips lightly touching, sat watching the Superintendent, quite unperturbed. When his nephew paused for breath, he turned his head, and said with something of his son's mildness: ''How much do you want, Kenneth?''

''I want five hundred pounds,'' replied Kenneth promptly. ''Three hundred is absolutely urgent, and if it won't run to five, I could make three do. But I want a hundred to buy a ring with, and another hundred for splurging about. I can buy a ring for a hundred, can't I, Giles?''

''Several, I should think,'' replied Giles.

''Must be diamonds,'' explained Kenneth. ''Large, flashy ones. You know: the kind of thing which makes you want to vomit. It's for Violet. I haven't given her one yet, and that's the deluded wench's taste. I wouldn't put it above her to hanker after a ruby tiara once I touch Arnold's millions, bless her vulgar little heart!''

Giles intervened. ''We'll talk it over later. I can lend you some money to tide you over. Is that all you came about?''

''That's enough, isn't it?'' said Kenneth. ''Murgatroyd's got it into her head that bailiffs will storm the place at any moment. I can't see what on earth it matters as long as they don't get in our way, but she won't listen to reason, and, as a matter of fact, I daresay they would be a bit of a nuisance. Because we've only got one sitting-room, you know.''

''All right, I'll come along this evening and arrange something,'' promised Giles. ''Meanwhile Superintendent Hannasyde wants to ask you some questions.''

"I just want to know what your movements were on Saturday evening," said Hannasyde pleasantly.

"I know you do, but according to Giles you won't believe a word of my story," replied Kenneth. "My point is that you can't disprove it. If you've got any sense you won't try. You'll simply arrest my sister, and be done with it. I call her behaviour fishy in the extreme. Moreover, any girl who gets engaged to a human wen like Mesurier deserves to be hanged. What did you make of him, Giles?"

"I hardly know him. Try to stick to the point."

"Well, I think he's a blister," said Kenneth frankly.

Hannasyde said patiently: "May I hear this story which I can't disprove?"

"Sorry, I'd forgotten you for the moment," said Kenneth, and seating himself on a corner of the desk which happened to be free from litter, related with unexpected conciseness the history of his movements on Saturday. "And that's that," he concluded, delving in his pocket for an evil-looking meerschaum. "My fiancée says it's such a rotten story you're bound to believe it. She ought to know. She reads about seven detective thrillers a week, so she's pretty well up in crime."

Hannasyde looked at him rather searchingly. "You don't remember the picture-theatre you visited, or even what street it is in, or what the film was about, Mr. Vereker?"

"No," said Kenneth, unrolling an oilskin tobacco pouch, and beginning, under his uncle's fermenting stare, to fill the meerschaum.

"That argues a singularly bad memory, doesn't it?"

"Vile," agreed Kenneth. "But anyone'll tell you I've no memory."

"I'm surprised that with such a bad memory you are able to tell me so exactly what you did that evening," said Hannasyde gently.

"Oh, I learned that off by heart!" replied Kenneth, putting his pipe in his mouth, and restoring the pouch to his pocket.

Superintendent Hannasyde was not a man to show surprise readily, but this ingenuous explanation bereft him momentarily of speech. Giles's slow voice filled the gap: "Don't try to be funny, I implore you. What do you mean?"

Charles Carrington, whose attention had been successfully switched from the meerschaum, watched Kenneth with an air of impersonal interest. "Yes, what do you mean?" he inquired.

"Just what I said," responded Kenneth, striking a match. Between puffs, he continued: "After Giles had gone, last night, it dawned on me that I'd better make sure I didn't forget what I did on Saturday. So I wrote it all down, and learned it by heart in case I lost the book of the words."

The Superintendent, recovering, put rather a stern question: "Do you remember anything at all of what you did, Mr. Vereker, or are you merely favouring me with a recitation?"

"Of course I remember," said Kenneth impatiently. "You can't go on repeating a saga without remembering it. If you mean, Did I make it up? certainly not! I should have thought out a much better story than that. Something really classy. As a matter of fact, my sister and I concocted a beauty, but we decided against using it because of the mental strain. If you make a thing up you keep forgetting some of the ramifications, and then you're in the soup."

"I'm glad you realize that," said Hannasyde dryly. "Will your memory go back as far as the third of June?"

"What's to-day?" asked Kenneth, willing to oblige, but cautious.

"To-day, Mr. Vereker, is the nineteenth of June."

"Then I shouldn't think it would. It all depends. Not if you're going to ask me what I had for breakfast that day, or whether I went out for a walk, or——"

"I am going to ask you whether you remember writing a letter to your half-brother, requesting him to give or to lend you five hundred pounds?"

"Did I write that on the third?"

"You remember writing the letter, even though you may not remember the date?"

"You bet I do," said Kenneth. "I've been kicking myself for having done it ever since I heard about the murder. Didn't I tell you the swine would keep my letter, Giles?"

"Do you also remember a second letter which you wrote your half-brother—presumably upon receipt of his refusal to send you any money?"

Kenneth frowned. "No, I'm afraid I don't. Did I write a second time?"

The Superintendent opened his pocket-book and took out a single sheet of notepaper. "Isn't that it, Mr. Vereker?"

Kenneth leaned forward to read it, and burst out laughing. "Oh lord, yes! Sorry! I'd forgotten that for a moment."

"You were angry enough to write a letter telling your half-brother that it would give you great pleasure to wring his neck——"

"Bloody neck," corrected Kenneth.

"Yes, his bloody neck is the term you used. You felt that strongly enough to write it, and then forgot all about it?"

"No, I forgot I'd written it," said Kenneth. "I didn't forget that I wanted to wring his neck. My memory's not as bad as that."

"I see. Am I to understand that this violent desire persisted?"

Giles made a slight movement as of protest, but Kenneth spoke before he could be stopped. "More or less. Whenever I happened to think about him. But it was only a beautiful dream. I couldn't have pulled it off. Arnold was too beefy for me to tackle single-handed."

There was an infinitesimal pause. Then the Superintendent said: "I see. I think you said you are engaged to be married?" Kenneth nodded: "Have you been engaged long, Mr. Vereker?"

"Three months, more or less."

"When do you mean to be married, if I may ask?"

"I think you mayn't, Superintendent," said Giles, shifting his shoulders against the mantelpiece.

"You must advise your client as you see fit, Mr. Carrington, but it is a question that will be asked," Hannasyde said.

"Let him ask me anything he likes," said Kenneth. "I don't mind. I haven't got any feeling against the police. I don't know when I'm going to be married. My betrothed has religious scruples."

"Has what?" asked Hannasyde, startled.

Kenneth waved his pipe vaguely in the air. "Religious scruples. Respect due to the dead. All against the funeral baked-meats coldly furnishing forth the marriage tables. *Romeo and Juliet,"* he added.

"*Hamlet,"* said the Superintendent coldly.

"Shakespeare, anyway."

"Do you mean that your fiancée wishes to postpone the wedding until you're out of mourning?"

"She can't. She knows perfectly well I'm not going into mourning."

"Mr. Vereker, had you arranged a date for your wedding before Saturday, or not?"

"Not."

"I'm going to ask you a very straightforward question, which your solicitor won't like," said Hannasyde, with a faint smile. "Was the wedding-day unsettled because of money troubles?"

"You needn't bother about my solicitor," said Kenneth amiably. "When a thing stands out a mile, you don't catch me queering my pitch by denying it. Money it was. The lady's not in favour of a two-pair back. By the way, that was something I wanted to ask you, Giles. What *is* a two-pair back?"

"I don't know," said Giles.

"Well, it doesn't really matter," said Kenneth, banishing the question. "Now Arnold's dead the point doesn't arise."

"No," agreed Giles, of intent. "Whatever a two-pair back may be it isn't anything like the Eaton Place house."

Kenneth took his pipe out of his mouth. "Let's get this straight!" he requested. "Nothing would make me live in that high-class mansion, or any other remotely resembling it! That's final, and you may tell Violet so with my loving compliments."

"All right. Where *do* you propose to live?"

"Where I'm living now. If Violet wants ropes of pearls, and a brocade bed, and a Rolls-Royce, she can have 'em, but there it ends. I utterly refuse to alter my habits." He stood up, and pushed the lock of hair back from his forehead. "You can also tell her," he said, his eyes very bright all at once, "that these hands"—he flung them out, the fingers spread wide—"are worth more than all Arnold's filthy money, and when he's been forgotten for centuries people will still be talking about me!"

Charles Carrington blinked, and looked to see how Hannasyde received this sudden outburst. Hannasyde was watching Kenneth. He said nothing. Kenneth's brilliant, challenging gaze came to rest on his impassive face. "That's what you don't yet grasp!" he said. "I might have killed Arnold because I loathed him, and his money-grubbing mind, and his vulgar tastes, but not for his two hundred and fifty thousand pounds!"

"Don't you want his two hundred and fifty thousand pounds?" asked Hannasyde conversationally.

"Don't ask me dam' silly questions," snapped Kenneth. "Of course I do! Who wouldn't?"

Hannasyde got up. "No one of my acquaintance," he answered. "I've no more questions to ask you at the moment, dam' silly or otherwise."

"Good," said Kenneth. "Then I'll depart. Don't forget to come round to-night, Giles. And mind the wolf! According to Murgatroyd it's at the door. Good-bye, Uncle. Give my love to Aunt Janet."

"I must be going too," said Hannasyde, as the door shut behind Kenneth. "I may act as I think fit with regard to this letter, Mr. Carrington?"

Charles Carrington nodded. "Use your discretion, Superintendent. I expect you've got a lot, hey?"

Hannasyde smiled. "I hope so," he said. He turned to Giles. "I shall see you to-morrow at the inquest, shan't I?"

Giles held out his hand. "Yes, I shall be there."

Hannasyde gripped the hand for a moment, a certain friendly warmth in his eyes. "I'll let you know if anything interesting transpires."

He went out, and Charles Carrington pushed back his chair from the desk. "Well, well, well!" he said. "Sheer waste of my time, of course, but not unamusing."

"I've half a mind to ask Kenneth to look for another solicitor," said Giles ruefully.

His father sat up, and resumed his search amongst the papers on his desk. "Nonsense!" he said briskly. "That boy is either an incorrigibly truthful young ass, or a brilliantly clever actor. He's got your Superintendent Hannasyde guessing, Giles. What's more, he's got you guessing as well. You don't know whether he did it or not.''

"No, I don't. I don't even know whether he'd be capable of doing it. He's a queer fish. Curiously cold-blooded.''

"He's capable of it, all right. But whether he did it or not I can't make out. Where the devil *are* my spectacles?''

CHAPTER 8

THE Deputy-manager of the Shan Hills Mining Company, Mr. Harold Fairfax, received Superintendent Hannasyde with anxious deference, and raised no objection at all to the Superintendent's request that he might be allowed to question certain members of the staff. Mr. Fairfax was a spare little man of middle age, and seemed to be in a perpetual state of being worried. He could throw no light on the mystery of Arnold Vereker's death. "You see," he said unhappily, "so many people disliked Mr. Vereker. He was a hard man, oh, a very hard man! I—I believe he trusted me. I like to think he did. We never quarrelled. Sometimes he would be very short with me, but I have known him a great many years, and I think I understood him. It is a dreadful thing, his murder; an appalling thing. And all, perhaps, because someone couldn't make allowances for his temper!"

Miss Miller, Arnold Vereker's secretary, was more helpful. She was a businesslike-looking woman, of an age hard to determine. She fixed her cold, competent eyes on the Superintendent, and answered his questions with a composure tinged with contempt. She told him the exact hour of Arnold Vereker's arrival at the office on Saturday morning; she recited a list of the engagements he had had, and described his callers. "At five-and-twenty minutes past ten," she said

71

briskly, "Mr. Vereker sent for Mr. Mesurier, who remained in his room for twenty-seven minutes."

"You are very exact, Miss Miller," said the Superintendent politely.

She smiled with tolerant superiority. "Certainly, I pride myself on being efficient. Mr. Mesurier was sent for immediately after the departure of Sir Henry Watson, whose appointment, as I have informed you, was at ten o'clock. Mr. Cedric Johnson, of Messrs. Johnson, Hayes & Heverside, had an appointment with Mr. Vereker at eleven, and arrived seven minutes early. I informed Mr. Vereker at once, through the medium of the house telephone, and Mr. Vereker then came out, and, I presume, returned to his own office."

"Thank you." said the Superintendent. "Can you tell me if there was any unpleasantness during any of Mr. Vereker's appointments that morning?"

"Yes; Mr. Vereker's interview with Mr. Mesurier was, I imagine, extremely unpleasant."

"Why do you imagine that, Miss Miller?"

She raised her brows. "The room which is my office communicates with the late Mr. Vereker's. I could hardly fail to be aware of a quarrel taking place behind the intervening doors."

"Do you know what the quarrel was about?"

"If I did I should immediately have volunteered the information, which must necessarily be of importance. But it is not my custom either to listen at keyholes, or to waste my employer's time. During Mr. Vereker's interview with Mr. Mesurier, and his subsequent one with Mr. Cedric Johnson, I occupied myself with Mr. Vereker's correspondence, using the dictaphone and a typewriter. What was said, therefore, I did not hear, or wish to hear. From time to time both voices were raised to what I can only describe as shouting-pitch. More than that I am not prepared to say."

He put one or two other questions to her, and then got rid of her, and asked to see Mr. Rudolph Mesurier.

Mesurier came in five minutes later. He looked rather white, but greeted Hannasyde easily and cheerfully. "Superintendent Hannasyde, isn't it? Good-morning. You're investigating the cause of Arnold Vereker's death, I understand. Rather an awful thing, isn't it? I mean, stabbed like that, in the back.

Anything I can tell you that might help you I shall be only too glad to—only I'm afraid I can't tell you much." He laughed apologetically, and sat down on one side of the bare mahogany table, carefully hitching up his beautifully creased trousers. "Just what is it you want to know?" he asked.

"Well, I want to know several things, Mr. Mesurier," answered the Superintendent. "Can you remember where you were on Saturday evening between the hours of—let us say eleven o'clock and two o'clock?"

Mesurier wrinkled his brow. "Let me see now: Saturday! Oh yes, of course! I was at home. Redclyffe Gardens, Earl's Court. I have digs there."

"Are you sure that you were at home then, Mr. Mesurier?"

"Well, really——!" Mesurier laughed again, a little nervously. "I was certainly under that impression! I had a bit of a head that night, and I went to bed early."

Hannasyde looked at him for a few moments. Mesurier stared back into his eyes, and moistened his lips. "Where do you garage your car?" asked Hannasyde.

"What an odd question! Just round the corner. I have a lock-up garage, you know, in a mews."

"Are you always careful to keep that garage locked, Mr. Mesurier?"

Mesurier replied a shade too quickly. "Oh, I'm afraid I'm rather casual sometimes! Of course, I do usually see that it's locked, but occasionally, when I've been in a hurry—you know how it is!"

"Did you use your car at all on Saturday?"

"No, I don't think I—— Oh yes, I did, though!"

"At what time?"

"Well, I don't really remember. In the afternoon."

"And when did you return it to the garage?"

Mesurier uncrossed his legs, and then crossed them again. "It must have been sometime during the early part of the evening. I'm afraid I'm a bit hazy about times. And of course, not knowing that it would be important—the time I garaged the car, I mean——"

"Are you sure, Mr. Mesurier, that when you say the early part of the evening, you don't mean the early part of the morning?"

"I—I don't understand you. I've already told you I went to bed early. I don't quite follow what you're driving at. I mean, if you think I had anything to do with Arnold Vereker's death it's too utterly absurd."

"The proprietor of the four lock-up garages in the mews," said Hannasyde, consulting his notes, "states that you took your car out at approximately five o'clock."

"I daresay he's quite right. I certainly shan't dispute it. I told you it was during the afternoon. What I don't understand is why you should be so interested in my movements. Frightfully thorough of you, and all that, but I must say I find it rather amusing that you should actually take the trouble to question them at the garage!"

"The proprietor further states," continued Hannasyde unemotionally, "that at one-forty a.m., on Sunday, he was awakened by the sound of one of the garages being opened. Apparently the garage you rent is immediately beneath his bedroom. He declares that he recognized the engine-note of the car being driven into the garage."

"Of course that's perfectly preposterous!" Mesurier said. "In any case, it wasn't my car. Unless, of course, someone else had her out. If I forget to lock the garage they might easily have done so, you know."

"Who?" asked Hannasyde.

"Who?" Mesurier looked quickly across at him, and away again. "I'm sure I don't know! Anybody!"

"Whoever took your car out on Saturday evening must have had a key to the garage, Mr. Mesurier. The proprietor states that when you had left the mews in the car shortly after five he himself shut the doors. When he went to bed at ten-thirty they were still locked."

"I daresay he was mistaken. Not that I'm saying anyone did take my car out. It's much more likely that the car he heard at one-forty-five was someone else's. I mean, he was probably half-asleep, and anyway he could not recognize the engine-note so positively as all that."

"You will agree, then, that it is highly improbable that anyone should have taken your car out of the garage on Saturday night?"

"Well, I—it looks like it, certainly, but I don't *know* that no one did. I mean. . . . Look here, I don't in the least see why you should bother so much about my car when I've told you——"

"I'm bothering about it, Mr. Mesurier, because your car was seen by a Constable on patrol-duty, at a point known as Dimbury Corner, ten miles from Hanborough, on the London Road, at twenty-six minutes to one on Sunday morning," said Hannasyde.

Again Mesurier moistened his lips, but for a moment or two he did not speak. The ticking of a solid-looking clock on the mantelpiece became suddenly audible. Mesurier glanced at it, as though the measured sound got on his nerves, and said: "He must have been mistaken, that's all I can say."

"Is the number of your car AMG240?" asked Hannasyde.

"Yes. Yes, it is."

"Then I don't think he was mistaken," said Hannasyde.

"He must have been. He misread the number. Probably ANG, or—or AHG. In any case, I wasn't on the Hanborough Road at that hour." He put up a hand to his head, and smoothed his sleek black hair. "If that's all the case you've got against me. . . . I mean, this Constable's memory against my word, I don't think much of it. Not that I wish to be offensive, you know. You detectives have to try everything, of course, but——"

"Quite so, Mr. Mesurier." The Superintendent's even voice effectually silenced Mesurier. "You are only being asked to account for your movements on Saturday night. If you were in your lodgings all the evening you can no doubt produce a witness to corroborate the truth of that statement?"

"No, I don't think I can," Mesurier said with an uneasy smile. "My landlady and her husband always go out on Saturday evening, so they wouldn't know whether I was in or out." He became aware of a piece of cotton on his sleeve and picked it off, and began to fidget with it.

"That is unfortunate," said Hannasyde, and once more consulted his notes. He said abruptly: "You had an interview with Arnold Vereker at ten-thirty on Saturday morning. Is that correct?"

"Well, I wouldn't swear to the exact time, but I did see him on Saturday."

"Was the interview an unpleasant one, Mr. Mesurier?"

"Unpleasant? I don't quite——"

"Did a quarrel take place between you and Mr. Vereker on that occasion?"

"Oh lord, no!" Mesurier cried. "Vereker was a bit peeved that morning, but we did not *quarrel*. I mean, why should we?"

Hannasyde laid his notes down. "I think," he said, "that we shall get along faster if I tell you at once, Mr. Mesurier, that I am in possession of a certain letter concerning you which Mr. Vereker wrote to the firm's solicitor on Saturday. You may read it, if you choose."

Mesurier held out his hand for the letter, and said: "This —this isn't Vereker's writing."

"No, it is mine," said Hannasyde. "That is a copy of the original."

Mesurier, a tinge of colour in his cheeks, read the letter, and put it down on the table. "I don't know what you expect me to say. It's an absolute misstatement——"

"Mr. Mesurier, please understand me! The particular point raised in that letter does not concern me. I am not investigating the accounts of this company but the murder of its chairman. The information contained in the letter tells me that your interview with Arnold Vereker on Saturday morning cannot have been a pleasant one. In addition, I have already ascertained that both your voices were heard raised in anger. Now——"

"That bloody cat, Rose Miller!" exclaimed Mesurier, flushing. "Of course, if you're going to believe what she says . . . ! She's always had her knife into me. It's a complete lie to say that we quarrelled. Vereker went for me, and I shan't attempt to deny that he was in a bad temper. In fact, he actually accused me of embezzling. Utterly ridiculous, I need hardly say. As a matter of fact I got into a bit of a mess—lost a packet racing, if you want to know how—and I—I borrowed a little from the firm, just to tide me over. Of course I know I oughtn't to have done it, but when you're hard pressed you do silly things. But to say I stole the money is—is positively laughable! I mean, if I'd wanted to do that I shouldn't be paying it back, which even Vereker admits I am doing. He simply had a down on me——''

"Because he had discovered that you had become engaged to his half-sister?"

"That had nothing to do with him at all!" Mesurier said quickly. "He didn't care a brass farthing about Tony."

"He seemed to think it had a great deal to do with him," said Hannasyde, a dry note in his voice. "He threatened you with exposure, didn't he?"

"Oh, he threatened me with all sorts of things!" said Mesurier. "I can't say I took him very seriously, though. I knew perfectly well he wouldn't prosecute when he'd had time to think it over. I mean, it would be too silly, on the face of it."

"Would it?" said Hannasyde. "You will admit, I imagine, that if he had prosecuted you for—er—borrowing the firm's money, your career would have been ruined."

"I don't know so much about that," Mesurier said uneasily. "Of course, it would have been damned unpleasant, but——"

"I am speaking entirely in your interests, Mr. Mesurier, when I say that the best thing you can do is to tell me the truth about your movements on Saturday night. Think it over."

"I don't need to. You can't prove it was my car that the bobby thought he saw—and even if it was it certainly wasn't me driving it." He got up. "That's absolutely all I have to say."

"Then I won't keep you any longer," said Hannasyde. "But I still advise you to think it over."

By the time the Superintendent left the Shan Hills Mining Company's premises it was past four o'clock. Awaiting him in the main hall of the building was his subordinate, one Sergeant Hemingway, a cheerful person with a bright eye and a persuasive manner. They went out together to the nearest tea-shop, and, over cups of strong tea, compared notes.

"The trouble is," remarked the Sergeant at length, "there's too many people with good motives. I never like that kind of case, Super. Do you remember the Ottershaw murder? Took ten years off my life, that did." He prodded one of the buns which the waitress had set before them, and shook his head. "Not at my age," he said. "You ought to be able to have 'em up for foisting that kind of food on the public. Keep me awake all night, that would. Take this young Vereker chap. He's a new one on me, Super. Make anything of him?"

"No," said Hannasyde slowly. "Nothing at all yet. He's a new one on me too. I suspect, a mighty slippery customer."

"He's got the biggest motive of the lot, I know that. Here, miss, you take these buns back where they came from, which was the dustbin, I should think, judging from the look of them, and bring a nice plate of bread-and-butter, there's a good girl."

"Sauce!" said the waitress, tossing her head.

The Sergeant winked at her, and turned back to Hannasyde. "Smart-looking girl, that. Well, now, I've got something for you. I went round to this studio, according to your instructions, and got talking to the skivvy there. Regular old cough-drop she is, too. Name of Murgatroyd. Used to be personal maid to the second Mrs. Vereker before she was married, *and* after. Stopped on after Mrs. Vereker died, and acted nurse to the kids. You get the layout, Super. She's the devoted family retainer all right. Well, I did what I could, jollying her along, but she was close as an oyster—— Thank you, miss." He waited until the waitress had removed herself out of earshot, and then continued: "Close as an oyster. Suspicious and wary. But one thing she did say and stuck to."

"What was it?"

The Sergeant folded one of the slices of bread-and-butter in half, and put it into his mouth. When it was possible for him to speak intelligibly, he said: "She told me that whatever anyone might say to the contrary she was ready to get up and swear her Master Kenneth was safely tucked up in his bed and sleeping like a lamb at midnight on Saturday."

"Did she really say that?" inquired Hannasyde, mildly curious.

"I won't swear to it those were her exact words," replied the Sergeant, unabashed. "I may have made it a bit more poetic. But that was the gist of it. Now you tell me that the said Master Kenneth admits he was rampaging round town up till four o'clock. Bit of a departmental muddle, Super. Looks like they haven't got together enough over the question of alibis.''

"I don't make much of it," said Hannasyde. "It's obvious that young Vereker's position is very weak, and if this Murgatroyd is a devoted old servant, that's just the sort of gallant attempt to protect him you'd expect her to make.''

"I'm not saying it isn't, Super. I'll go so far as to say it is. But what I'll say is that the old girl's scared. She's afraid young Vereker did it. If she was plumb-sure he didn't she'd have bitten my head off for daring to come round suspecting her darling boy.''

Hannasyde put down his cup. "Look here, did she talk like that or not?''

"She did not," said the Sergeant. "That's my point, Super. I figured she would.''

"Why?''

"Psychology," said the Sergeant, vaguely waving his fourth slice of bread-and-butter in the air.

"Cut it out," said his superior unkindly. "What did you find out about Vereker's chauffeur?''

"It wasn't him. You'll have to rule him out, Super. No good at all. I'll tell you what he was doing on Saturday.''

"You needn't bother. Put it in a report. I think I'll pay a call on Miss Vereker.''

The Sergeant cocked a wise eyebrow. "All on account of Light-fingered Rudolph? She gets a letter from Arnold, spilling the beans about him cooking the accounts, and threatening to ruin him, so down she goes to plead for Rudolph, and when that turns out to be no use, sticks a knife in the cruel half-brother. I haven't worked out how she got him in the stocks, but from what I can make out about these Verekers that's just the sort of joke they would pull, and think a proper scream. Myself I haven't got that type of humour, but it takes all sorts to make a world. It's a wonder anyone ever gets out of these tea and bun bazaars, the trouble it is to get the girls to come across with the bill. I've been trying to catch Henna'ed Hannah's eye for the past ten minutes. I know what my job is now, Super. I've got to check up on Friend Rudolph.'' He looked shrewdly at his chief, for he had worked with him often before, and knew him. "Worried about Rudolph, aren't you, Super?"

"Yes, I am," replied Hannasyde. "He fits, and yet he doesn't fit. See what you can find out, Hemingway."

The Sergeant nodded. "I will that, sir. But he can't have done it. Not to my way of thinking. Here, Gladys—Maud—Gwendolyn, whatever your name is—tell me this: Are you standing us this tea?"

"I never did! You haven't half got a nerve!" said the waitress, giggling.

"I only asked because you seemed kind of shy of bringing the bill," said the Sergeant.

"You *are* a one!" said the waitress, greatly diverted.

CHAPTER 9

MURGATROYD, opening the door to Superintendent Hannasyde, stood squarely in the aperture and asked him aggressively what he wanted. He asked if Miss Vereker was in and she said: "That's as may be. Your name, please, and business."

His eyes twinkled. "My name is Hannasyde, and my business is with Miss Vereker."

"I know very well what you are," said Murgatroyd. "I've had another of you here to-day, and I've had enough. If the police would let well alone it would be a good thing for everyone." She stood aside to allow him to enter, and led him across the tiny hall to the studio. "It's the police again, Miss Tony," she announced. "I suppose you'd better see him."

Antonia was sitting by the window with two of her dogs at her feet. One of them, Bill, recognized an acquaintance in the Superintendent, and wildly thumped his tail; his daughter, Juno, however, got up growling.

"Ah, who says dogs have no sense?" said Murgatroyd darkly.

"Shut up, Juno!" commanded Antonio. "Oh, it's the Superintendent! That means I'm going to be interrogated all over again. Have some tea?"

"Thank you, Miss Vereker, but I've had tea," said Hannasyde, his eyes on a big canvas on the easel.

Antonia said kindly: *"Dawn Wind,* but it isn't finished yet. My brother's new picture."

Hannasyde went up to look more closely at it. "Your brother told me to-day that his hands are worth more than all your half-brother's money," he remarked.

"Yes, he does think a lot of himself," agreed Antonia. "You'll have to get used to that sort of swank if you mean to see much of him."

"Well, I was thinking that he's probably right," said Hannasyde. "I don't pretend to know much about art, but——"

"Don't say that!" besought Antonia. "Every well-meaning idiot says it. What on earth are you standing there for, Murgatroyd?"

"You may be glad of me staying," said Murgatroyd grimly.

"Well, I shan't. Not after the way you shoved your finger into Kenneth's pie with all that rot about him being in bed at midnight."

"What I've said I stand by," replied Murgatroyd.

"What's the use of standing by it when nobody believes you?" said Antonia reasonably. "Anyway, don't stand there, because it puts me off."

"Well, you know where I am if you want me," Murgatroyd replied, and withdrew.

"Sit down," invited Antonia. "What do you want to know?"

"What was in that letter?" replied the Superintendent promptly.

"Which letter?—Oh, Arnold's! Nothing much."

"If there was nothing much in it why did you destroy it?" asked Hannasyde.

"It was that sort of letter."

"What sort of letter?"

"The sort you destroy—— Look here, we're beginning to sound like a pair of cross-talk comedians!" Antonia pointed out.

"Very like," agreed the Superintendent evenly. "Did you destroy the letter because it contained a rather serious accusation against Mr. Rudolph Mesurier?"

Antonia looked defensive. "It didn't."

"Quite sure, Miss Vereker?"

Antonia propped her chin in her hands and frowned. "I wish I could remember what I said in that ghoulish Police Station," she said. "I almost wish I hadn't burned the letter, too. Because you seem to think it was frightfully important, and as a matter of fact it wasn't. It was just a general hate against Rudolph."

"No specific charge?"

"No. He just ran through Roget's Thesaurus for synonyms of Scoundrel, and put them all into the letter."

"You say that there was no specific charge, Miss Vereker, but does a business man like your half-brother threaten to take legal proceedings against another man without any definite reason?"

"The whole point is, did he mean it, or was he merely woffling?" Antonia said, off her guard. "That's what I went to find out." She broke off and flushed angrily. "Damn you, you don't play fair!"

"I am not playing, Miss Vereker."

She looked up quickly, for there was a hint of sternness in his voice. Before she had time to speak he went on: "Arnold Vereker wrote to you forbidding your engagement to Mesurier. According to you, he gave no definite reason for this. But you have admitted that he threatened to prosecute Mesurier for some offence or other, and you have also admitted that his letter made you exceedingly angry."

"Of course it did!" she said impatiently. "It would make anybody angry!"

"I expect so. Perhaps it may also have alarmed you?"

"No, why should it? I wasn't afraid of Arnold."

"Not on your own account, but you were alarmed for Mesurier?"

"No, because I didn't take the letter seriously."

"You took it seriously enough to drive all the way to Ashleigh Green that day."

"Only because I wanted to know just what Arnold had against Rudolph, and to stop him spreading any filthy story about him."

"How did you propose to do that, Miss Vereker?"

She considered this. "I don't know. I mean, I don't think I'd worked it out."

"In fact, you were so angry with him that you got straight into your car and drove to Ashleigh Green without having the least idea what you would do when you got there?"

"Oh no!" said Antonia sarcastically. "I took a knife and stuck it into Arnold, and then went and spent the night in his house just to make sure you'd know I was the murderess; and finally told your silly policeman there were bloodstains on my skirt." She broke off, her ill humour suddenly vanishing. "Which isn't as idiotic as it sounds," she said. "Now I come to think of it, that wouldn't have been at all a bad plan if I'd murdered Arnold. In fact, definitely brilliant, because no jury would ever believe I could have been fool enough to loiter round the scene of the crime and brandish blood-stained garments about. I must put that to Giles." At this moment Kenneth strolled into the studio. Antonia immediately propounded her notions to him.

Superintendent Hannasyde had seen enough of the Verekers by this time to feel very little surprise at the enthusiasm with which Kenneth at once entered into a discussion.

"That's all very well," Kenneth said, "but what about the dog-fight?"

"I could easily have staged that," his sister said napoleonically.

"Not at that hour of night," objected Kenneth. "If you murdered Arnold and got blood on your clothes, meeting the retriever, or whatever it was, was sheer luck. Also you haven't piled up enough evidence against yourself. Obviously if you were clever enough to commit a murder and plant yourself down in the murdered man's house afterwards you ought to have told as many people as you could that you were going down to have it out with Arnold. No one'ld believe you killed him after that. What do you think, Superintendent?"

"I think," replied Hannasyde, exasperated, "that your tongues are likely to lead you into serious trouble."

"Ah!" said Kenneth, a wicked gleam in his eye. "That means you don't know what to make of us."

"Quite possibly," said Hannasyde, unsmiling, and took his leave. But he admitted later to his subordinate that the young devil had gauged the situation correctly.

Meanwhile Antonia had summoned her fiancé to come to see her as soon as he left the office. When he arrived, which was shortly after six o'clock, he found brother and sister arguing over the correct amount of absinthe to be put into the cocktail-shaker. Neither paid much attention to him until a decision had been reached, but when Kenneth had finally won his point on the score of being several years Antonia's senior, and the mixture had been well shaken and poured into the glasses, Antonia nodded to her betrothed and said: "I'm glad you were able to come. I've had the Superintendent-man here, and I think we ought to talk things over."

Rudolph shot her one quick glance and said: "How very serious you look, darling! You mustn't let all this get on your nerves, you know. What has the worthy Superintendent got in his bonnet now?"

"This is a bloody cocktail," said Kenneth dispassionately. "You can't have mixed it as I told you. If you think the human sleuth is interested in you you're wrong. He's hot on my trail, and I won't have him diverted. Oh here's Leslie! Leslie, my sweet, come on up!" He leaned out of the window and addressed Miss Rivers at the top of his voice. "The gyves are practically on my wrists, darling, so come up for a last cocktail. No, on second thoughts, don't. Tony mixed it. I'll stand you a drink at the Clarence Arms." He drew in his head, set his glass down on the table and vanished precipitately from the studio.

Antonia, her attention once more distracted from her fiancé, hung out of the window and conferred with Miss Rivers until Kenneth presently emerged into the mews and swept the visitor off in the direction of the Clarence Arms. She then turned back to Rudolph and demanded to know what they had been talking about.

"Oh, I think you were worried about the Superintendent, weren't you?" Mesurier said. "It's all frightfully upsetting for you, dearest."

"No, it isn't," said Antonia bluntly. "But what I want to

know is, what have you been up to, Rudolph?"

He changed colour, but replied with an amused laugh: "Up to, Tony? How do you mean?"

"Well," said Antonia, finishing her cocktail, "the impression I've got is that you've been forging Arnold's name or something."

"Tony!" he cried indignantly. "If *that's* the opinion you have of me——"

"Do shut up!" begged Antonia. "This is serious. It's why I went down to see Arnold on Saturday night. He said he was going to prosecute you."

"Swine!"

"I know, but what was it all about?"

Mesurier took a turn round the studio, his hands thrust into his pockets. "I'm in a damned awkward position!" he said suddenly. "God knows I didn't want you to be dragged into it, but if I don't tell you some one else will. Think me what you like, but——"

"Sorry to interrupt, but just open that cupboard and see if there's a bottle of salted almonds, will you?" asked Antonia. "I've suddenly remembered buying some and putting them either there or——"

"They aren't here," said Rudolph in an offended voice. "Of course, if salted almonds are more important to you than my——"

"No, but I distinctly remember getting some," said Antonia. "And if we've got some it seems a pity—— However, it doesn't really matter. Go on about the forgery."

"There is no forgery. Though God knows I've been through such a hell of anxiety about money that it's a wonder I'm *not* a forger!"

"Bad luck!" said Antonia, with polite but damping sympathy.

Mesurier said in a more natural voice: "They've found out something. Not that it can harm me. What I mean is, it doesn't prove I murdered Arnold, though it naturally makes the police suspicious. I—you see, Tony, I've been in the devil of a jam. Had to raise some cash somehow or other, and raise it quick, so I—sort of borrowed a spot from the firm—Arnold's firm, you know. Of course I need hardly tell you it was nothing but a loan, to tide me over, and as a matter of fact I've been steadily paying it back. You do understand, don't you, darling?"

"Yes, absolutely," replied Antonia. "You cooked the accounts, and Arnold found out. I've often wondered how that's done, by the way. How do you do it, Rudolph?"

He flushed. "Please——! It—this isn't very pleasant for me, Tony. I ought not to have done it, but I thought I could pay it all back before the next audit. I never dreamed Arnold had his eye on me. Then he sprang it on me—actually on Saturday morning. He was filthily offensive—you know what he could be like! We—we had a bit of a row, and he threatened to take the whole thing into court, largely, I'm afraid, because you'd told him of our engagement, darling. Not that I'm blaming you, but it was rather unfortunate, all things considered. And the devil of it is that we were heard—well—quarrelling—by that foul Miller girl, and, of course, she pitched in a highly exaggerated story to the Superintendent. And on top of that——" He paused, and studied his well-manicured nails for a moment, a pucker between his brows. "The most extraordinary thing," he said slowly. "I confess I don't understand it. Some idiot of a village Constable imagines he saw my car ten miles from Hanborough on Saturday night. It's utterly absurd, of course, but you can see what an ugly complexion it puts on things."

She sat up suddenly. "Rudolph, how did you know which day Arnold was murdered?"

He blinked at her. "I don't understand what you mean."

"Yes, you do. On Sunday, when you came here to supper, you said you'd quarrelled with Arnold on the very day he was murdered."

"Did I? I expect you'd told me, then. I don't know how else I could have known."

"I wish you'd stop being guarded," Antonia complained. "If you killed Arnold you might just as well say so, because Kenneth and I don't mind a bit about that, and we shouldn't dream of giving you away."

"I didn't kill him. For God's sake don't go about talking like that!"

"Well, what's all this about your car being seen near Hanborough?"

"It wasn't! I mean, I don't know whether it was or not, but *I* wasn't in it. I was in my digs all the evening. I can't prove that, but if they're going to take one sleepy bobby's word against mine——"

"The fact of the matter is none of us can prove anything," said Antonia cheerfully. "You've merely joined the noble army of suspects. Kenneth'll be rather fed-up if you become chief suspect. He thinks he's being awfully clever, and I daresay he is. He can be when he likes."

Rudolph let himself sink down into one of the big armchairs, and dropped his head in his hands. "You can treat it as a joke, but I tell you it's damned serious," he said, his voice a little unsteady. "That Superintendent thinks I did it. He doesn't believe anything I say. I can see he doesn't. I don't know what the hell to do, Tony!"

He sounded helpless, frightened, and although such a mood of panic was alien to her nature she responded at once as well as she could. "I shouldn't worry," she said, patting his knee. "I'll ask Giles what he thinks. He's coming here this evening to talk business with Kenneth. You don't mind, do you?"

He seemed undecided. "He knows anyway," he said. "Arnold wrote a letter about me to his uncle, and the Superintendent got it. Of course your cousin must have seen it. I don't know that I exactly *mind* consulting him, because I haven't anything to conceal. I mean—"

At this moment the studio door opened, and Giles Carrington came in, accompanied by Kenneth. Antonia greeted him with a friendly smile, but desired her brother to tell her what he had done with Miss Rivers.

"She pushed off homewards," answered Kenneth. "Cigarette, Giles?—if there are any, which I doubt."

"Oh, well, in that case we can talk!" said Antonia briskly. "Giles, do you know about Rudolph cooking the firm's accounts, or not?"

"What?" ejaculated Kenneth, pausing in his search for the

cigarettes, and turning to stare at Mesurier. "Actually embezzling funds? Did you really?"

His manner was partly interested, partly critical, and it goaded Rudolph, deeply flushed, to defend himself. His explanation was met with so derisive a laugh that Antonia at once took up the cudgels, and told her brother he needn't be offensive, because for one reason she wouldn't put it above him to cook accounts, and for another it had nothing to do with him.

"Oh yes, it has!" objected Kenneth. "You seem to forget I'm the heir. I daresay I could prosecute, if I wanted to. Not that I do, of course, though I do rather draw the line at embezzling. It's one thing to bump a man off, but quite another to monkey with his accounts. However, don't think I'm being captious. I expect it seemed good to you at the time,' Rudolph."

Mesurier said angrily: "I don't care for your tone! I'm willing to admit I shouldn't have borrowed the money, but when you accuse me of——"

"My bonny lad, I haven't accused you of anything," said Kenneth, beginning to fill a pipe. "Tony said you'd been cooking the firm's accounts; I merely displayed the proper amount of surprise, interest and disapproval."

Antonia had drawn her cousin over to the window, and stood there facing him, with one hand lightly grasping his sleeve. She looked gravely up at him and asked quietly: "He's in a mess, isn't he?"

"I don't know, Tony."

"Well, I think he is. You will help him, won't you, Giles?" He did not answer immediately, and she added after a moment: "You see, I'm engaged to be married to him."

"That isn't an inducement to me, Tony."

Her candid eyes were a trifle puzzled; they searched his unavailingly. "Isn't it?" she asked, seeking enlightenment. "No."

"Oh! Well—well—will you do it for me, Giles?"

He looked down at her, and at her hand, still clasping his sleeve. "I suppose so, Tony," he said in his level way, and glanced across the big room to where Mesurier and Kenneth were arguing. "Shut up, Kenneth," he said pleasantly. "Yes, I know about the letter my cousin wrote before his death, Mesurier. It doesn't prove, you know, that you had anything to do with his murder."

"No," agreed Antonia, "but the bit about the car is not so good. Tell my cousin, Rudolph; he really is quite helpful."

Mesurier gave a shrug to his shoulders. "Oh, that's nothing but a ridiculous mistake on the part of the police. Some local bobby imagines he saw my car near Hanborough on the night of the murder, Carrington."

"Policemen haven't got imaginations," said Kenneth, who had stretched himself along the sofa, his pipe between his teeth.

Giles was frowning slightly. "Where was your car?" he asked.

"In the garage, I suppose. I mean, I spent the evening at home."

"I see. Can you produce anyone to corroborate that statement?"

"No, as a matter of fact, I can't," said Mesurier, with a slight uncomfortable laugh. "Seems silly, but the truth is I had a bad headache, and I went to bed early."

"You are a rotten liar," observed Kenneth lazily. "Why bother? *We* won't give you away. I might even bestow a suitable reward on you. Or would that be indelicate?"

Giles said rather sternly: "Your own story is just as thin, Kenneth."

"Admittedly, but I tell it with a much better grace," Kenneth pointed out. "What do you think, Tony? Did he do it? I don't believe he had the nerve."

"Of course he had the nerve!" said Antonia indignantly. "The trouble with you is that you're so taken up with admiring your own cleverness in baffling the police that you don't think anyone else is capable of doing anything."

Giles, who had ignored this interchange, was looking steadily at Mesurier. "When you say that a bobby saw your car on the night of the murder, do you mean that he saw a car of the same make as yours, or that he actually read your number on its plate?"

"My number," Mesurier answered, "or so he thinks. But

he could easily have muddled it up with another, which is, of course, what he did do."

"I can so readily picture our friend the Superintendent lapping that story up," remarked Kenneth. "Tony, your young man promised well at one time, but he begins to bore me now."

Giles took out his cigarette-case and opened it. "It isn't for me to question your story, Mesurier. I can only say that if it's true I'm sorry."

"Sorry?" Rudolph ejaculated. "I don't understand you!"

Giles lit a cigarette and pitched the dead match into the grate. "For your sake, very. You had an excellent alibi there, Mesurier."

"Alibi! Where?"

"In the car," replied Giles. "For if you had been driving your car back to London from Hanborough that night I don't think you could very well have been the murderer."

CHAPTER 10

THE effect of this calm pronouncement was slightly ludicrous. Rudolph Mesurier blinked at him in a bewildered manner and said: "Then—then I might just as well have admitted I was out? But I don't understand what you're driving at!"

"It is always better to speak the truth," said Kenneth smugly. "Witness my own masterly conduct of this highly intricate case."

"I daresay," responded his sister. "But did you speak the truth?"

"That, my love," said Kenneth, "is for the police to find out."

"Oh, I wish you'd shut up!" Mesurier said, exasperated. "It's all very well for you to lie there and sneer, but I'm in a damned awkward position."

"So are we all," replied Kenneth, quite unmoved. "Moreover, this new development gives Tony a nice, pure motive for murdering Arnold. Tell me, Tony, would you really murder Arnold to protect Rudolph's fair name?"

"Yes, of course I would!" said Antonia bristling. "I don't mean that I approve of him embezzling funds, because, as a matter of fact, I think it's a poor show, but I wouldn't let Arnold prosecute him if I could stop it. If it comes to that, wouldn't you have murdered him for Violet's sake?"

"Don't confuse the motives. I murdered him for the sake of his money. You've got the noble motives: and Rudolph's is the sordid one."

"No more sordid than yours!"

"Oh yes, darling! Comes under the same heading as card-sharping and shop-lifting."

Giles interposed. "Shut up, Kenneth. None of this leads anywhere, and it isn't particularly pleasant for Mesurier. Were you out in your car on the night of the murder, Mesurier?"

Rudolph looked uncertainly from one to the other. "Don't be coy," recommended Kenneth. "We all know you were by this time."

"Well, as a matter of fact, I was," Rudolph said, taking the plunge. "That's what makes it so frightful." He began to walk jerkily up and down the studio. "When that detective asked me, I denied it. I mean, what else could I do? They can't *prove* I was out. It would be absolutely circumstantial evidence, and it seemed to me my best plan was to stick to it that I was at home. Only now *you*"—he looked at Giles—"say if I was out in my car I couldn't have done the murder, so . . ." He stopped and gave a nervous little laugh. "So now I don't know what to do."

"With any luck," remarked Kenneth, "we'll foist this murder on to Rudolph."

"I don't call that funny," said Mesurier stiffly.

"Depends on the point of view. It would be much funnier than having you as a brother-in-law."

Antonia bounced up out of her chair. "Damn you, shut up!" she said fiercely. "If it comes to that I'd a lot sooner foist the murder on to Violet than have her as a sister-in-law! I don't see that Rudolph's any worse than she is."

"Thank you, dear," said a smooth voice from the doorway. "How sweet of you! And what am I supposed to have done?"

Kenneth sat up and swung his legs off the sofa. "Darling!" he said. "Come right in and join the party. A good time is being had by all."

Violet Williams still held the door-knob in one gloved hand.

She was charmingly dressed in a flowered frock and a becoming picture-hat, and carried a sunshade. She raised her plucked eyebrows and said: "Are you sure I shan't be *de trop?*"

"You couldn't be. Tony was only retaliating in kind. You know Giles, don't you? Come and sit down, ducky, and listen to the new revelations."

Mesurier made a movement as of protest but Antonia very sensibly pointed out to him that Kenneth was bound to tell Violet all about it anyway, so he might as well get it over. As Kenneth's attention seemed for the moment to be engaged by Violet, who had gone over to the sofa, and was speaking to him in a low voice, Mesurier seized the opportunity to ask Giles why his car should be supposed to constitute an alibi.

"Well," Giles answered, "if you murdered Arnold and drove back to Town in your own car, who disposed of Arnold's car?"

This unfortunately caught Kenneth's ear and he instantly said: "Accomplice."

"I hadn't got an accom—I mean—Oh, for God's sake stop shoving your oar in!"

"An accomplice, if you like," said Giles. "But who?"

"Tony, of course."

"Kenneth dear, you really oughtn't to say things like that, even in fun," Violet reproved him gently.

Antonia, however, was inclined to regard her brother's suggestion with interest. "You mean we hatched the plot between us, and I lured Arnold to the stocks while Rudolph followed in his own car and did him in? That's no use, because I spent the night at the cottage, and I shouldn't think I'd have had time to burst up to town again with Arnold's car *and* have motored back. Anyway, I didn't, so that's out. I knew Giles would think of something."

Mesurier drew a long breath. "What a fool I was not to think of that myself! Thanks a lot. Of course it absolutely lets me out!"

"Oh no, it doesn't!" said Kenneth. "You might have had another accomplice, or tacked your own number-plate on to Arnold's car."

"Too clever," objected Antonia. "Rudolph would never

have thought of anything as wily as that, would you, Rudolph?''

"That's the worst of these people who set out to commit a murder and leave everything to chance,'' said Kenneth.

Mesurier decided to ignore this, and, turning to Giles, asked him if he was sure the alibi was good enough. Giles rather damped his optimism by replying that he was not sure of anything.

Violet, who had been playing idly with the clasp of her handbag, raised her large, unfathomable eyes to Mesurier's face, and asked in her well-modulated voice why he had been at Hanborough that night. "Please don't think I'm being impertinent!'' she said. "But I couldn't help wondering. It seems so funny of you, somehow.''

It was plain that her question took him aback, quite plain enough for Kenneth, who mounted on to the back of the sofa and said: "Now, infidel, I have you on the hip!''

Mesurier cast him a look of goaded hatred and answered: "I can't see what that has to do with it.''

This somewhat weak rejoinder had the effect of setting his betrothed against him. Antonia said severely: "Giles can't possibly help you if you're going to behave like an idiot. You must have had some reason for going to Hanborough that night and it merely makes you look very fishy if you won't say what it was.''

"Very well, then!'' said Mesurier. "If you *will* have it, I went down with a mad idea of throwing myself on Vereker's generosity, but I thought better of it, and came back again.''

"The only thing I have to say is that I must have another drink,'' said Kenneth, getting off the sofa and strolling over to the sideboard. "The more I hear of Rudolph's story the more convinced I am that we can push all the blood-guilt on to him with very little trouble.'' He measured out a whisky-and-soda. "Anyone else have a drink?'' As no one answered he raised his own glass to his lips, drank half the whisky, and came back to the sofa. "The theory I'm working on at the moment is that Arnold's car never left London,'' he said.

Antonia frowned. "Yes, but that means he must have motored down with Rudolph, and he wouldn't have.''

"Of course he wouldn't, and, considering all things, who shall blame him? The point is that Rudolph murdered him first."

"Oh, how ghastly!" shuddered Violet. "Please don't!"

Mesurier was looking rather pale and very angry.

"Very clever!" he said. "And pray, how do you account for the fact that there are no bloodstains in my car?"

Kenneth took another drink. "You wrapped the body in an old mackintosh," he replied.

"Which he afterwards burned in his bedroom grate," interpolated Giles dryly.

"Oh no, he didn't. He cut the maker's name out of it, tied it round a boulder and dropped it into the Hammerpond at Huxley Heath," said Kenneth.

"That's good," approved Antonia. "But you haven't told us how he managed to murder Arnold without being seen, and get his body into the car!"

"When you have quite finished amusing yourselves at my expense," said Rudolph furiously, "perhaps you will allow me to tell you that I very much resent your attitude!"

Antonia opened her eyes at him. "I can't see what on earth there is to get annoyed about. After all, Arnold was our relative, and if we don't mind discussing the murder, why should you? We weren't even going to be shirty about it if you did do it."

"It seems to me," Rudolph said, his voice trembling a little, "that I am to be cast for the rôle of scapegoat!"

"I'm afraid," said Giles in his calm way, "that you don't quite understand my cousins'—er—purely intellectual interest in the crime. If you'd prefer not to talk about it there's no sort of reason why you should."

"Except, of course," put in Kenneth, "that when I'm put into the witness-box I shall be bound to say that I thought your manner hellish secretive when we talked it over."

"You're more likely to be in the dock," said his sister unkindly.

"In that case," replied Kenneth, finishing his whisky-and-soda, "I shall bring in the embezzlement-*motif*. *Sauve qui peut.*"

Mesurier thrust his hands into his pockets and forced his lips to smile. "I rather fancy a jury would see that occurrence in a more reasonable light," he remarked. "I don't pretend that I was justified in doing what I did, but there's no question of—of theft. I've already paid back a great deal of what I borrowed."

"The point is, Arnold didn't look at it in a reasonable light at all," said Antonia.

"There I take issue with you," said Kenneth immediately. "I don't hold any brief for Arnold, but I can't see why he should be expected to be pleasant about it. You can't pinch a man's money, and then say, 'Thank you for the loan' and pay it back in driblets. I don't in the least blame Arnold for cutting up rough, and, what's more, no jury would either. They'll see that Rudolph's got a motive for murder that makes mine look childish."

"I'm perfectly well aware that I'm in an awkward hole," Mesurier said. "But it's no use you or anyone else trying to fasten the murder on to me. I never owned a knife like that in my life, for one thing, and for another——"

"Just a moment," interrupted Giles. "A knife like what?"

A wave of colour mounted to Mesurier's face. "A—a knife capable of killing a man. I naturally assume it must have been some sort of a dagger. I mean, an ordinary knife could hardly——"

"You saw Arnold Vereker after he was dead, didn't you?" said Giles.

There was a moment's silence. Violet gave a shiver. "You're making me feel sick. Do, do let's talk of something else!"

"You can't be sick yet, darling. Rudolph's going to make a full confession."

Mesurier's eyes were fixed on Giles's face, but at this he veiled them suddenly, and put a hand to his breastpocket and drew out his cigarette-case. He opened it, took out a cigarette, and put it between his lips. There was a match-box on the table, and he walked over to pick it up. "Yes," he said, lighting his cigarette. "You're quite right. I did see Vereker after he was dead."

"Just happened to be passing that way," nodded Kenneth.

"No. I went down to Ashleigh Green on purpose to see him. When I got to the village my headlights lit up the stocks. I didn't know it was Arnold then. I got out and went to inspect."

"And finding it was Arnold, came home again."

"Well, why not?" demanded Antonia. "If Arnold was dead there was no point in staying."

"He might have tried to *do* something," Violet said in a low voice. "He might have called for help."

"A womanly thought, sweetheart. Rudolph, why didn't you?"

"I didn't want to get mixed up in it. I saw there was nothing to be done."

"What time was all this?" inquired Giles.

"I don't know. I mean, I'm not sure. Somewhere between twelve and one in the morning."

"At which salubrious hour you were going to knock Arnold up for a friendly chat," observed Kenneth. "The whole story seems to me to want revision. Personally I should jettison it, and think out a new one. The moths have got at this one pretty badly."

"Well, I wasn't going to knock Arnold up," Mesurier said, throwing away his cigarette. "I've—I've been through a pretty bad time over this, I don't mind telling you. Vereker meant to ruin me. He could have, easily. Even if he didn't win his case, the mere fact of my being in such a case would absolutely finish me. I—I was utterly desperate. Didn't know which way to turn. I knew Vereker was going down to Riverside Cottage; I heard him tell Miss Miller so. Of course, I was mad, but I meant to follow him there and shoot him, making it look like a burglary. I'd been to the cottage once. I knew it was fairly remote, and I knew a place where I could hide my car. I thought—if I broke into the place—I could conceal myself behind the bookcase in the hall, and when Vereker came down to investigate, I could shoot him from there and make a getaway before anyone else came on the scene. That's my story, and if you don't like it you can just do the other thing!"

"You've only to tell me what the other thing is and I'll go and do it at once," promised Kenneth. "The story makes me want to weep. My poor sister!"

"Yes, but there's just one thing," said Antonia seriously. "It's so dam' silly that people are quite likely to think it's true. Don't you agree, Giles?"

"It's quite possible," said her cousin.

"Well, if that's your opinion why not let us all in on it?" said Kenneth. "Let's all say we burgeoned off to kill Arnold, but found someone else had done it for us."

"I shouldn't advise it," replied Giles. "It's not the sort of story that bears being told a second time."

"Second time!" exclaimed Kenneth scornfully. "It had whiskers on it when Rudolph dug it up."

"It happens to be true," said Rudolph. "And it isn't any weaker than the story you told. Personally I thought that the thinnest thing I'd ever heard."

"Yes, I quite see that," said Antonia, trying to be fair, "but Kenneth's story was a much better one, all the same, because you can't disprove it, and it doesn't place him anywhere near Ashleigh Green. I really don't think much of yours, Rudolph. Can't you think of something better? We'll all help, won't we?"

"Speaking for myself, no," replied Giles.

"Then I think it's pretty mouldy of you. Kenneth, what do you think Rudolph had better say?"

"I won't have a hand in it," said Kenneth. "My first idea was the best: let Rudolph be the scapegoat. It's the best solution all round. He's only a nuisance as it is."

"He may be a nuisance, but you needn't think I'm going to let him carry the blame for you!" Antonia flashed.

"Who said it was for me? Aren't you in on this?"

Giles intervened once more, his eyes on his wrist-watch. "This is all very enthralling, but may I remind you, Kenneth, that I came here to talk of something quite different? I suggest that we close this entirely arid discussion."

"Certainly!" said Mesurier, his eyes smouldering. "I'm leaving in any case. I may say that if I'd known the sort of thing I was going to be treated to I should never have come. Though I suppose I might have guessed! Oh, please don't trouble to show me out!" This last savagely polite remark was cast at Antonia, who, however, paid no heed to it, but followed him into the hall, carefully shutting the door behind her.

Kenneth drifted back to the sofa. "Well, with any luck that ought to bust up the engagement," he observed.

"What you need is kicking," replied Giles, without heat.

"Oh no, I don't! You can't pretend that you think it would be a good thing for Tony to marry that sickening lizard. Besides, Murgatroyd doesn't like him."

"Mr. Carrington," said Violet suddenly, "what did you think of his story?"

He glanced down at her. "Nothing much. I've heard more improbable ones."

"Somehow I don't like him," she said. "And if he really had nothing to do with it why didn't he call for help?"

"Panic, Miss Williams."

She looked rather contemptuous. "Yes, I suppose so. Personally I've no use for people who lose their heads in emergencies. Do you want to talk privately to Kenneth?"

"Lord, no!" said Kenneth. "It's only about money. How much can I have, Giles?"

"I'll lend you what you want for your immediate needs," replied Giles.

"Are you trying to put the wind up me?" demanded Kenneth. "Has anything gone wrong with the Will?"

"No, nothing at all," said Giles. "But apart from the fact that it wouldn't look too well for you to draw on the estate within three days of Arnold's death, there's a little formality to be attended to before the executors will advance you any money. We must prove Roger's death."

"What a bore!" said Kenneth. "How long is that likely to take?"

"Not very long, I hope. How much do you want?"

"Would three hundred break you?" asked Kenneth persuasively.

"I can stand it. I'll make out a cheque for that amount now, and you can write a formal receipt while I'm doing it."

In the middle of this labour Antonia came back into the room and announced that Rudolph had gone.

"Well, that's one good thing, anyway," remarked Kenneth. "Still adhering to his story?"

"He swears it's perfectly true."

"He'd better go and swear it to old Hannasyde and see how he takes it. You've got to have faith to swallow a chestnut like that."

"I must say I thought it was pretty fatuous myself," admitted Antonia. "I didn't like to pour much more scorn on it, though, because he was a trifle ruffled. The trouble is, he doesn't altogether understand us when we speak, Kenneth."

Giles looked up, half smiling: "Rather a grave disadvantage in a life-partner, Tony."

"I know. It occurred to me about half an hour ago. I do hope I haven't made another mistake."

"It would be rather difficult for the average man to understand you when you speak, as you call it," said Violet. "I must say, I think a great many of your remarks are extremely odd, to say the least of it."

"Bless you, darling," said Kenneth, blotting his receipt. "What a commonplace mind there is behind that lovely face!"

She flushed. "If you think me commonplace I wonder you want to marry me."

"I've explained it to you before, my sweet. I worship beauty."

"Yes, so you say, but I notice that doesn't hinder you from running after perfectly ordinary-looking girls like Leslie Rivers."

"Jealous little cat," he remarked. "I've known Leslie for years. There you are, Giles. I'll pay it back as soon as I touch. Thanks, by the way. I can now buy you a vulgar ring, beloved."

"I don't want a vulgar ring, I can assure you. Simply because I happen to prefer diamonds to any other stone——"

"You shall have a slab of a diamond, my pet. A large, table-cut one, which no one could possibly suppose a fake because it's so improbable."

"Are you going to blue the whole of that on a ring?" inquired Giles.

"I should think so," replied Kenneth. "Because if I'm the

heir the bills can wait over. And when I get my hands on the Vereker fortune, Violet, you shall have a string of pearls as well, and some carved jade ear-rings. How's that?''

"I shall love the pearls, but I don't know that I care awfully for jade. You see such a lot of it about.''

"God help the poor wench!" groaned Kenneth.

Giles screwed on the cap of his fountain-pen. "Postpone hostilities till I've gone," he requested. "You haven't forgotten it's the Inquest to-morrow, have you, Tony?''

"As a matter of fact, I had, but I remember now that you mention it. You said you'd run me down in your car. Do you mind if I bring one of the dogs?''

"Yes, I do. I'll call for you round about ten o'clock. Show me out, please. Good-bye, Miss Williams: so long, Kenneth.''

Antonia took him out into the hall. "Giles, I've made the most shattering discovery," she said awe-inspiringly.

"Good God, Tony, what is it?" he asked, amused.

"Rudolph and Violet. Soul-mates. I can't think why I didn't realize it before. They've got the same type of mind. Do you think I ought to point it out to them?''

"No, I don't," he said firmly. "I should leave them to find it out for themselves. Do you really mean to marry Mesurier?''

"Well, I thought I did," she replied, wrinkling her brow. "He can be awfully attractive, you know, though I must say he doesn't shine much under adversity.''

"Tony, you impossible brat, are you in the least in love with him?''

"I don't quite know," said Antonia sadly. "To tell you the truth, Giles, I'm not at all sure what being in love is like. I thought I was at one time, but I seem to have gone off Rudolph a bit lately. It's really very difficult.''

"I should give him the push if I were you," he recommended.

"No, you wouldn't. Not when he's in trouble," said Antonia.

"Then the sooner he gets out of trouble the better.''

"Yes," she agreed. "But the question is, will he get out of it? That car alibi is all very well, but the more you think of it the more you can't help suspecting that there's a snag in it if only you could find it. You know, this rotten murder's beginning to be a scourge instead of a blessing. Who did it, Giles? Have you got any idea?''

"No, none at all. I have a feeling that we aren't anywhere near the truth yet. It wouldn't surprise me if something totally unexpected cropped up suddenly.''

"Oh, why?'' she asked, interested.

"I don't know,'' said Giles Carrington. "Just a pricking in my toes.''

CHAPTER 11

THE Inquest, held at Hanborough next morning, was not productive of any new evidence. Antonia professed herself frankly disappointed, though she listened with interest to the news that the murdered man's hands had borne traces of having done some repair work on a car. When it was disclosed that the spare wheel on Arnold Vereker's car was flat, and showed a bad puncture, she leaned towards her cousin and whispered: "That dishes Kenneth's theory, anyway."

She gave her own evidence with a cheerfulness which, combined with the absence of decent mourning, rather shocked the members of the jury. To Giles Carrington's relief she was not at all truculent. She answered the Coroner with a friendliness which was due, as she afterwards explained to Giles, to his likeness to the veterinary surgeon who had attended Juno's last accouchement.

It was evident that neither the Coroner nor the jury knew what to make of her, but her unconventional attitude towards Superintendent Hannasyde, whom she greeted, when he rose to put a question to her, as an old and valued acquaintance, made quite a good impression.

Rudolph Mesurier was not called, nor was his name mentioned, and the proceedings terminated, as had been foreseen, in a verdict of Murder against a Person or Persons Unknown.

Coming out of the Court-room Giles Carrington fell in beside Hannasyde, and murmured pensively: "It's the perfect crime, Superintendent."

Hannasyde's slow smile crept into his eyes. "Nasty case, isn't it? What's happened to your disarming client?"

"Gone to the Police Station," replied Giles, with complete gravity, "to give Sergeant—I'm afraid I've forgotten his name, but he breeds Airedales—an infallible prescription for the cure of eczema. Mesurier turned out to be a bit of a red herring, didn't he?"

"Oh, you spotted the snag, did you?" returned the Superintendent. "I thought you would. I'm satisfied, by the way, that he was not in his rooms between twelve and two that night, but at first glance that doesn't seem to help much. Sergeant Hemingway here, however"—he indicated his bright-eyed subordinate—"thinks there might be a way out of it. We shall see."

"Several ways," said Giles, nodding to the Sergeant. "We discussed them all *ad nauseam* last night. But, speaking for myself, I don't like the idea of an accomplice."

"No, sir," said the Sergeant instantly. "Not in a murder case. That's what I say. But that isn't to say it couldn't have been done without, not by a long chalk."

Giles was looking at Hannasyde. "You don't much fancy Mesurier, do you?" he said.

"I don't know that I fancy anybody much," answered Hannasyde. "One thing seems fairly certain, though. Whoever murdered Arnold Vereker was a very cool, clever customer."

"I rather think that rules out Mesurier then," said Giles. "He's neither cool nor clever."

"You can't go by how he acts now, sir," said the Sergeant. "Some of the wiliest of 'em lead you up the orchard by making out they're so silly they couldn't tread on a black beetle without carrying bits of it all over the house for hours after. He was cute enough, the way he cooked the Company accounts."

Giles took out his cigarette-case and opened it. "All carefully planned," he said. "Not done in the heat of the moment."

The Superintendent nodded but Sergeant Hemingway

pursed up his lips. "It looks like it was cold-blooded," he said, "but you can go astray on that line of reasoning. Some people lose their heads when they're all worked up, but there's others as don't. Seem to get needle-sharp. Same effect as taking a pinch of cocaine—not that I've ever done so, but that's the effect they say it has. Comes in psychology—which the Superintendent here doesn't hold with."

Hannasyde smiled, but declined the gambit. His shrewd grey eyes were on Giles's face. "What have you got up your sleeve, Mr. Carrington? Are you going to spring something new on us?"

"Oh, no!" said Giles. "But I became prophetic yesterday, and the fit hasn't passed yet. Something is going to turn up."

The Sergeant was interested. "Kind of premonition?"

"Premonition!" snorted the Superintendent. "A very safe bet! Of course something's going to turn up. All I hope is that it'll have an alibi I can check up on, and won't have spent the night walking to Richmond, or in bed with a headache, or alone in somebody else's house!"

Giles's eyes were alight. "I'm afraid you're feeling ruffled, Superintendent."

Hannasyde laughed and held out his hand. "Can you wonder at it? I must be getting along now. That minx of a client of yours! The idea of saying 'Oh, hullo!' to me in Court! Did she tell you we parted yesterday not on the best of terms? You can warn that young brother of hers, if you like, that it isn't always wise to be too clever with the police. Good-bye!"

They shook hands. "Come to my chambers, and smoke a cigar this evening, and talk it over," invited Giles. "Without prejudice, you know."

"Without prejudice I will, gladly," replied Hannasyde. "Thanks!"

On this they parted, Hannasyde and the Sergeant to catch a train, Giles to extricate his cousin from the Police Station, and take her to have lunch before motoring back to town.

She was in a cheerful mood, and appeared to consider herself safely out of the wood. Giles disillusioned her, and she at once declared that to arrest her now would be an extremely dirty trick, and one of which she did not believe Superintendent Hannasyde capable.

"Except for an occasional brush we don't get on at all badly," she said. "In fact, I think he quite likes me."

"That won't stop him doing what he believes to be his duty."

"No, but I don't think I'm really one of his suspects," said Antonia. "He's got his eye more on Kenneth, or, rather, he had till Rudolph cropped up. I wish I could make up my mind about Rudolph, by the way."

"Whether to marry him or not? Let me help you."

"Oh no, not that! As a matter of fact," she added candidly, "I shouldn't be surprised if he called the engagement off. He was considerably peeved last night, you know. What I meant was, did he do it, or not?"

"You know him better than I do, Tony. It doesn't look as though he did."

"No, but I'm not so sure. I didn't think he'd be so rattled, somehow. Because the only time I've ever seen him in a tight corner, which was when a motor lorry shot out of a side-turning one day, he was as cool as a cucumber, and completely and utterly efficient. That was partly why I fell for him. The ordinary person would have jammed on his brakes and we'd have been smashed into, but he just trod on the accelerator, and sort of skimmed by in a huge semicircle, and then went on with what he'd been saying before it happened."

Giles was unimpressed. "The biggest ass of my acquaintance is an expert driver," he said. "It's one thing to keep your head at the wheel of a car, and quite another to keep it when confronted by the shadow of the gallows, so to speak. My own impression of your elegant young man is that he wouldn't—to put it vulgarly—have had the guts to do it."

"That's what I'm not sure about," said Antonia, quite unresentful of this slur upon her betrothed's character. "His mother was foreign—at least, half, because she had an Italian father or mother or something—and occasionally Rudolph reverts a bit. He has white rages. You never know with people like that. They might do anything. Of course, that story he told might have been true, though I admit it sounded thin, but, on the other hand, it might be a masterpiece of low cunning. Same as me now. For all you know I'm being cunning talking like this."

"Yes, that had occurred to me," agreed Giles.

"Kenneth too," pursued his cousin. "Kenneth won't say one way or the other, because partly, I think, he's enjoying himself, and partly he holds that it's no use saying he didn't do it, because naturally he'd be bound to say that. But I'll tell you one thing, Giles." She paused, frowning, and when he looked inquiringly at her, said in a serious tone: "If it was Kenneth I'll bet every penny I've got no one'll ever find it out."

"I shouldn't, Tony."

"Well, I would. Because generally murderers get found out because they did something silly, or left some important detail to chance. Kenneth never does."

"My dear girl, Kenneth is hopelessly casual."

"Oh no, he's not! About things that he doesn't think matter he may be, but when he gets interested in anything, or thinks something worth while, he concentrates on it in a dark and secret way which Murgatroyd says is like our grandfather—not the Vereker one, but the other. By the way, ought he to go to the funeral?"

"Yes, of course. He must."

"Well, that's what Murgatroyd and Violet say. It's about the only thing they've ever agreed on. But Kenneth says no. He says it would be artistically wrong. However, I'll tell him what you think."

Her method of conveying this information was characteristic, and wholly lacking in tact. Set down at the entrance to the mews shortly before four o'clock, she ran up the outside stairway to the front door, let herself into the flat, and went at once to the studio. Undeterred by the presence not only of Violet Williams, but of Leslie Rivers, who was curled up on the divan watching Kenneth at work, and of a tall, fair man in the early thirties, who was smoking a cigarette in the window-embrasure, she said: "It was a rotten Inquest, so you didn't miss anything. But Giles says of course you must show up at the funeral, Kenneth. Hullo, Leslie! Hullo, Philip, I didn't see you. Has anyone taken the dogs out?"

"Yes, I did," replied Leslie, in her slow, serious way. "You asked me to."

"Well, thanks. Giles says you can hire the proper clothes."

"I daresay, but I won't," replied Kenneth, somewhat inarticulately, because he was holding a paint-brush between his lips. "Get rid of these people, will you? They think they've come to tea."

"They may as well stay, then," said Antonia.

"Is that a vague instinct of hospitality, or mere supineness?" inquired Philip Courtenay.

"Supineness. What have you come for, anyway?"

"Curiosity. Moreover, my dear, I've been interviewed by a bird-like policeman in plain clothes who asked me the most embarrassing questions about Arnold's private affairs. I can't be too thankful I relinquished the post of secretary when I did."

"Well, at least, Eaton Place was more or less bearable when you were there," said Antonia. "How's Maud? And the baby?"

"Both very fit, thanks. Maud sent her love."

Violet said: "But do tell us! What did the detective want to know?"

"Hidden scandals. I hinted that subsequent secretaries might be of more use to him, but it transpired that the longest tenure of office since my departure had been five weeks, so that wasn't much use."

Kenneth removed the brush from his mouth. "Subsequent secretaries is good," he remarked. "Had Arnold got a *mie?*"

"Dozens, I believe, but out of my ken. I wasn't as private as that."

"I don't quite understand," Violet said, fixing her eyes on his face. "Do the police suspect a *crime passionnel?*"

" 'He done her wrong' *motif,*" said Kenneth, screwing up his eyes at the canvas before him. "What sordid minds policemen have!"

"Blackmail," said Courtenay, looking round for an ashtray, and finally throwing the stub of the cigarette out of the window. "Seventy pounds and a seedy stranger were the main subjects of my policeman's discourse. I was regretfully unable to throw light."

"I object!" Kenneth said. "I won't have seedy strangers butting in on a family crime. It lowers the whole tone of the thing, which has, up to now, been highly artistic, and in some ways even precious. Go away, Murgatroyd: no one wants any tea."

"You speak for yourself, Master Kenneth, and let others do likewise," replied Murgatroyd, who had come into the studio with her usual purposeful tread, and was ruthlessly clearing the table of its load of impedimenta. "Well, Miss Tony, so you're back, I see. Where's Mr. Giles?"

"He wouldn't come in. He says Kenneth will have to go to the funeral, by the way."

"There's others could have told him that. *And* a decent suit of blacks," said Murgatroyd cryptically.

"Be damned to you: I won't."

"That's quite enough from you, Master Kenneth, thank you. You'll be chief mourner, what's more. Don't put any of your nasty wet brushes down on the tablecloth, and not that smelly turps neither."

"Kenneth," said Leslie Rivers, "could I have the sketch?"

He glanced down at her, his brilliant, slightly inhuman gaze softening. "You can."

"Thanks," she said.

"You really ought not to give your sketches away," said Violet, overhearing this interchange. "I mean, of course, as a general rule. They may become quite valuable one day."

"Who cares?" said Kenneth, wiping his brushes.

Leslie flushed, and said gruffly: "Sorry. I didn't think."

He smiled lovingly at her, but said nothing. Violet got up, and shaking out her skirt, said graciously: "Oh, naturally, it's different with such an old friend as you, dear. Shall I pour out, Tony, or would you rather?"

"Anyone can pour out as far as I'm concerned," said Antonia, with complete indifference. "We may as well have the loaf in while we're about it, Murgatroyd. I'll come and get it."

She went out and was followed in a few minutes by Leslie Rivers, who came into the kitchen, and said unhappily: "I hate her and hate her."

Neither Antonia nor Murgatroyd experienced the least difficulty in interpreting this remark. Murgatroyd set the loaf down on the wooden bread-board with a thud. "Her!" she said darkly. "Doing the hostess all over our flat! A beauty, is she? Well, handsome is as handsome does, and brown eyes are what I never did trust and never will, not without more reason than I've had yet."

"I shouldn't mind—at least not nearly as much—if only I thought she'd look after him, and understand about his painting," pursued Miss Rivers. "But I can't see that she cares about anything except being admired, and having the best of everything."

"Ah!" said Murgatroyd, emerging from the pantry to collect an errant knife, "still waters run deep. You mark my words!"

"Yes," agreed Leslie, when Murgatroyd had vanished again. "But she doesn't run deep. She's purely mercenary, and she'll hurt Kenneth."

"Not she," replied Antonia. "He knows she's a money-grubber. Kenneth isn't extraordinarily vulnerable, as a matter of fact."

Miss Rivers blew her nose rather fiercely. "She's the sort that would wear away a stone," she said. "Quiet persistence. Hard and cold and calculating. And even if I dyed my hair it wouldn't do any good." With which sibyllic utterance she picked up the bread-board and marched back to the studio.

From the pantry doorway Murgatroyd watched her go, and remarked that that was what she called a lady. "Why Master Kenneth can't see what's been under his nose ever since you was all of you in the nursery is what beats me," she declared. "A proper little wife Miss Leslie would make him, but that's men all over. What happened at that Inquest, Miss Tony?"

"Oh, pretty much what Giles said. It was very dull, and they brought in a verdict of Murder against Person or Persons Unknown. The Superintendent's going to go and have a friendly talk with Giles this evening, so probably Giles will put in a good word for us."

"Hm!" said Murgatroyd grimly. "I don't doubt that's what he thinks, but it's a lot likelier that policeman will get him talking about the family, and go fastening on to something that'll land us all in gaol."

"Good lord!" said Antonia. "I didn't know there was anything."

"There's always something if you look for it," replied

Murgatroyd. "And the more smooth-spoken the police are the more you want to mistrust them. Always on the look-out to trip you up. Cat and mouse, they call it."

The simile, as applied to Superintendent Hannasyde and Giles Carrington, was not strikingly apt, nor, if Giles was full of mistrust and Hannasyde on the watch for an unguarded remark, were these respective attitudes at all apparent when Giles's servant ushered the Superintendent into the comfortable book-lined sitting-room that evening. Hannasyde said as he shook hands: "Nice of you to ask me to look in. I envy you your quarters. They tell me you can't get one of these Temple flats for love or money nowadays."

Murgatroyd might have detected a sinister trap in these seemingly harmless remarks, but Giles Carrington accepted them at their face-value, invited the Superintendent to sit down in one of the deep leather chairs, and supplied him with a drink and a cigar. He had been idly engaged on a chess problem when his visitor arrived, and the sight of the board on the table, with a few pieces set out, naturally inspired Hannasyde, also a humble follower of the game, to inspect the problem narrowly. There was no room for any other thought in either man's head until Black had been successfully mated in the requisite three moves, but when this had been worked out, the pieces put away, a few chess reminiscences exchanged, the scarcity of really keen players deplored, a pause ensued and Giles said: "Well, what about this tiresome murder? Is it going to be an unsolved crime?"

"Not if I can help it," replied Hannasyde. "It's early days yet—though I won't deny that I don't altogether like the look of it." He scrutinized the long ash on the end of his cigar, debating whether to tip it off or to wait a little longer. "Hemingway—the chap with me to-day—is feeling aggrieved." He smiled. "Says there oughtn't to be any mystery about the murder of a man like Vereker. You expect to be baffled when it's a case of some unfortunate girl being taken for a ride and bumped off, but when a prominent City man is stabbed it ought to be fairly plain sailing. You have what Hemingway calls the full décor. His hobby is amateur theatricals—it's the worst thing I know of him. Well, we've got plenty of décor, and we've got dramatis personae, and the net result"—he paused, and at last tipped off the ash of his cigar—"is that we seem most of the time to have got mixed up in a Chekov play instead of the Edgar Wallace we thought we were engaged for."

Giles grinned. "My deplorable cousins. I'm really very sorry about it. It would be interesting to know what you make of them."

"I haven't the least objection to telling you that I don't know what to make of them," replied Hannasyde calmly. "On the face of it, things point young Vereker's way. The motive is there, the opportunity is there, and unless I'm very much mistaken in my reading of his character, the nerve is there, too."

"I agree with you," said Giles.

"Yes," said Hannasyde, with a kind of grim humour. "I know you do. I'm perfectly well aware that you're as much in the dark over him as I am, and equally well aware that you think things look rather black for him. Well, they do, but I'll be quite frank with you: I wouldn't apply for a warrant for that young man's arrest until I had a cast-iron case against him. His story is the weakest I've ever had to listen to—and I wouldn't let him tell it to a jury for anything you could offer me. Which reminds me, by the way, that Mesurier came up to see me at the Yard this afternoon, with yet another weak story. But I daresay you know about that."

"I believe I know the story, but I didn't know he'd been to see you."

"Oh yes!" said Hannasyde. "He went down to that cottage to shoot Vereker, but found him already dead, so returned to town. What I should really welcome would be some suspicious character with a good, strong, probable alibi. I believe it would be easier to disprove. Hemingway fancies Mesurier more than I do. He will have it the man's a dago. I've set him to work on that car alibi, but I don't myself see a way round it. So leaving Mesurier out of it for the time being, we're left with a chauffeur whose alibi I don't altogether trust, as it's supplied by his wife, but whom I don't really think had sufficient motive to murder Vereker; with one unknown man who vis-

ited Vereker on Saturday, possibly with the idea of blackmail
(and blackmailers don't kill the goose that lays the golden
eggs); and with Miss Vereker and her brother.'' He stopped
and drank some of the whisky-and-soda in his glass. ''Taking
Miss Vereker first,'' he continued, ''if I were to set the facts
down on paper, and show them to any one man, I should
think he'd wonder why I haven't had her arrested on suspicion
long since. But so far I've nothing to show that she murdered
her brother, and that particular kind of candour she treats me
to, which looks at first glance to be so damning, is the sort of
candour that would get her off with ninety-nine juries out of a
hundred. Mesurier's type—trying to conceal facts he thinks
might tell against him, contradicting himself, hedging—is far
easier to deal with. Ask him if he quarrelled with Vereker, and
he says he would hardly call it a quarrel—with any number of
people ready to swear that they heard him quarrelling. Ask
Miss Vereker whether she got on with her half-brother, and
she says she hated the sight of him. She doesn't appear to conceal a thing. It's the same with her brother; you don't know
whether they're very clever, or completely innocent, or a pair
of lunatics.''

''I can set your mind at rest on one point: they're quite
sane,'' said Giles. ''And since you've been so frank with me
—admitting what I've known from the start—I'll tell you in
return that Miss Vereker, who knows her brother as well as
anyone, is willing to bet her whole fortune that if he committed the murder it will never be proved against him.''

The Superintendent's eyes had twinkled appreciatively at
one part of this speech, and he replied at once: ''That piece of
information ought to be very useful—to Miss Vereker, if not
to me. But I'm too old a hand to accept it quite as you'd like
me to.''

Giles got up to replenish both glasses. ''As a matter of fact,
I didn't mean it like that at all,'' he confessed. ''Whatever I
may or may not think about Kenneth, I am quite convinced in
my own mind that his sister had nothing whatsoever to do with
it.''

''That doesn't surprise me at all,'' said Hannasyde dryly.
''Moreover, I very much hope you're right—for both your
sakes.''

Giles handed him his glass without comment. A slight flush had crept up under his tan, and the Superintendent, repenting, said with superb inappropriateness: "And why—perhaps the most important question of all—was the body placed in the stocks?"

CHAPTER 12

GILES CARRINGTON, in the act of raising his glass to his lips, lowered it again, and looked down at the Superintendent with a startled frown. "Yes, of course, that's an important point," he said. "Stupid of me, but I really don't think I've considered it. Does it mean anything, I wonder?"

"Yes, I think so," said Hannasyde. "Without going to the length of searching for some obscure incident in Vereker's past which had a bearing on stocks, I imagine that there must have been some reason for putting the body there."

"Unless it was the murderer's idea of humour," said Giles, before he had time to stop himself.

The two pairs of eyes met. Giles Carrington's quite limpid and expressionless, the Superintendent's full of a kind of amused comprehension.

"Quite so," said Hannasyde. "I'd already thought of that. And now I'm going to be really frank. It's the kind of humour I can easily imagine young Vereker indulging in."

Giles smoked for a moment in silence. Then he said: "No. I'm speaking now merely as one who—to a certain extent—knows Kenneth Vereker. It may be helpful to you. Kenneth would not place his half-brother's body in the stocks as a senseless practical joke. If he did it, it would be for some very good, and probably rather subtle reason. That is my honest opinion.''

The Superintendent nodded. "All right. But you'll admit you can visualize circumstances under which he might have done it.''

"Yes, I'll admit that. But you're assuming that the body was placed there after death.''

"At the moment I am, because it seems the more likely hypothesis.''

"No blood on the grass round the stocks,'' Giles reminded him.

"There was very little external bleeding—and no signs of any struggle,'' replied Hannasyde. "So that if you incline to the theory that Vereker was stabbed after his feet were put in the stocks you must work on the assumption that he sat there quite willingly. Now the time was somewhere between eleven at night, or thereabouts, and two o'clock in the morning. We know from the medical evidence that Vereker can't have been drunk. Does it seem to you credible that he should choose that hour of night to try what sitting in the stocks felt like—when he could have done it any day he happened to be in the village?''

"No, I can't say it does,'' admitted Giles. "Though I can conceive of situations where it might be entirely credible.''

"So can I,'' agreed Hannasyde. "If he was motoring down with a gay party after the theatre, and they were all in a light-hearted mood. Or even if he was with one person alone, whom we'll assume to have been a woman. We know he had a puncture on the way down; suppose he picked it up at Ashleigh Green; and after changing the tyre sat down on the bench to admire the moonlight, or cool off, or anything else you like. I can picture him being induced to put his feet in the stocks, but what I can't picture is the woman then stabbing him. It can't have been Miss Vereker, for whatever I disbelieve about her I entirely believe that she was on the worst possible terms with her half-brother. Very well, then, was it some lady of easy virtue motoring down to spend the week-end with him at his cottage?''

"Quite likely,'' Giles said. "I see what's coming, though,

and I confess I can't offer a solution."

"Of course you see it. What should induce any such woman to murder him? You've seen the knife. It's a curious sort of dagger—might have come from Spain, or South America. Not the sort of thing you carry about with you in the normal course of events. That proves the murder was premeditated."

"Some woman who had a grudge against him," suggested Giles.

"Must have been a pretty large size in grudges," said Hannasyde. "And one, moreover, that Vereker didn't set much store by. If he'd done any woman an injury big enough to give her a motive for cold-blooded murder, do you suppose he would quite unsuspectingly have put himself into a helpless position at her instigation?"

"No. On the whole he had rather a suspicious nature," replied Giles. "And in justice to a somewhat maligned man I'm bound to say that I don't think he would have done a woman any serious injury. He was amorous, but not ungenerous to his fancies, and not unkindly."

"That's rather the impression I gathered," said Hannasyde. "I don't rule out the possibility of an unknown woman in the case—but my department hasn't been idle, you know, and so far we can't discover any woman who had the least reason for wanting to murder Vereker. I don't mind telling you that we checked up on several, too. That shabby stranger the butler described to us made me think there might be some woman who'd been got into trouble, because there's a smell of blackmail about that odd visit, but I haven't discovered anything of the kind. On the contrary, Vereker seems to have been pretty decent, and his women were the sort who can look after themselves."

Giles sat down on the arm of his chair. "Yes, I should think they were. Arnold was no fool. And I'm ready to admit that you've made it seem highly improbable that the murder was done after Arnold was in the stocks. But do you mind looking at the other side of the picture? Does it seem to you probable that having stabbed a man to death the murderer conveyed his body to the stocks—the most conspicuous place he could well think of—and arranged it carefully in a natural position there, which I imagine must have been not only a gruesome but also a somewhat difficult task? Impossible for Miss Vereker to have done it; too macabre for Mesurier; too senseless for Kenneth."

"It may not have been senseless," said Hannasyde. He glanced at his wrist-watch, and got up. "That's what I've got to try and find out—amongst other things. By the way, we've been trying to trace those notes Vereker had on him the day he was killed. You remember we found the counterfoil of a cheque for a hundred pounds drawn to self, and only thirty pounds in his pocket? Well, only one of these has come in, to date, and that one is a ten-pound note which a man in a blue suit handed to a waiter at the Trocadero Grill in payment of his bill for dinner on Saturday evening. The suit might have been a dark grey, I may mention, and the waiter really couldn't call the gentleman's face to mind, because there were a lot of people dining that night. You can't say we policemen get much help! Look here, I must be going! Many thanks for by far the most pleasant hours I've spent on this case yet."

Giles laughed. "Well, I hope they'll prove to have been profitable ones."

"You never know," said Hannasyde. "It's always good to get another point of view."

Mr. Charles Carrington, hearing something of the visit next day from his son, paused in his search for the pencil he distinctly remembered placing on his desk not five minutes earlier, and said: "Absurd! You can't run with the hare and hunt with the hounds, or if you can you shouldn't. An Eversharp pencil—you must have seen me use it hundreds of times! Use your eyes, Giles! Use your eyes! So Superintendent Hannasyde doesn't know what to make of those Vereker brats? Now I come to think of it the boy baffled me too. More in him than I thought. God bless my soul, a pencil can't *walk* away!"

Kenneth, getting wind of Hannasyde's visit, loudly endorsed his uncle's verdict, adding a rider to the effect that if there was any double-crossing going on he should immediately change his solicitor. When Giles gave every evidence of regarding such a happening in the light of a Utopian dream, he forgot his original complaint in pointing out his own virtues as a client. He was in one of his more incalculable moods at the time, and his cousin's somewhat unwise rejoinder that the vaunted virtues had escaped his notice provoked him to give a trenchant résumé of his own case. He walked up and down the studio, with his eyes very bright, and with what Antonia called his elf-smile on his lips, and held his cousin partly in dismay, partly in admiration, of the ingenuity with which he postulated various fantastic ways in which he might, had he been feeling like it at the time, have murdered his half-brother.

With the Superintendent's remarks in mind, Giles demanded a reason for putting Arnold Vereker's body in the stocks. The result of this, though entertaining, was not helpful, for Kenneth threw himself into what he conceived to be the spirit of the inquiry with huge zest, and, abandoning the dramatization of himself as the murderer, advanced a quantity of the most astonishing theories, not the least brilliant of which involved the reputation of the Vicar of Ashleigh Green, a gentleman entirely unknown to him.

Giles gave it up. There was nothing to be made of Kenneth, who, if he were indeed playing a dangerous game, obviously preferred (and Giles could only applaud his wisdom) to play it alone.

A more immediately pressing anxiety than the question of whether or not he was guilty of murder was, in the estimation of his entourage, the problem of how to induce him to attend Arnold Vereker's funeral. Exhaustive, and at times heated, discussions, into which Giles was dragged, raged throughout the evening, Murgatroyd, Violet, Leslie and Giles being banded upon the side of respectability, against Kenneth, who was supported by his sister, and his own quite irrefutably logical arguments. The contest was won eventually by Violet, who, though lacking Murgatroyd's stern piety, was quite as insistent that Kenneth must at least appear to accord a proper respect to the dead. Finding that he was unmoved by argument or entreaty, she got up in a cold anger that was only partly feigned, and signified her intention of departing without permitting him to kiss her, or even to touch her hand. Some spark of wrath kindled in his eyes, but was quenched by the closing of the door behind her. He hurried after her; what passed between them in the hall the others had no means of knowing; but in a few moments they came back together, Kenneth meekly bound by his word to attend the funeral, and Violet as charming and as sweet-tempered as she had been angry before.

"If Kenneth marries that young woman he won't be able to call his soul his own," Giles remarked later to Antonia at the door of the flat.

"I know; it's sickening," she agreed. "He isn't really in love with her, either. He's in love with what she looks like."

"Which reminds me," said Giles. "What has become of your intended?"

"I don't know, but I'm beginning to be afraid he's going to jilt me," replied Antonia, with undiminished cheerfulness.

This theory, however, proved to be incorrect, for Mesurier attended the funeral the following afternoon, and returned with Kenneth to the flat afterwards. He had recovered his poise, and nothing could have been more graceful than his apology for having left Antonia in anger when they had last met. He apparently considered that his apology action in seeking out Superintendent Hannasyde at Scotland Yard with the revised version of his story exempted him from any future inquiry, but Kenneth did what he could to disillusion him on this point, and succeeded so well that within two days of being reconciled to his fiancée, Rudolph's nerves began to show signs of fraying, and he exclaimed, in exasperation at the Verekers' absorption in other and more everyday matters: "I don't know how you two can go on as though nothing had happened, or was likely to happen!"

"What is likely to happen?" inquired Antonia, looking up from a collection of guide-books and railway time-tables. "We could quite well go to Sweden, Ken. I've worked it all out."

"What's the use of talking about trips abroad when you may be in prison?" said Rudolph, with an attempt at a laugh.

"Oh, that!" she said, dismissing it. "Of course we shan't be in prison. Anyway, I'm getting sick of the murder."

"I wish we knew what the police were doing!"

"They're working like a pack of bloodhounds on our trails," said Kenneth, leaning over the back of Antonia's chair to look at Baedeker. "And talking of bloodhounds, why's all my bedroom furniture in the hall?"

"Murgatroyd. She says she's going to turn the whole flat out."

"What, not this room too?" cried Kenneth, in such tones of dismay as not the gloomiest of Rudolph's forebodings could wring from him.

"Yes, but not till to-morrow. Leslie said she'd come and help, so I daresay she'll take care of your pictures," said his sister, omitting, however, to add the information that Murgatroyd's bitterly expressed object was to keep the place free from that Violet Williams for one day, even though she had to make the studio floor wringing wet to do it.

It was as well for Murgatroyd's temper that this was not really her main object, for when Violet walked into the flat after luncheon on the following day (a habit which she had lately acquired) and found the studio in a state of glorious disorder, with one dishevelled damsel polishing the handles of a bow-fronted chest, the other turning out the contents of an overloaded bureau, and Kenneth, sitting on the window-seat, reading aloud to them snatches from *The Oxford Book of Seventeenth Century Verse,* she displayed an unexpectedly domesticated trait in her character, demanded an overall from Murgatroyd, and within ten minutes of entering the studio had taken complete charge of operations. By the time she had shown Leslie a better way to polish brass, convinced Antonia that what she wanted was a large box to put all the waste paper in, and rehung all the pictures which had been taken down to be washed, one only of the original four in the studio remained unruffled. This was, of course, Kenneth, who paid not the least attention either to requests that he should move, or that he should shut up for a moment, but continued to delve into the pages of the *Oxford Book,* emerging always with a fresh extract which he read aloud, heedless of the fact that no one was listening to him. The only time he vouchsafed any answer to the various things that were said to him was when Violet, in the voice of one at the limit of her patience, said: *"Will* you stop reading Milton aloud?" To this he replied: "No," in a perfectly calm way as soon as he got to the end of a line.

Any failure on Kenneth's part to treat her with that adoring respect which she demanded from him always impaired the smoothness of Violet's temper, so neither Antonia nor Leslie was surprised when she seized on the opportunity afforded by the discovery of an automatic pistol in the bureau to say with a sting behind her sweetness: "Yours, Tony dear? Perhaps it's as well the police know nothing about that."

"I don't know why," replied Antonia. "It's fully loaded, and hasn't been fired for months."

"Why so touchy, darling?" said Violet, raising her delicate brows. "Of course, now I daren't ask why you keep such a very odd weapon."

"That's a good thing," said Antonia.

Conversation waned after that, but Violet's capable assistance so soon reduced the studio to order that Antonia repented of her momentary ill-temper, took the *Oxford Book* away from Kenneth, and told Murgatroyd to go and make tea.

They were in the middle of this repast when the door was opened, and a man who might have been any age between thirty-five and forty-five, looked in. He had a good-humoured, if somewhat weak countenance, from which a pair of rather bloodshot grey eyes looked out with a certain amiable vagueness.

The party gathered round the table stared at him blankly and unhelpfully.

He smiled deprecatingly. "Hullo!" he said, in the slightly husky tones of one in the habit of indulging his penchant for spirits too often. "Door was on the latch, so I thought I'd walk in. How's everybody?"

Antonia glanced inquiringly at her brother, and was startled to see his face suddenly whiten. A look of mingled incredulity, horror, and anger came into his eyes. "My God in Heaven!" he said chokingly. *"Roger!"*

CHAPTER 13

A SLICE of bread and butter dropped from Violet's fingers on to the floor. Leslie, seated beside her, heard her say numbly: "But he's dead. They *said* he was dead!"

Antonia looked the visitor over frowningly. "Is it really? Yes, now I come to think of it, that's whom you reminded me of. We thought you were dead."

"Thought!" Kenneth cried. "We knew he was dead! He's been dead for years!"

"Well, as a matter of fact, I never was dead," said Roger Vereker, with the air of one making a confidence. "Just at the time it seemed a good thing on the whole to be dead, because there was a bit of trouble over some money. I forget the rights of it now, but people were very unpleasant, very."

"But why on earth did you go on being dead all this time?" demanded Antonia.

"Oh, I don't know," replied Roger, with the vagueness which characterized him. "There wasn't much point in coming to life again, really. It would have meant a lot of bother one way and another. I did think of it, but I was getting on quite well as I was. Fancy you being Tony! I shouldn't have known you. Kenneth's altered too. Wants his hair cutting."

"Leave my hair alone!" said Kenneth angrily. "If you——"

"It's all right. I wasn't going to touch it. You know, it seems very funny to me to find you two grown up. Tony had a pigtail when I saw her last—at least, I may be confusing her with someone else, but I think it was she. Long one, with a bow on the end. You were a horrid little beast. You haven't changed as much as Tony, now I come to look at you. I remember you messing about with a lot of smelly paints."

"Well, he still does that. He's an artist," said Antonia.

Roger heard this with a faint show of surprise, as fleeting as it was mild. "No, is he really? Well, I'm sorry I spoke about his hair, then. One gets out of touch, that's how it is. I'm going to settle down at home now. After all, why not? You get sick roaming about, and the man they mistook for me in that Cuban dust-up was called Harry Fisher. The man who was killed, I mean. I didn't mind at first: one name seemed as good as another. But you've no idea how tired you can get of being called Fisher. I've had seven years of it, and it's very irritating. I thought I'd come home."

"It seems to me," said Antonia, who had listened to this rambling speech with a good deal of impatience, "that you might have called yourself Vereker again without coming home."

"That's just it. It wouldn't have been safe. Bloodsuckers, and things," explained Roger. "Besides, why shouldn't I come home?"

"Because you're not wanted!" Kenneth said tersely. "God, it makes me sick!" He began to pace up and down, shaking his clenched fists. "For seven years we've been living in a fool's paradise, believing you dead and buried, and you turn up now—*now* of all accursed moments! and ruin everything!"

"Good lord, I hadn't thought of that!" exclaimed Antonia. "I must say, it is a bit thick!"

"Thick! It's damnable!" Kenneth shot out. "What's the use of Arnold's being murdered if we're saddled with Roger?"

Violet, who had been sitting in a kind of frozen silence, now said, in a sharpened voice: "Please! *Must* you talk like that?"

No one paid any attention her; Antonia sat glowering at Roger, Kenneth continued to walk up and down, and Roger, glancing from one to the other, said cautiously: "What was that you said? Sometimes I think I'm getting a bit deaf. I wish you wouldn't tramp about so; it's a fidgeting sort of habit. Makes me giddy."

"Arnold's dead," said Antonia briefly.

He blinked at her, apparently incredulous. "My brother Arnold?"

"Yes, of course. Do you think we know hundreds of Arnolds?"

"But he can't be dead."

"I tell you he is."

"Well, that's a very extraordinary thing. Of course, if you say he is, I daresay you may be right, but I don't understand it at all. What did he die of?"

"He died of a knife in the back!" Kenneth flung over his shoulder.

Roger looked startled, and tut-tutted several times. "I can't understand it at all. I call it very shocking, very shocking indeed. Who did that to the poor fellow?"

"We don't know," replied his sister. "Kenneth or I, probably."

"You shouldn't joke about it," said Roger. "How would you like to have a knife stuck in your back? When did it all happen?"

"Last Saturday," said Antonia.

Roger stared at her, and then looked round for a chair. He sat down. "Well, I'm surprised," he said. "Extremely surprised."

Kenneth paused in his pacing. "Just how long have you been in England?" he demanded.

"I'll tell you," answered Roger obligingly. "I landed yesterday. Extraordinary coincidence. I mean, I come home expecting to see poor old Arnold, and I find he's just been killed."

"If that was what you expected to do why didn't you go to Eaton Place instead of coming here?"

"Figure of speech," explained Roger. "When I said that I expected to see Arnold, what I meant was that I didn't think he'd be dead." He drew Antonia's attention to Leslie Rivers, who had risen from the table, and was putting on her hat before the mirror. "Someone's going. Nobody need go on my account, you know."

"I think I will, though," Leslie said. "I expect you've got a lot to say to each other,"

"Nice girl," observed Roger, when she had departed. "Who's the other one?"

"Violet Williams. She's engaged to Kenneth," answered Antonia.

"Oh!" said Roger dubiously. He found that Violet was bowing slightly, and half rose to return this civil greeting. Sinking back again into his chair he became lost in thought, from which he presently emerged to say: "If Arnold's dead who gets all the money?"

"Oh, give me air!" besought Kenneth, beginning to tramp up and down again.

Antonia replied somewhat scornfully: "You know jolly well you get it. That's why we're so disgusted you've turned up."

"Well, I thought I did," said Roger. "I must say I could do with it. I was a bit shocked at the news at first, but I see it's not so bad. Mind you, I quite appreciate your point of view."

"If you don't clear out of this damned quick there'll be another murder in the family!" Kenneth said through his teeth.

"Now, don't get worked up," Roger advised him kindly. "You'll soon get used to me being back. When you've lived as long as I have you'll find it's extraordinary what you can get used to. And talking of clearing out, my idea was that I'd stay with you for a day or two, till I get my bearings."

"No!" cried his half-brother and sister in unison.

"That's all very well," said Roger, "but if I don't stay here, where am I going?"

"Anywhere. We don't mind," replied Antonia.

"Yes, but to tell you the truth," confided Roger, "I'm a bit hard-up just at the moment."

"You've got two hundred and fifty thousand pounds," said Kenneth bitterly.

"Is that what Arnold left? You don't mean it. If I'd known that——" He paused, and shook his head.

"What on earth do you mean—if you'd known it?" asked Antonia.

He looked at her in his hazy way. "Forgotten what I was going to say. Trouble is, I haven't got any clothes."

"You must have some clothes," replied Antonia.

"That's just it: you might think so, and as a matter of fact I did have some, only I had to pawn my suit-case."

"Well?" said Antonia unsympathetically.

"Well, that's the whole thing in a nutshell. It's no use hanging on to a lot of shirts and things if you haven't anything to carry them about in. You see my point?"

"Oh, God!" groaned Kenneth. "I can't bear it!"

"I call that very unreasonable," said Roger. "After all, they weren't your clothes. If I started putting your shirts up the spout you'd have a perfect right to complain. It's coming to something if I can't pop my own belongings. Moreover, if I inherit all Arnold's money I shall be able to buy a lot of new clothes, and no harm done. But don't run away with the idea that I particularly want to stay with you, because I don't at all mind putting up at a hotel as long as I've got money. Supposing you were to lend me a few pounds—say fifty to tide me over?"

"Let's pretend!" said Kenneth sarcastically. "You've never paid a debt in your life!"

"That's perfectly true," agreed Roger, with unimpaired affability, "but I wouldn't mind paying you back if I had two hundred and fifty thousand pounds."

"Well, I won't take the risk," replied Kenneth. "Go and touch Giles. You won't get anything out of me."

At this moment the door opened to admit Murgatroyd, who came in to clear away the tea. Antonia said gloomily: "Look what's happened, Murgatroyd. Isn't it damnable?"

Murgatroyd started to say: "How many times have I told you I won't have you use such——" Then she caught sight of Roger, and gave a scream.

"Hullo, Murgatroyd!" said Roger, with his sleepy, apologetic smile. "You still alive?"

Murgatroyd seemed to find difficulty in speaking. She swallowed once or twice, and in the end said in a hollow voice: "I knew it. You ask Miss Leslie if I didn't see bad news in my teacup yesterday, plain as plain. Mark my words, I said, something awful is on its way to this house."

"A lot of people scoff at reading fortunes in teacups," said Roger, interested. "I've always thought there was something in it myself. It just shows. You haven't changed much. Fatter, of course, but I should have known you anywhere."

"I'll thank you not to make personal remarks about me, Mr. Roger! What have you come home for, that's what I'd like to know? Not that I need to ask. Trust you to come nosing round after pickings! Talk about hyenas!" Wrath swelled her voice. She said strongly: "Just like you it is to try and take what's Master Kenneth's away from him! Don't tell me! If I had my way, back you'd go to where you came from, double-quick!"

"Yes," said Antonia, "but he hasn't got any clothes, and he says he's going to stay with us."

"Not in this house, he isn't," said Murgatroyd.

"I shan't get in the way," Roger assured her. "You'll hardly notice me."

"No, not once you're the other side of the front door, I won't," was the grim reply.

Violet got up from the table, and came slowly across the room. "Don't you think this is all a little undignified?" she said in her calm way. "Kenneth dear, please stop prowling, and try to be reasonable. Poor Mr. Vereker can't help not being dead, after all!" She smiled at Roger, and added prettily: "They're an awful couple, aren't they? You mustn't pay any attention to what they say. And no one's offered you any tea! Would you like some?"

"No," said Roger frankly, "but I shouldn't mind a whisky-and-soda if it happened to be handy."

"Of course," she said. "I'll get you one—since these rude people have forgotten their manners!"

Kenneth gazed at her in blank astonishment. "My good girl, do you realize what this means?" he asked. "Have you by any chance grasped who he is?"

"Yes, dear, perfectly," replied Violet, going over to the sideboard and opening one of the cupboards. "And if I can put a decent face on it, I think you might too. Will you say when, Mr. Vereker?"

"If he does it'll be a record," remarked Kenneth.

"That'll do, Kenneth," Violet said, in a tone of authority. "There, is that how you like it, Mr. Vereker?"

"I like it almost anyhow," replied Roger simply. "I've

forgotten your name, but thank you."

"Williams," she said. "Violet Williams. A very ordinary name, I'm afraid."

"Yes, they're always the worst to keep in your head," agreed Roger. "Well, here's luck, everybody! Chin-chin!"

His relatives received this in unresponsive silence. Murgatroyd, whose indignation had been diverted by the sight of Violet doing the honours of the flat, said suddenly: "Well, what's to be done, that's what I want to know?"

"Don't worry about me," said Roger. "I'm very adaptable. I don't suppose I shall be here long either. My idea is to take a flat on my own."

"Why bother?" said Kenneth. "Isn't Arnold's house enough for you?"

"I shouldn't like it," replied Roger, with more decision than he had yet shown. "Not my style at all. I'll tell you what, though: I'll give it to you and Tony."

"Thanks. We don't want it."

Murgatroyd, who had been thinking, said in a somewhat mollified voice: "I suppose he'll have to stay. It won't do any good to have him trapesing around town like a regular tramp. He can have the camp-bed in the boxroom."

"I shall want a pair of Kenneth's pyjamas as well," said Roger helpfully.

"If you stay in this flat I shall clear out," announced Kenneth.

"No, you won't," said his sister. "I'm not going to be left to cope with him."

"All right, then, let's both go. Let's go to Sweden at once!"

"I can't. Who'd look after the dogs?"

"Damn the dogs!"

"Have you got a lot of dogs?" inquired Roger, looking round for some sign of them. "What sort of dogs?"

"Bull-terriers," replied Antonia briefly.

"I don't know that I like the sound of that. I got bitten by a dog once, and they told me it was a bull-terrier. Not that I wanted to know."

"Let's have the dogs in," said Kenneth, brightening. "You never know your luck."

"Don't be childish, Kenneth," interposed Violet. "It isn't

for me to make a suggestion, but don't you think Mr. Carrington ought to be told what's happened?"

"You don't mean to tell me Uncle Charles isn't dead yet?" said Roger. "I don't want to see him. The last time I set eyes on him he said a whole lot of things I'm glad I can't remember."

"You won't have to see him," replied Antonia. "Giles took over all our affairs years ago."

"Oh, Giles!" said Roger. "Well, I don't mind him. Do just as you like about it. Now I come to think of it, he wasn't a bad chap at all. I was at school with him."

"Yes, till they sacked you," said Kenneth.

"You've got that muddled up," said Roger. "You're thinking of Oxford. Now, there I did get into trouble. I forget the rights of it, but there was a lot of unpleasantness one way and another. As a matter of fact, I've been very unlucky all my life. Not that I'm complaining."

Antonia, apparently thinking that Violet's suggestion was a good one, had walked across the studio to the telephone, and was dialling her cousin's number. He answered the call himself, and as soon as Antonia heard his voice, she said without any preamble: "Giles, are you doing anything? Because if not you'd better come round at once."

"Had I?" he said. "What's happened now?"

"Something utterly sickening. Roger's turned up."

"*What?*"

"Roger. He isn't dead, at all. He's here."

There was a moment's startled silence; then Giles said in a voice quivering with amusement: "But what a disaster!"

"Yes, it's awful. We don't in the least know what to do about it."

"My poor Tony, I'm afraid there's nothing you can do."

"It's all very well for you to laugh, but he says he's going to stay with us till you advance him some money. So do you think you could bring round some at once? He wants fifty pounds, but I should think twenty would do. He hasn't got any clothes."

"What, none at all?"

"No—that is, yes, you idiot, of course he has! But no pyjamas, or things."

"How very like him!" said Giles.

"I daresay, but the point is we don't want him here, and he won't go unless he has some cash."

"My dear girl, *I* can't possibly do anything about it at a moment's notice!"

"I suppose you wouldn't like to lend him some money?" Antonia said, without much hope.

"I shouldn't," replied Giles.

"No, I didn't think you would. But it's pretty grim if we've got to have him here, you know."

"Where is he?"

"I keep on telling you! *Here.*"

Giles's voice was brimful of laughter. "Not in the room?"

"Yes, of course," said Antonia impatiently.

"How he must be enjoying this conversation!"

At this point Roger, who had been listening with his usual placidity, interrupted to say: "Give old Giles my love."

"He wants me to give you his love. He's just like that."

"He always was. I can't rise to those affectionate heights, but tell him I congratulate him on not being dead. Where did he spring from?"

"South America, I suppose. I didn't ask. Anyway, he landed yesterday. *Do* come round!"

"I can't do any good if I do, Tony; but I'll look in after dinner, if you like."

With this she had to be content. At the other end of the telephone Giles Carrington sat for a moment after he had laid down the receiver, thinking. Then, with a faint smile hovering about his mouth, he picked the receiver up again, and rang up Scotland Yard.

Superintendent Hannasyde was still in the building, and after a few minutes Giles was put through to him.

"Is that you, Hannasyde?"

"It is," replied the Superintendent.

"Do you remember, I wonder, that I prophesied something unexpected would turn up?"

"I do." The Superintendent's voice quickened with interest.

"Well, I thought perhaps you'd like to know that it has," said Giles. "Roger Vereker has come home."

"Roger—Who's he?"

"Roger Vereker," said Giles, "is the brother who ought to have died seven years ago!"

"Good lord!" The Superintendent sounded startled. "When?"

"I'm informed that he landed yesterday—I believe from South America, but I'm not certain on that point. At the moment he's staying at the studio. I'm going round to see him this evening."

"Do you mind if I come with you?" asked Hannasyde.

"Not in the least," replied Giles cheerfully.

CHAPTER 14

VIOLET, who made a show of leaving the studio shortly before dinner, was easily persuaded to remain. Kenneth said that since she seemed to like Roger so much she had better stay and entertain him, as neither he nor Tony felt at all capable of doing it. She took this in good part, merely smiling at him in a rather aloof way, and continuing to ask Roger civil questions about his journey. Presently, when Murgatroyd, with an ill grace, came to show Roger the way to the box-room which was to be his temporary abode, she took the Verekers to task, and told them that she felt so sorry for Roger at meeting with such a reception that she felt she had to do something about it. Antonia pointed out to her that as far as Roger was concerned it was all water off a duck's back: an observation so patently true that even Violet could not gainsay it. Antonia saw more point in her second argument, which was that by showing his disgust so plainly Kenneth was placing himself in a very suspicious light. Antonia was inclined to agree with this, but Kenneth at once started to argue that his attitude was entirely consistent, and would be more likely to puzzle the police than to convince them that he was Arnold's murderer. In the middle of the inevitable discussion that followed, Roger came back into the room, and Kenneth, to whom, once he was embarked on an argument, all persons were alike, immediately put the case to him.

Roger listened attentively, and without embarrassment, and said in a painstaking way: "You mean, if you go about saying what a damnable thing it is I've come home, the police will think you stuck that knife into Arnold?"

"No, that's what Violet thinks. I say that if I pretended not to mind they'd be far more likely to be suspicious."

"Well, I don't know," said Roger. "They might, of course, but you can't be too careful with policemen. I've had a lot of trouble with them in my time, all sorts of policemen. Sometimes I think the English ones are the worst, but at others I'm not so sure. By the way, did you murder Arnold? I don't want to be inquisitive, but I wondered."

"What do you suppose I'm likely to answer?" retorted Kenneth.

"Quite so," said Roger. "Silly of me. What I mean is, it's a nuisance for you if you did, now I've come home. Waste of time."

"Unless I murder you too," said Kenneth thoughtfully.

"Now, don't start talking like that," said Roger. "Before you know where you are you'll be doing it. I never could stand impulsive people, never."

Kenneth eyed him speculatively. "The best thing, of course, would be to foist Arnold's murder on to you," he said. "I don't quite see how, at the moment, but I may think of something."

"That's not a bad idea," remarked Antonia. "You wouldn't have to make up a motive, either, because he's got one."

"Well, I don't like it," said Roger, a shade of uneasiness in his voice. "And it's no use going on with it, because I've already told you I only landed yesterday."

"Moreover," continued Antonia, brightening, "the knife was a foreign dagger or stiletto (I forget which), common in Spain and South America. They said so at the Inquest."

"You never told me that," Kenneth reproached her. "It's very important. Naturally, that's just the sort of thing Roger would use."

"Now there you're wrong," said Roger. "If there is one thing that I wouldn't use it's that. I don't believe in knifing people. You see a lot of it in some of the places I've been in but that isn't to say you get into the way of doing it yourself. At least, I don't. Besides, I didn't know anything about the murder till you told me. As a matter of fact, now I come to think of it, I don't know much about it now. I don't even approve of it."

However, Kenneth was not easily to be diverted from his chosen train of thought, and he continued to pursue it until dinner was brought in. Murgatroyd waited on them in silence, and only occasionally threw Roger a hostile look. She confided to Antonia, later, that it might be as well to keep in with Roger. "For, whatever his faults, Miss Tony—and it would take me till to-morrow to tell you them—he's not mean. That I will say for him."

"You needn't think I'm going to sponge on Roger," replied Antonia.

"You never know what you may do till you come to it," said Murgatroyd.

It was not until after nine o'clock that Giles Carrington entered the flat, and when she admitted him, and recognized his companion, Murgatroyd gave a disparaging sniff, and remarked that it never rained but what it poured.

The small party gathered together in the studio was not being a success, in spite of all Violet's efforts to make it one. She had managed to stop Kenneth trying to evolve some method by which Roger might have contrived to commit the murder and yet appear to have been on the high seas at the time, but she could not induce him either to take part in the sort of general conversation she was trying to promote, or to be polite to his half-brother. She had taken pains to draw Roger out on the subject of his travels, but Kenneth, who was invariably made irritable when she bestowed her attention on another man, blighted most of Roger's reminiscences by interpolating now and then the remark that he didn't believe a word of it. He sat slouched in the largest arm-chair, with an expression of brooding anger in his eyes; and the only interest he displayed during Roger's rambling narration was in the story of the beautiful Spaniard who had twice tried to kill him.

Antonia, frankly bored, had curled herself up on the divan with two of her dogs at her feet, and was reading a novel. She put it down when the door opened to admit her cousin, and greeted him with relief. "Oh, good!" she said. "Now you can come and tell us how to get rid of him! *Hullo!* What have you brought the police for?"

Kenneth's scowl vanished. He sprang up, exclaiming: "You see how right my theory is, Roger! They've come for you already!"

Roger, too, had risen, and was looking greatly disturbed: "If policemen are going to infest the place I shall have to go," he said. "It isn't that I'm afraid I shan't be comfortable, because I've tried the camp-bed and it isn't bad. What I mean is, I've slept in many worse. But I don't like policemen. Some people feel the same about cats. Always know the instant one comes into the room, and begin to get creepy. Not that I've any objection to cats, mind you. Far from it. In fact, if I had to be bothered with any sort of an animal, I think I should choose a cat."

"Well, I wouldn't," said Antonia, who had happened to listen to this. "They're inhuman things—though I suppose there are cats *and* cats."

"There you are, then," Roger pointed out. "But it's no use telling me there are policemen *and* policemen, because it wouldn't be true. It's always puzzled me what anyone ever wanted policemen for except to stand about at cross-roads, sticking out their hands, and even that seems to me the kind of job anyone else could do as well, if not better."

"I wish you wouldn't talk such drivel," said Antonia. "Anybody would think you were going to have one as a pet. And if other people directed traffic instead *they'd* be policemen, so I don't see that it would make much difference."

Roger followed this argument carefully. "There's a fallacy in that," he said. "I'm not sure where it is, and I'm not going to work it out, but the thing doesn't sound right to me, somehow."

Any faint hope Hannasyde might have cherished for finding in Roger one normal member of the Vereker family vanished.

He sighed, and transferred his attention to Kenneth.

Giles interposed before Antonia could continue the argument. "Shut up, Tony. Well, Roger, how are you? When did you arrive?"

"I'm getting tired of answering that question," replied Roger, shaking hands. "I keep on telling everyone I landed yesterday—I'm glad you've come around, because it's a very awkward predicament, mine. I've run out of cash. They tell me you're one of Arnold's executors, so you'll be able to advance me some of the money. How much have you brought?"

"I haven't brought any," answered Giles. "I can't advance you money in that haphazard fashion."

The interest which had gleamed for a few moments in Roger's eye was effectually banished by this pronouncement. He relapsed into his usual quiescence, merely remarking in a discouraged way that if that was so, he couldn't see why Giles had troubled to come. "Not that I don't want to see you," he added. "But there doesn't seem to me to be much point in it."

"If he succeeds in ridding us of you there'll be a great deal of point in it," said Kenneth savagely. "Sit down, my friend-the-Superintendent, sit down! What can I offer you? Whisky? Lager?"

The Superintendent declined any refreshment. "I'm sorry to interrupt a—a family party," he said, "but——"

"Not at all," said Kenneth. "We're charmed to see you. At least, my half-brother isn't, but that's probably because his conscience isn't clear. But the rest of us are delighted. Aren't we, Violet? By the way, I don't think you've met our friend-the-Superintendent, darling. This is he. Superintendent, my fiancée—Miss Williams."

Violet bowed slightly, and bestowed on Hannasyde the small mechanical smile she reserved for her social inferiors. Turning from him, she suggested to Kenneth in a low voice that she should go. He instantly quashed this, so she compromised by withdrawing tactfully to the other end of the room under pretence of opening a window.

Meanwhile Giles had introduced the Superintendent to Roger, and Hannasyde, in his good-humoured way, was explaining the ostensible reason for his visit. "As I expect you have been told, Mr. Vereker, your brother, Mr. Arnold

Vereker, was stabbed at Ashleigh Green last Saturday," he began, "so I'm sure you will——"

"Yes, I've been told that," replied Roger, "but it has nothing to do with me. Naturally I was shocked to hear it. In fact, I didn't at first believe it."

"It must have been a terrible shock," agreed Hannasyde sympathetically.

"Well, it was. If they'd said he'd been shot, or been found with his head stuck in a gas-oven, it would have been another matter, because there's nothing surprising about that in these days. But a knife in the back is a very unusual thing in England. Took me back to Colombia in a flash."

"Really?" said Hannasyde. "Have you just come from Colombia?"

"Oh no," said Roger vaguely. "But I was there for a spell once. Didn't care for it, but you'd be surprised at the amount of quiet knifing that goes on. At least, it did in my day, but of course it may have changed by now."

"I've always understood that those parts were somewhat uncivilized," said Hannasyde. "Though they say South America is the country of the future."

"They'll say anything," replied Roger dampingly.

Hannasyde persevered. "Which part have you come from?" he inquired.

"B.A.," said Roger. "But it's no use making a lot of inquiries about me there, because I've been living under another name. More convenient," he added, in explanation.

"I see," said Hannasyde. "And so you're just back. When did you land?"

"Yesterday," said Roger, eyeing him suspiciously.

Hannasyde smiled. "That sounds to me like a remarkably good alibi," he said lightly. "What was your ship?"

"Well, I've forgotten," said Roger, "if I ever knew, which I rather doubt. To tell you the truth, I don't take much interest in ships. There are some people who no sooner get on board than they start making friends with the Chief Engineer so that they can go down and have a look at the engine-room, which as a matter of fact, is a nasty, smelly place. I'm not like that at all."

Giles, who had been inquiring of Antonia half-laughingly,

half-anxiously, whether she was reconciled to Mesurier, turned his head and said: "You must remember the name of the ship, surely?"

"There's no must about it," replied Roger. "I can forget much more important things than that. Though I don't say it won't come back to me. Very often things do, and, what's more, things that happened years and years ago."

"That'll be useful," remarked Kenneth, lighting a cigarette. "What a fool you were to tell us what your assumed name was! You could have forgotten that too."

"Oh no, I couldn't," Roger contradicted with sudden bitterness. "If you'd ever been called Fisher for years on end, you wouldn't forget it either."

"I've just had a horrible thought," said Antonia suddenly. "Are you married?"

"It doesn't matter if he is," snapped Kenneth. "The mere fact of his being alive has ditched the whole thing."

"Not *absolutely*," Antonia answered. "After all, he's bound to die ages before you, because he's nearly forty now. Only if he's got hordes of children it all becomes a complete washout."

"You needn't worry about that," said Roger, "because I'm not married. I've done a lot of silly things in my time, but I never let anyone marry me."

"Wonderful!" mocked Kenneth. "One can so readily picture the eager queue of maidens——"

"Now, don't try to be witty," besought Roger. "It's a very unrestful habit. All I want is a quiet life, but how I'm going to get it with you being clever and policemen dancing in and out like——"

"And all I wanted," Kenneth struck in savagely, "was for you to remain decently interred!"

"Antipathy, Mr. Vereker? or are you making the discovery that the acquisition of a large fortune is not a matter of such indifference as you would have had us believe?"

There was a note of irony in the Superintendent's level voice, and at the sound of it Kenneth turned, not put out of countenance, but alert and with his sullen ill-humour gone in a flash. His eyes held a challenge, his elf-smile reappeared. " 'A hit, a very palpable hit!' And yet, my friend-the-Super-intendent, you would suspect me more if I didn't seem to care whether I inherited Arnold's fortune or not."

"Perhaps," Hannasyde acknowledged. "But you should consider whether perhaps I may not suspect you of assuming a greater degree of annoyance than you really feel, on purpose to throw dust in my eyes." He paused, and then, as Kenneth did not immediately answer him, added gently: " 'Another hit. What say you?' "

Kenneth laughed, and said with a good deal of delight: " 'A touch, a touch, I do confess.' You know, I'm beginning to like you quite a lot."

"I might return that compliment, if it occurs to you to stop trying to hoodwink me. You are fond of quoting from *Hamlet* (though not always sure of your source), so I will give you one more line to digest: 'Take care that you don't become as a woodcock to your own springe.' "

"Ah, 'justly kill'd with mine own treachery!' I'll take such care—Osric—that I won't let this conversation alter my attitude by so much as a hair's-breadth."

Roger leaned sideways in his chair to say confidentially to Giles: "It's getting a bit too high-brow for me. Is his name Osric? I thought you said it was Harrington."

"There is such a thing as being too clever, Mr. Vereker."

"I'll take your word for it. But I am only being honest. Didn't you come here to-night to see how I was reacting to the prodigal's return?"

Hannasyde smiled faintly. Antonia, watching him, said dispassionately: " 'They bleed on both sides.' I hoped I'd be able to get that one off sooner or later."

This sally seemed to complete Roger's bewilderment. He had been trying to follow the dialogue, but he gave it up at that point, and shut his eyes.

"You're not being exactly helpful, Kenneth," said his cousin.

"Why should I be? I don't want the murderer to be un-masked—unless it was Roger, of course. I approve of him."

Roger opened his eyes again. "Now, that's a very sensible remark," he said. "I don't mean the bit about me, but the rest of it. I don't want to know either, and if we don't, what's it got to do with anyone else? That's what I complain about in policemen. Always poking their noses into other people's business.''

"You can't blame them for that," said Antonia reasonably. "They pretty well have to. But it does seem to me much more important at the moment to decide what's to be done about you. It's all very well for you to say you can't advance any money, Giles, but you needn't think we're going to let Roger wear all Kenneth's clothes while you sit on the cash.''

"No," said Roger, his interest reviving. "Because I don't like any of his shirts, for one thing.''

Antonia at once took up the cudgels in defence of her brother's taste, and since the argument showed signs of developing swiftly into an abstract discussion on sartorial matters, Hannasyde apparently judged it wisest to go away. The Verekers paid very little attention to his departure, but Giles escorted him to the front door, and said that he had all his sympathy.

"Thanks," returned Hannasyde. "Was Roger Vereker deported, by any chance?''

"Probably," said Giles, with perfect equanimity. "At all events, he's been cast up penniless on our hands.''

Hannasyde looked at him under his brows. "Are you acting for him, Mr. Carrington?''

"Not if I know it," answered Giles.

A few moments later, having sped the Superintendent on his way, he returned to the studio to find that the argument had been interrupted by Violet, who throughout Hannasyde's visit had sat quietly at the other end of the room turning over the leaves of a magazine. "I held my tongue while that man was here, because, of course, I realize that it isn't my affair," she was saying. "But I really was shocked at the way you went on, Kenneth. It's so silly of you, and childish. We know you didn't kill your half-brother, but you're simply asking for trouble, talking as you did. And I must say I don't think it's particularly nice of you, or sporting, to be so unkind to Mr. Vereker.''

"Don't bother about me," said Roger. "I don't mind him, as long as he doesn't start sticking knives into me."

"I think that's extremely generous of you, Mr. Vereker," said Violet. "And whatever Kenneth may say, I hope you'll believe that I at least don't share his feelings." She picked up her hat and gloves, and held out her hand. "I'm going now. Good-bye—and please don't pay any attention to Kenneth or to Tony."

"Aren't you going to kiss him?" inquired Antonia ruthlessly.

"Shut up!" said Kenneth, an edge to his voice. "I'll see you home, Violet."

They had barely left the studio when Roger remarked with sudden and unexpected shrewdness: "I'll tell you what she is: she's a gold-digger. I've met lots of them. He'd better not marry her."

Antonia regarded him for the first time with a friendly eye. "Yes, she is a gold-digger, and I'll bet anything she's trying to vamp you so that you'll do something handsome for Kenneth."

"Well, I shan't," said Roger simply. "Not," he added, "that I've got much chance to do anything for anybody so far, even myself. When can I have some money, Giles?"

"I'll get on to Gordon Truelove to-morrow," replied Giles. "He's the other executor. I don't think you ever knew him."

"No, and I don't want to," said Roger. "All I want is some money, and I don't see why I can't have it."

"You can," said Giles. "I'll let you know as soon as I've had a word with Truelove."

"Come and have tea," invited Antonia. "Kenneth's taking Violet out to a matinée."

"He needn't do that," said Roger. "Just ring me up."

Giles paid no heed to this somewhat tactless suggestion. He was looking at Antonia. "Do you want me to, Tony?"

She raised her candid eyes to his face. "Yes, I do," she answered.

So Giles Carrington, making vague excuses to his suspicious and somewhat incensed parent, left the office shortly after half-past three the next day, drove himself to Chelsea, and arrived at his cousin's flat just as Superintendent Hannasyde was preparing to mount the stairs to the front door. "Hullo, what brings you here again so soon?" he inquired. "Have you discovered a startling new development?"

"Yes," said Hannasyde, "I have."

CHAPTER 15

THE smile vanished from Giles Carrington's eyes, but it was in the same lazy, rather humorous voice that he said: "That sounds exciting. What has happened?"

They began to walk up the stairs together. The Superintendent said with a twinkle: "Don't worry; neither of your clients is implicated in the new developments."

"I'm glad of that," replied Giles, pressing the front door bell. "Roger was in England at the time of the murder. Is that it?"

"Yes," said Hannasyde. "That is it."

"Poor old Roger!" remarked Giles. "I rather suspected he was when he forgot the name of his ship."

Hannasyde bent an accusing stare upon him. "You're as bad as the rest of them," he said severely. "The instant you set eyes on Roger Vereker you not only suspected that he'd been in England some time longer than he admitted, but you were pretty sure also that he was the shabby stranger who visited Arnold Vereker that Saturday. Isn't that true?"

"Not quite," said Giles. "I suspected it several hours before I set eyes on him. As soon as I heard he had turned up, in fact. Good afternoon, Murgatroyd. Miss Tony in?"

"Oh yes, she's expecting you, sir," said Murgatroyd holding the door wide. "But what call you've got to bring the police back again I'm sure I don't know. Seems as though we can't call the place our own these days. They're both in the studio, Mr. Giles.''

Giles Carrington nodded, and walked across the little hall, followed by the Superintendent. In the studio Roger Vereker was apparently working some problem out on scraps of paper, critically but not unamiably watched by his half-sister, who sat with her chin in her hands, looking over his calculations. She glanced up quickly as the door opened, and, when she saw Giles, smiled in her confiding way. "Hullo!" she said. "Roger's trying to work out a System. I think it's all rot myself.''

"Long may you continue to think so," said Giles.

Antonia perceived Superintendent Hannasyde, and raised her brows. "I didn't know you were coming too," she said. "I rather wish you hadn't, because, to tell you the truth, I'm getting awfully sick of the Family Crime. However, come in if you must.''

"I'm afraid I shall have to," Hannasyde answered, closing the door. "I want to ask your half-brother a few questions.''

Roger, who had started violently at sight of him, said: "It's no good anyone asking me questions, because I'm very busy at the moment. As a matter of fact, I was hoping for a quiet afternoon, now we've got rid of Kenneth.''

A rough sketch in pastels, propped on the mantelpiece, caught Giles's attention. "Good lord, that's clever!" he said involuntarily. "Kenneth's?''

"I don't see anything clever in it at all," said Roger. "In fact, if I weren't a very easy-going man, I might be quite annoyed by it.''

"Yes," said Giles. "I—I should think you might.''

"Moreover, it isn't anything like me," pursued Roger. "Can't be, because Kenneth had to tell me who it was meant to be.''

"He's caught the look, hasn't he?" said Antonia. "He did it this morning. After saying portrait painting's a debased art, too. It is good, isn't it?''

"Wicked!" said Giles, under his breath. "Really, it's indecent, Tony!''

Hannasyde, who had also been looking in considerable

astonishment at the sketch, overheard this, and found himself in complete agreement, and wondered whether it was fanciful to feel convinced that the man who could perpetrate so merciless a portrait would be capable of anything, even murder. He transferred his gaze from it to the original, and said without preamble: "You informed me last night, Mr. Vereker, that you landed in England two days ago."

"I daresay I did," admitted Roger. "One way and another there was a lot of chatter going on last night, and I don't remember all I said. But I don't want to start an argument, so have it your own way."

"Do you still adhere to that statement?"

"Why shouldn't I?" said Roger cautiously.

"Principally because it is untrue," replied the Superintendent, with disconcerting directness.

"I object to that," said Roger. "That's a very damaging thing to say, and if you think that just because you're a detective you can go round giving people the lie you'll find you're mistaken." He paused, and reflected for a moment. "Well, as a matter of fact, you probably won't," he said gloomily, "because it seems to me there's no limit to what the police can get away with in this country."

"There is a limit," said Hannasyde, "but your cousin is here to see that I don't overstep it. Your name, Mr. Vereker, does not figure on the lists of passengers on board any vessel arriving from South America two days ago."

"Well, that's a very extraordinary thing," said Roger. "But when I said I landed two days ago, I didn't say I landed from South America."

"You said that you had come from Buenos Aires," Hannasyde reminded him.

"That's true enough," agreed Roger. "So I did. Of course, if I'd known you were interested I could have told you the whole story. The fact of the matter is, I got off at Lisbon."

"What on earth for?" demanded Antonia.

"There was a man I wanted to see," said Roger vaguely.

"About a dog, I should think," said Antonia, with considerable scorn.

"No, it wasn't about a dog. It was about a lot of parrots," said Roger, improvising cleverly.

"You got off at Lisbon to see a man about a lot of parrots?" repeated the Superintendent.

"That's right," nodded Roger. "Amazon parrots. Not those grey ones with pink tails, but green ones. The sort that screech." The story began to grip him; warming to the theme, he continued: "Thought I could do a deal. You'd be surprised at the demand there is for parrots in Portugal."

"I should," interpolated Hannasyde grimly.

"Anyone would be," said Roger. "I was myself. But there it is. The idea was to ship a lot over to this man I was telling you about. Only the trouble was we couldn't come to terms, so the best thing for me to do was to see him in person."

"I trust you arrived at an agreement," said Hannasyde, with heavy sarcasm.

"Well, no," said Roger, ever fertile. "We didn't, and the whole thing is more or less in abeyance, because he wanted to buy the parrots in bulk, which is ridiculous, of course. However, now I've come into money I shan't bother any more about it."

"I say, what a shame Kenneth's missing all this!" said Antonia. "Where are the parrots supposed to be?"

"Round about the Amazon," said Roger. "You have to catch them."

"Yes, I can just see you penetrating into forests and laying snares for parrots. You are an ass!"

"Well, I shouldn't do that myself. I should employ people," said Roger. "Of course, if the business grew, and I daresay it would, the idea was to start a farm and breed them, the same way that people breed silver foxes and things. Properly managed there might be a lot of money in it, because if the purchaser has to pay ten pounds for a parrot (and very often a good parrot costs more than that), you can see for yourself that the profit per parrot is pretty considerable." He decided that the parrots had served their turn, and jettisoned them. "But, as I say, I've given up thinking of it now that I've come into money. They're really beside the point."

"I agree with you," said Hannasyde. "I have ascertained, Mr. Vereker, that you were a passenger on board the SS. *Pride of London* which docked at Liverpool on 16th June—the day before that on which your brother was murdered."

Roger leaned back in his chair. "Well, if you've ascertained it, that's that," he observed. "It's silly to argue points like that with detectives, so I'll tell you right away that the parrots were just a little joke of mine."

"I am aware of that," replied Hannasyde. "We shall get on better and faster if you don't make any more jokes."

"A lot of people think speed is the curse of the age," said Roger. "I can't say I'm keen on it myself. Mind you, I'm not at all sure there isn't something in that parrot scheme. The more I think of it the more I think there might be. Supposing people started trimming hats with parrot-feathers, for instance?"

"Mr. Vereker, *I* am not quite fool enough to believe that *you* are the fool you pretend to be. Shall we abandon the subject of parrots?"

"Just as you like," said Roger amiably.

"You admit that you landed in Liverpool on Friday, 16th June?"

"If you've been nosing around at shipping-agents, there's no point in asking me whether I admit it or not. It's a great pity you've been so inquisitive, because you're bound to waste a lot of time trying to make out I murdered Arnold, and I can tell you at the start I didn't."

"If you are so sure that I shall be wasting my time, Mr. Vereker, why did you try to conceal the fact that you were in England on the 17th June?"

"Now that's what I call a damned silly question," said Roger. "It's obvious that if it was known that I was in England then I should have had the police after me like a pack of bloodhounds. Well, what I mean is, look at the way you're behaving now! Not that I blame you, because naturally you're bound to do it. But that's just it. I turn up one day, broke to the wide, and Arnold gets himself murdered the day after. I should be a bigger fool than any I've ever met with if I didn't see who was going to be suspected once that leaked out. I don't like unpleasantness, and I don't like policemen. What's more, I find all this sort of thing very exhausting, because I'm not one of these people who always want to be using their brains, trying to remember a lot of unimportant details. It makes my head ache. All I want is peace and quiet."

"Nevertheless, Mr. Vereker, I must ask you to cast your mind back to the day you landed, and tell me just what you did."

Roger sighed, but he seemed to be more or less resigned to the necessity of answering, and said in a weary voice: "Well, I came to London. Naturally. What else should I do?"

"On the Friday?"

"If you've been making a lot of inquiries, you must know as well as I do that we didn't dock till late," said Roger.

"Certainly I know it, but you could still have journeyed to London that day."

"Well, I didn't. I don't like night travel. Never did. Some people sleep better on a train than anywhere. All I can say is, I don't."

"When did you come to London, then?"

"Next day, of course. But it's no use asking me what time the train got in, because I don't remember. I had lunch on it."

"And when you arrived in London, what did you do?"

Roger thought this over for a moment, and then asked: "Do you know what I did?"

"I am asking you," replied Hannasyde.

"I know you are, and that's just the trouble. The point is, if I know just how much you know it'll save a great deal of bother. I mean, it's no use my telling you I went to the Zoo if you're going to prove I spent the day in the British Museum. At the same time, I don't want to tell you anything I needn't. You see my difficulty?"

Giles Carrington interposed before Hannasyde could reply. "May I give you a piece of advice, Roger?"

"Anybody can do whatever they like as far as I'm concerned," said Roger. "Mind you, I don't particularly want your advice, because as far as I can see you're hand in glove with this Superintendent Osric—no, not Osric, but, anyway, whatever his name is."

Giles disregarded this. "Don't play the fool. You're not dealing with a fool."

"Is that your advice?" demanded Roger incredulously.

"It is."

"Well, I don't think much of it. You can't expect me to

change my habits at my time of life. I've always had a gift for taking things cheerfully."

"This particular brand of cheerfulness is likely to land you in trouble," said Giles rather sternly.

There was a distinct gleam of intelligence in the hazy, blood-shot eyes. "Oh no, it isn't!" said Roger. "Nobody's going to land me in trouble. Of course, I don't say that there may not be a great deal of unpleasantness. I daresay there will be. But Tony's been telling me all about this murder, and it looks pretty water-tight to me. You haven't got any clues at all, not even a finger print; you don't know who was with Arnold that night—in fact, you don't know anything at all, except that he was murdered."

"We have one clue," said Hannasyde. "The weapon which was used."

"Well, you prove that it belonged to me and you'll be cleverer than I take you for," retorted Roger. "You won't do it, because it didn't belong to me. Then where are you? Back at the beginning again. You'd much better give it up now."

"Thank you," said Hannasyde. "If you don't mind, I'll stick to it a little longer. I should take your cousin's advice, if I were you. What did you do when you reached London?"

"This and that," said Roger airily.

"For one who is so convinced that nothing will land him in trouble you are singularly reluctant to admit that you went to call on your brother, Mr. Vereker."

"Ah, you did know that, did you?" nodded Roger. "Oh, well, that makes it easier, I must say. I was getting very tired of hedging. Yes, I went to call on Arnold."

"A very natural thing to do," agreed Hannasyde.

"Of course it was a natural thing to do. I hadn't any money left."

"I see. Am I to understand that you shared your half-brother's and sister's dislike of him?"

"No, I didn't dislike him," said Roger, reflecting. "Not that I've really considered the matter."

"You were, in fact, indifferent?"

"That's it," said Roger. "Just the word I wanted. Though I must say that now I know what he was worth I'm not at all surprised he was disliked. Mean, very mean. You'd hardly believe it, but fifty pounds was all I could get out of him and he only gave me that because he didn't want it to get about that a brother of his was spending the night on the Embankment. He'd picked up a lot of very respectable ideas, I thought. Didn't like me coming to his house at all. If I were one of these sensitive people, which thank God I'm not, I should have been quite offended at the way he took it. You'd hardly believe it, but he only gave me that miserable fifty pounds on condition I didn't come near him again.''

"I'm surprised you were satisfied with fifty pounds, Mr. Vereker.''

"I wasn't at all satisfied with it, but I'm a reasonable man, and you can't expect people to carry much more than fifty pounds on them. Besides, I didn't know he'd made such a packet out of the old mine.''

Antonia suddenly elected to take part in the conversation, and said forcefully: "Look here, I don't want to crab your story, but if it's got to be Kenneth or you or me (the murderer, I mean), I'd rather it was you. So don't tell me you were going to fade out of Arnold's life for fifty pounds!''

"Certainly not,'' replied her imperturbable half-brother. "As a matter of fact the story is rather funny. Because I hadn't actually thought out how much Arnold was probably good for. The poor fellow was very upset at seeing me; oh, very upset! Well, you can't really blame him, because I've always been the disreputable member of the family, and I daresay he was afraid I might drag the name in the mud, or something. Naturally, as soon as I saw how green he was looking I realized that this was where I tried my hand at a little polite blackmail. You'd be surprised how easily he fell for it. I said I'd come to stay with him. He didn't like that at all. In fact, he got a bit violent at one time. However, he cooled down after a bit and offered me fifty pounds to clear out. So I pocketed that, and said I'd think it over. Then he came out with what he thought was a very good idea, though I wasn't so struck with it myself. He was to give me a ticket to Australia, or any other place I liked at the other side of the world, and pay me two hundred pounds a year for as long as I stopped there.''

"I call that a good offer," said Antonia.

"Yes, only I don't want to go to Australia," explained Roger.

"What has become of the money your father left you?" asked Giles.

Roger looked faintly surprised. "I don't know. That was a long time ago. You don't expect money to last forever. Anyway, it didn't."

"Good lord!" said Giles. "Well, go on!"

"Forgotten where I was. All this talk is making me very thirsty," said Roger, getting up and going across the room to the sideboard. "Anyone else join me in a spot?" Receiving no answer to this invitation, he said: "Oh, well!" and poured himself out a double whisky. Armed with this he returned to his chair.

"That's better," he said. "Where was I?"

"Two hundred pounds a year to stay in Australia," prompted Hannasyde.

"Yes, that's right. Well, I said I'd think it over, and Arnold said I could take it or leave it. I may have been a trifle rash—though I don't think so, because from all I've heard Australia wouldn't suit me at all—but I said I'd leave it. That was more or less the end of the meeting. Arnold had a date, and wanted to be off."

"With whom?" asked Hannasyde quickly.

"How on earth should I know? I didn't ask him."

"Do you know where he meant to dine?"

"Look here," said Roger, "you don't seem to have got the hang of things at all. We weren't having a friendly chat."

"Very well," said Hannasyde. "What happened next?"

"Oh, nothing much! I told Arnold he could give me a lift as far as Piccadilly, and we got into his car and drove off. He didn't much want to give me a lift, but he seemed to be afraid I might tell his butler who I was, or something, if he refused. On the way he said his offer would stand open till Monday, and I could think it over. However, the more I thought about it the less I liked the scheme. Besides, I'd got fifty pounds."

The Superintendent was watching him closely. "So what did you do, Mr. Vereker?"

"I went to Monte Carlo," replied Roger.

"You went to *Monte Carlo?*" repeated the Superintendent.

"Seemed an obvious thing to do," said Roger. "I've been wanting to try out a System for some time."

"You threw away a certain two hundred a year for a flimsy chance of making money gambling?"

"Why not?" said Roger, eyeing him blandly.

The Superintendent glanced rather helplessly at Giles. Giles's lips quivered.

"Yes, that's in the part," he said.

Hannasyde turned back to Roger. "When did you leave for Monte Carlo?"

"Next morning," Roger replied.

"On Sunday?"

"I daresay it may have been a Sunday. I didn't notice."

"So that on the night of 17th June you were in England?"

"That's right," agreed Roger. "If I'd known Arnold was going to be murdered I wouldn't have been, but it can't be helped now."

"Where did you spend that night, Mr. Vereker?"

Roger finished what was left in his glass and set it down. His sleepy gaze travelled from one intent face to the other. "Well, that's a very awkward question," he confessed.

"Why is it an awkward question?"

"Because I don't know what to say," answered Roger.

The Superintendent's brows began to draw together. "You can say where you were on the night of 17th June, Mr. Vereker!"

"Well, that's where you're wrong," said Roger. "I can't."

"Why not?"

"Because," said Roger simply, "I don't know."

CHAPTER 16

HIS words produced an astonished silence. He smiled in his apologetic way and took advantage of his audience's surprise to get up and replenish his empty glass. "We shall be needing some more whisky, Tony," he remarked. "Thought I'd better mention it."

The Superintendent found his voice. "You don't *know* where you spent the night of 17th June?" he repeated.

"No," said Roger. "I don't."

"Come, Mr. Vereker, that is not quite good enough!"

There was a note of anger in Hannasyde's voice, but it left Roger unmoved. "Well, I was in London. That I *can* tell you."

"For God's sake, Roger, pull yourself together!" his cousin besought him. "You dined at the Trocadero, didn't you?"

Roger thought this over. "Wasn't it the Monico?" he inquired.

"Did you pay for your dinner with a ten-pound note?" demanded Hannasyde.

"Now you come to mention it, I believe I did," Roger admitted. "Wanted change, you see."

"Very well, then, we can assume that you dined at the Trocadero," said Hannasyde. "What time was it when you left the restaurant?"

"I don't know," said Roger.

There was no trace of his usual kindliness in the Superintendent's face by this time. His grey eyes were stern, his mouth set rather rigidly. "Very well, Mr. Vereker. Do you happen to know what you did when you left the Trocadero?"

Roger performed a vague gesture with one hand. "Just drifted about here and there," he said.

"Did you spend the night in a hotel or a boardinghouse?"

"No," said Roger.

"You booked no room anywhere?"

"No," repeated Roger, still amiably smiling. "Left my bag at the station."

"Mr. Vereker, you cannot have walked about London all night. Will you be good enough to put an end to this farce, and tell me without any more trifling—where you were?"

"The trouble is I don't know where I was," replied Roger, with the air of one making a fresh disclosure. "You see, I didn't give the address to the taxi-driver, which accounts for it."

"You were with someone, then?"

"That's it," said Roger. "I was with a friend."

"And your friend's name?"

"Flossie," said Roger. "At least it may have been Florence, but that's what I called her."

At this point Giles turned away rather hastily, and walked over to the window. The Superintendent was in no mood to share his obvious amusement, and merely rapped out: "Flossie who?"

"Well, there you rather have me," said Roger. "I didn't ask her. I mean, why should I?"

"I see," said the Superintendent. "You spent the night at an address you don't know, with a woman whose name you don't know. Is that what you expect me to believe?"

"It doesn't matter to me what you believe," said Roger. "You can do as you like about it. The point is you can't prove I didn't. And don't go rounding up all the Flossies in London for me to identify, because, though I'm not a shy man, I'll be damned if I'll do that."

Antonia, joining her cousin by the window, said wistfully: "I do wish Kenneth were here."

"I'm thankful he isn't," said Giles.

She said more softly: "Do you think Roger did it, Giles?"

"God knows!"

At the other end of the studio Superintendent Hannasyde was speaking. "Was it the news of your brother's death which brought you back from Monte Carlo, Mr. Vereker?"

"Oh no!" said Roger. "I didn't know anything about that. As a matter of fact, that particular System didn't work out right. Of course, I may have muddled it, but I'm inclined to think it wasn't a good one. However, it's made me think of something that I rather fancy may be pretty useful, so it doesn't much matter. Only it was a pity they would insist on sending me home, because I might have raised some money somehow or other. I told them I wasn't going to commit suicide—well, do I look the sort of man who'd shoot himself? Of course I don't!—but it was no use."

"Do you never read the papers, Mr. Vereker? Your brother's death was widely reported."

"I wouldn't say never," replied Roger conscientiously. "Occasionally one hasn't anything better to do, but there's always something better to do at Monte Carlo. And if you think it over you'll see that if I read the papers, and knew about Arnold being murdered, I shouldn't have come home."

"As far as I can make out you had no choice in the matter," said Hannasyde tartly.

"Now, don't start losing your temper," advised Roger. "No one forced me to come and look my relations up, so I could quite easily have laid low till it all blew over."

"You had to look your relations up, as you call it, because you were badly in need of money," said Hannasyde.

"That's perfectly true," conceded Roger, "but if you'd been broke as many times as I have you'd know that there are always ways of rubbing along somehow. You don't suppose I should go shoving my head into a noose just because I wanted some money, do you?"

"I think," said Hannasyde, getting up, "that, in common with your half-brother, you suffer from a delusion that you are clever enough to get away with anything. Therefore I judge that you are very likely to have done just that."

"Have it your own way," said Roger equably. "And, talking of money, I want to talk business with my cousin when you're quite finished asking me questions.''

"I have finished," said Hannasyde. He turned. "Good-bye, Miss Vereker. I'm sorry to have interrupted your tea-party.'' He nodded to Giles Carrington and walked over to the door.

"You don't understand me at all," complained Roger. "I don't pretend to be clever. In fact, most people seem to think I'm a bit of a fool. Not that I agree with that, because I'm not a fool by any means. And while we're on the subject, it's my belief Kenneth isn't half what he's cracked up to be either. You may think he's very bright, but all I can say is——''

The door closed behind the Superintendent. Roger looked slightly pained, but quite resigned. "Gone off in a huff," he remarked. "One of those touchy people."

However, there were no signs of ill-temper about Hannasyde when, some hours later, he faced Giles Carrington across the dinner-table. He had accepted Giles's invitation to dinner without any hesitation, and the twinkle in his eye was clearly discernible as he remarked: "I can't make up my mind which of your cousins I would most like to convict of this murder. Are you letting that—that lunatic get his hands on the Vereker fortune?''

"What can we do?" shrugged Giles. "He's the heir all right. How does he strike you?''

"I should hate to be rude about any relative of yours," replied Hannasyde grimly.

"Do you believe his story?"

"No. But I can't say I disbelieve it either. I'm doing what I can to check up on it, of course—without much hope of success. I'm also making inquiries at all the likely restaurants—so far without any success at all. I can't discover where Arnold Vereker dined on the night of his death. That's what I really want to know. All these suspects, promising as they seem to be, with their motives and their lack of alibis, are nothing but a lot of blind alleys. If Kenneth Vereker didn't exist, everything would point to Roger. But Kenneth does exist, and there's not a penny to choose between him and Roger. Both had the same motive, neither has a credible alibi. But which am I to arrest?" He took a salted almond from the dish in front of him and ate it. "I'm pinning my hopes to the finding of the restaurant where Arnold Vereker dined that night, if he did dine at one. Hemingway has a photograph of him, which he's trotting round, and of course we've made inquiries at all his usual haunts. But we have to face the fact that he may have dined at a private house—with one of his lady-loves probably. I think I've seen most of them, but you never know. At Cavelli's, where he seems to have been a pretty frequent visitor, they tell me that he had been in the habit, lately, of bringing a new lady to dine there—dark, good-looking girl, unknown to Cavelli. On the other hand, the head waiter at the Café Morny says that the last time Vereker was there he had an ash-blonde in tow. It isn't very helpful, is it?"

"The trouble is, it was too simple a murder," said Giles. "Now, had you found my cousin's body in a locked room, the key on the inside, all the windows bolted——"

Hannasyde smiled. "Oh yes, that would have been easy compared with this," he said. "We should at least have had something to go on. It's always the straight-forward killings that present the worst difficulties. Once people start being too clever, and try to present us with insoluble mysteries, they are apt to give themselves away. These apparently impossible murders are like a good chess problem—mate in three moves, and only one possible solution. But when you get a perfectly simple murder like this, you can see at least half a dozen ways of bringing off a mate, and the Lord only knows which is the right one!"

Giles picked up the decanter, and refilled both the glasses. "I see I shall have to take a hand in this myself," he said meditatively.

The Superintendent laughed. "Talented amateur, eh? I wish you luck!"

"You never know," murmured Giles.

Hannasyde looked up quickly. "Have you got hold of something?"

"No," said Giles. "I can't say I have."

"I don't trust you," said Hannasyde bluntly. "For two pins you'd conceal some vital clue from me—if you could."

"Oh no!" said Giles. "Not unless I thought divulging it would lead to a family scandal. But don't be alarmed: I haven't discovered a vital clue."

Hannasyde looked suspicious, but beyond requesting his host not to attempt to pull any Quick-Watson! stunts during the course of his amateur investigations, he said no more about it.

Almost immediately after dinner he took his leave, and nearly collided on the stairs, on his way out, with Antonia Vereker, who was being towed up at a great rate by one of her dogs.

She betrayed no embarrassment at meeting Hannasyde, but said "Hullo," in her casual way, adding darkly that she always knew her cousin was playing a double game.

"I shouldn't be surprised," agreed Hannasyde, stooping to pat Bill. "I've just told him I don't trust him myself."

She smiled. "He's nice, isn't he?" she said ingenuously.

"Very nice."

There was a quizzical look in Hannasyde's eye, though his voice remained perfectly grave. Antonia was quite impervious to it. "Rather a bore for him, all this," she said. "Specially as he's always disapproved of us more or less. However, it can't be helped." She nodded in a friendly way, and went on up the stairs.

The Superintendent resumed his progress down the stairs, wondering by what sign (hidden from his own trained eye) Miss Vereker deduced that her cousin disapproved of her.

Disapproval was certainly not the predominant emotion visible in Giles Carrington's face when Antonia was ushered into his sitting-room. He got up quickly from a deep chair, and stretched out his hand. "Tony! My dear child, what on earth brings you here? Has anything happened?"

"Oh no!" replied Antonia. "Only I got fed-up with everybody at the flat, and thought I'd come and see if you were in. Can I have some coffee?"

Giles said: "Yes, of course. But you ought not to be here at all, you know. In fact, as soon as you've had your coffee I'm going to take you home again."

Antonia sighed. "Sorry; I'll go now if you want me to. It was only that I suddenly couldn't bear it any longer, and there wasn't anyone but you I could come to. Except Leslie, I suppose; but she's so livid about Roger turning up, and dishing

Kenneth, that she's almost as bad as the rest of them. However, if you're bored with our rotten affairs it doesn't matter."

"Sit down," said Giles, pulling up another chair. "You know I'm not bored. What's the matter, chicken?"

She looked up at him, flushing, sudden surprise in her eyes. "Oh, Giles, you haven't called me that for years!" she said.

"Haven't I?" he said, smiling down at her. "No, perhaps I haven't."

"You know jolly well you've had a hate against me ever since you were such a vile beast about John Fotheringham!" said Antonia.

"Well, that's one way of putting it," said Giles.

"It's the only way of putting it," said Antonia firmly. "In fact, I practically made up my mind never to speak to you again, after the things you said to me."

"You didn't speak to me again, Tony, for over a year."

"Yes, I did," contradicted Antonia. "I spoke to you at the Dawsons' dance, and once I had to ring you up about my Insurance shares. All the same, I wouldn't have, if I could have helped it. Only then I got myself into this ghastly mess, and I had to send for you to get me out of it."

Giles was watching her inscrutably. "Why, Tony?"

She smiled at him. "Well—whom else could I have sent for?" she asked, puzzled.

"Brother—fiancé—?" suggested Giles.

It was evident that this had not previously occurred to her. "Oh!" she said doubtfully. "Yes, I suppose I could, not that they'd have been much use. Anyway, I didn't think of them. And I'm glad I did send for you, because really and truly I was quite sick of the hate, and—and you have been frightfully decent to me ever since all this happened. So I don't mind admitting that actually I made a mistake about John—though I still think you were utterly rancid about the whole affair." She paused, and then added: "I've been rather wanting to bury that hatchet absolutely ever since Arnold was killed, I did mean to have it all out with you at Hanborough, that day, only when you turned up it didn't seem as though we ever had had a hate, and I forgot. Only if you did happen to be still feeling stuffy about me, I thought I'd just mention the matter.''

"Tony," Giles said abruptly, "are you still engaged to Mesurier?"

"Yes, and it's the most unutterable bore," she replied, with her usual shattering honesty. "To tell you the truth, it was partly because he turned up at the flat to-night that I cleared out."

"Tony, what in the world did you get engaged to that fellow for?"

"I can't make out. It's all most odd, and I'm inclined to think I must have been slightly deranged when I did it. But really, Giles, I thought I liked him awfully. And Kenneth had just picked up Violet, and life seemed fairly moth-eaten anyway, so—so I got engaged to Rudolph. And the funny part of it is I went on thinking he'd do for ages, and never noticed the things Kenneth kept on pointing out, like showing his teeth too much when he smiled, and wearing the sort of smart clothes that one's own men don't wear. And I didn't see that he was on the flashy side, till all of a sudden it dawned on me. I mean, absolutely in a burst. I can tell you the exact date. It was that Sunday—the day after Arnold was murdered—when we were all in the studio. You were there too, and Violet. It came over me like a—like a tidal wave, for no reason at all. And now I feel rather rotten about it, because really he didn't do anything to make me go clean off him like that."

"It doesn't matter how rotten you feel about it, Tony. You've got to break it off. Understand?"

"Well, of course I understand. But I can't break it off while there's a chance of him being pinched for the murder. It would be a frightfully mean trick."

"It's a much meaner trick to keep him dangling when you've no intention of marrying him."

She considered this. "No, I don't think it is," she answered presently. "It's bound to look a bit fishy if I throw him over while he's a suspect."

"Tony, what if he did it?" Giles asked.

"Oh well, then I shall just have to stick to him!" she said. "However, I left him proving to everybody how he couldn't possibly have done it, so perhaps he didn't. He's being rather pleased with himself at the moment, and that, coming on top of all the rest, was too much for me, so I bolted." She turned, as Giles's man came into the room with the coffee-tray, and waited until it had been arranged on a low table beside her chair. "Thank you. Is that cream? Because, if so, lovely!"

"All the rest of what, Tony?" Giles asked, as the door closed again.

"I'll tell you. I've put two lumps into yours. Is that enough? Well, to start with, Leslie Rivers drifted in after you left this afternoon, so I sent Roger out to order more whisky—it's completely incredible the amount he puts away, you know —and then she let fly. Usually she's a quiet sort of creature, and definitely sensible, but—this is absolutely private, Giles —she's not sane when it comes to Kenneth, and from the way she talked about Roger, you'd think he'd come home on purpose to do Kenneth an injury. Well, I got rather bored with that, because really and truly it's Violet who wants the Vereker fortune, much more than Kenneth, and I've got a distinct hope that she may throw him over now that he's poor again. Though I'm bound to say that he hadn't any expectations at all when she got engaged to him, so perhaps she won't. Leslie says she doesn't care tuppence for him, but then she's prejudiced. I admit I haven't much time for Violet myself—in fact, I can't stand her—but I daresay she feels a lot more than she shows. She's the sort that doesn't give herself away at all, so you can never tell what she's thinking. But that's not the point. The point is I got bored with Leslie being intense about the whole situation. She went away after a bit then Kenneth and Violet came back from that matinée in the middle of a most drivelling row. Apparently some fat old man with a pearl tie-pin came up to speak to her in the theatre and, according to Kenneth, called her Vi, and pawed her shoulder, and was quite obviously one of her past conquests. Well, you know what Kenneth is. He promptly went off the deep end, and came home in one of his moods, and pranced up and down the studio raving at Violet. And Violet made things worse by saying the Tie-pin was a Big Man in the City, and she'd met him quite by accident when she was waiting for a friend in the lounge of some hotel or other. Well, that didn't go with a swing by any means, and Kenneth was extraordinarily rude, and talked about Pickups and things. I hoped Violet would break off the engagement then and there, but she didn't. And, of course, I went and said the wrong thing without in the least meaning to, so Violet then had a shot at withering me.''

Giles laughed. ''What a hopeless task! What did you say?''

''Well, I meant it really to be on her side, because Kenneth was being such an ass, and I said I couldn't see what he was making such a song and dance about when he knew perfectly well that Violet was always getting off with rich men. I honestly didn't mean it cattily, but I quite see it may have sounded like that. All the same, Kenneth must know that she used to pick up men who could trot her round and give her a good time, because she's never made any secret of the fact. However, he wouldn't look at it in a reasonable light at all, and it went on and on till I got so fed-up I could have screamed. And then Roger came in, and it was quite obvious he'd been at a pub all the time, because he was just nicely.''

''Where did he get the money?'' inquired Giles.

''Took it out of my bag. He said so. Anyway, he was in a ghastly state.''

Giles was frowning. ''Really blind?''

''No, not in the least. That wouldn't have mattered, because we could have put him to bed. I don't think he *can* get decently tight: he's pickled by this time. He was just himself, only much more so, and he said the most outrageous things. He started on poor old Murgatroyd, and kept on asking her if she remembered the milkman—which is apparently the skeleton in her cupboard, but before my time. She was fearfully upset, but nothing would stop Roger telling us the whole story, because, though Kenneth might have thrown him out, he was glooming about Violet, and wouldn't pay any attention. So Violet took a hand, and was excessively sweet and charming to Roger, and I'm damned if he didn't say it was no use her making up to him, because he was too experienced to be caught, and didn't admire her type anyway. I will say this for Violet: she took it very well; but even she looked pretty peeved when Roger told Kenneth he could cut him out with her if he wanted to, but didn't.''

''What a party!'' Giles exclaimed. ''How long did this go on?''

"Oh, till Rudolph turned up after dinner. Roger started on him then. He wanted to know why he had such wavy hair, and said he didn't like it; and when he heard he was engaged to me he asked me what on earth I could possibly see in him. That sort of thing. Rudolph realized he was a trifle screwed, of course, and pretended not to listen. The last I saw of them, Roger was still going on about my being batty to marry Rudolph, and Rudolph was holding forth about not having murdered Arnold, and Kenneth was snapping at everybody in turn. So I cleared out, and came to talk to you. This is very good coffee."

"I'm glad. When is Roger going to leave the studio?"

"As soon as he can. I must say, I'm thankful to you and Gordon Truelove for letting him have some cash. I don't mind him as much as Kenneth does, but I couldn't stand much more of him. He's going to take a service flat."

"A service-flat! Why the devil can't he go and stay in Eaton Place?"

"He says it isn't his style. Kenneth had a friendly spasm when he heard that, but it turned out that he meant he couldn't stand having a lot of servants about. He said it would fidget him. So Violet—who badly wants Eaton Place—backed him up, and said she knew of a very good block. I gather she means to take him by the hand and lead him to a flat."

"Is Violet behaving with real nobility of character, or is she actually trying to catch Roger?"

"I don't know. I shouldn't think she can be trying to catch him, because she needn't have got engaged to Kenneth in the first place if she was set on marrying a rich man."

"Rich men aren't always so keen on marriage, Tony."

"No, I daresay they aren't. But I think myself that she's making up to Roger in the hope of getting him to give Kenneth a large allowance. Not that Kenneth would accept it, because he wouldn't."

"Kenneth seems to be taking this pretty badly," Giles said. "Yet I shouldn't have said that he cared much about money."

"He doesn't, but of course he is rather hard-up at the moment, and after thinking you're next door to being a millionaire, it must be fairly sickening to find you're just as poor as you always were." She got up, and fastened his leash to

Bill's collar. "I'd better go, I suppose. Do you know, Giles, I'm almost beginning to wish Arnold hadn't been murdered?"

"Tony, you're atrocious!"

"Well, but it did look good at first, you must admit. Only now we all seem to be in a mess over it, and everything's rather wearing. I'm glad we've got you. You're about the only dependable thing we have got."

"Thank you, Tony," he said, smiling a little.

"And I'm glad we've definitely buried the hatchet. I like you, Giles."

"Think again," he said.

She frowned. "Why? Don't you believe me?"

"Oh yes, I believe you," he replied. "But I've never thought half a loaf better than no bread, my dear."

CHAPTER 17

UPON the following morning, his inebriety having worn off, Roger cheerfully explained his condition as having been due to enforced abstinence for so long. This roused Kenneth to tell him exactly how many bottles of whisky he had consumed since his arrival at the studio, but Roger merely said: "Well, you don't call that anything, do you?" and the conversation dropped.

Violet came in soon after breakfast, a circumstance which induced Kenneth, still in a bitter mood, to ask her savagely whether she ever did any work at all. He himself was in his overall, scowling at the half-finished canvas on the easel. Violet refused to take offence at his tone, and replied that she had already sent off a couple of fashion-drawings by post, and thought that she was entitled to a holiday.

"I see," Kenneth said. "Devoting it to me, of course."

"No, dear, I'm not," replied Violet calmly. "You are far too disagreeable, let me tell you. I am going to try and fix your half-brother up in a place of his own."

"Sweet of you, my pet. I hope he'll appreciate all this pure altruism."

Violet stood for a moment, her lips slightly compressed. Then she walked across the room to Kenneth's side, and laid her hand on his arm. "Kenneth dear, will you try and be rea-

sonable?'' she begged. "We must get Roger away from here.
He's making you impossible to live with. You know quite well
he'll never move unless he's made to, and if neither you nor
Tony will do anything about it, it's up to me. I think you
might be a little grateful, I must say."

"You're doing it for what you can get out of him," Kenneth
said.

She was silent for a moment. Then she said: "Well, what
if I am? Why shouldn't he do something for us? I don't want
to be poor, if you do."

He looked at her with narrowed eyes. "Gold-digging, eh?
Do you care for anything else, my girl? Do you?"

She stiffened. "I'm not going to be spoken to like that, Kenneth. I'll go."

There was a pause. Kenneth had turned back to his work,
for the first time indifferent to her anger. She moved towards
the door, but looked back before she opened it. Her voice
changed. She said gently: "If you want to break off our
engagement, please tell me! Do you, Kenneth?"

He did not answer for a moment, but swung round, and
stood looking at her under scowling brows. "I don't know,"
he said at last.

She remained quite still, fixing her great eyes on his. He put
down his palette suddenly, and strode across the floor to her
side, and pulled her roughly into his arms. "No. No, I don't.
Damn you, you've no heart, but I'm going to paint you like
that, against the door, with the light falling just *so.*"

She returned his embrace, and took his face between her
slender hands. "Try not to mistrust me, darling. It hurts."

"Leave Roger alone, then," he replied.

"Yes, dear, as soon as I've got him out of this place I will,"
she promised. "You can't really suppose that he's of any interest to me!"

He let the subject drop, but might well have pursued it more
rigorously had he but heard what his half-brother was saying
to Antonia at that very moment.

Roger, who said that the sight of Kenneth dabbing at a
picture was very unrestful, had sought refuge in the kitchen,
where he found Antonia busily engaged in ironing handker-
chiefs. This was a hardly less disturbing sight than that of an

artist at work, but it had the advantage of being unaccompanied by the smell of turpentine. Having ascertained that Murgatroyd had gone out to do the marketing, Roger sank into the basket-chair by the fire, and lit a cigarette.

"You'll catch it if Murgatroyd comes in," Antonia warned him.

"I daresay she won't for a bit," said Roger hopefully. "That girl's here again."

"Who? Violet?"

"She's going to find me a service flat."

"Good," said Antonia. "The sooner the better."

"Now, don't you get spiteful!" said Roger. "Because for one thing I quite like you, and for another I've got a good idea."

"Why on earth do you like me?" demanded Antonia, curious but ungrateful.

"I don't know. You can't account for these things. Mind you, I don't like that pimple you've got yourself engaged to, but that's neither here nor there, and as far as I can see you won't marry him. However, that wasn't what I wanted to say. This Violet-girl."

"Well, I think it would be a good idea to get rid of her. I mean, do you want her joining the family?"

"Not particularly."

"Of course not. Who would? I know her type. Give her three months, and she'll be managing the lot of us, and talking me into giving Kenneth more money than I've got. You may think I don't bother my head over these things, but that's where you're wrong. When I haven't got anything else to do I think a lot, and, of course, it's quite obvious that she's not at all the sort of girl Kenneth ought to marry."

"How do you propose to stop him?"

"Well," said Roger, tipping the ash of his cigarette vaguely in the direction of the stove, "Kenneth seems to be a jealous young cub. Flies off the handle at nothing. My idea was that if I took Violet about a bit it might lead to the engagement's being broken off."

"Yes," said Antonia. "But it might lead to a new one's being formed."

A gleam crept into Roger's eyes. "If she's clever enough to

catch me, she can keep me," he said. "She won't be the first to try, not by a long chalk."

"It's not a bad idea," Antonia said slowly. "Only I doubt if you'll succeed in taking Violet in. She's no fool."

"Anyway," said Roger, "she might just as well be useful as not, and there's bound to be a lot to do settling me into a flat."

"Are you trying to lure Violet just to move you into a flat?" Antonia inquired scornfully.

"Well, someone's got to do it," he pointed out. "Not that that's my only reason, because it isn't. Far from it. Now I've come into all this money I shall go about a bit here and there, and she's a very good sort of a girl to take around. What I mean is, she's smart, and she won't want me to think out what she'd like to eat. If there's one thing that wears me out quicker than anything it's having to choose a lot of food for someone else to eat. Besides, if she's supposed to be going to be my sister-in-law I shan't have to be polite. Not that I want to be rude, but I find ceremony very exhausting. And, talking of things being exhausting, they tell me I own the mine now."

"I thought it was a limited company."

"Yes, but I've got all Arnold's shares, which apparently gives me control. Of course I've nothing against holding the shares, but I'm not going to control the mine. It's absurd. I suppose Kenneth wouldn't like to be chairman?"

"I shouldn't think so," said Antonia indifferently. "But why worry? You may be arrested for murdering Arnold before you have to think about appointing chairmen."

Roger blinked at her, and said uneasily: "I don't see why you need bring that up, just when I'd forgotten about it. The fact of the matter is I don't like it. Not that I did murder Arnold, because such an idea never entered my head, but it's no good saying people don't get convicted of crimes they didn't commit. Very often they do. Let alone that it's very disturbing to have a lot of detectives with their eyes glued on you. That's one reason why I shall be glad to get out of this place. I can't stand having that Superintendent bobbing in and out like a dog at a fair. It's not my idea of comfort, by any means. If he thinks he's going to treat my flat like his own house he's mistaken, and that's all there is to it."

Antonia put the iron back on the stove. "Giles wants to know why you can't live in Eaton Place," she observed.

"Because I don't want to be bothered with a great house like that, and a lot of servants worrying me to know whether I'll be in to lunch, and what I'd like to wear. Besides, if you run a pack of servants you have to look after them. I've already told Kenneth he can have Eaton Place, which, of course, is why Violet's so keen on fixing me up in a flat."

"One thing I will say for you, Roger," remarked Antonia, preparing to depart, "you may be an ass in some ways, but there aren't many flies on you. All the same, there aren't many on Violet either, so don't be too optimistic about cutting Kenneth out." She paused, as a thought occurred to her, and added: "I suppose you couldn't see your way to marrying her? Then Kenneth could marry Leslie, and everything would be splendid. Violet would make you rather a good wife, too."

"No one would make me a good wife," replied Roger simply. "Moreover, if by Leslie you mean that girl who was here yesterday, I don't think it would be splendid at all. We shouldn't get on. Every time I meet her she looks at me as though she'd like to murder me. It's very unnerving, I can tell you."

At this moment the door opened and Violet looked into the kitchen. "Oh, you are here!" she said. "I heard someone talking, so I thought it must be you two."

Antonia could not help wondering how much she had heard, and had the grace to blush. However, Violet was not paying any attention to her. She suggested to Roger that they should go out together to look at flats, and added, with a thoughtful glance at his suit, that she knew of a very good tailor if he had not already got one of his own.

Antonia, seeing Roger go off meekly in Violet's wake, was more than ever convinced that she would be the very person for him to marry.

The events of the next few days did nothing to weaken this conviction. Not only was Roger installed in a furnished flat, but an entire wardrobe was purchased for him, so that Kenneth regained possession of his shirts and pyjamas, and Murgatroyd was induced to look upon Violet for the first time with approval.

Roger was so well pleased with his flat that he roused himself sufficiently to give a dinner-party as a sort of housewarming, and invited not only his half-brother and sister, but Violet and Giles as well. He did not invite Mesurier, for various comprehensive reasons which he was quite ready to expound to any and everybody. It had naturally been impossible to keep Mesurier's financial antics a secret from him, and he was only deterred from dismissing him from the firm by Kenneth's warning that to do so would be tantamount to fixing the date of his wedding to Antonia. "If you want that tailor's dummy for a brother-in-law, let me tell you that I don't!" said Kenneth.

"Certainly not," said Roger. "In fact, that was why I thought I'd sack him. Though, mind you, I should like to sack him on my own account, because for one thing I don't care for him, and for another I'm all for sacking someone just to see what it feels like."

"I suppose you only know what it feels like to be sacked," remarked Kenneth waspishly.

"Exactly," nodded Roger, utterly impervious to this or any other insult. "And, funnily enough, the last time I got the boot it was for almost the same thing. Only, as it happens, I wasn't thinking of paying the money back. I don't say I mightn't have thought of it if I'd had any means of doing it, but I hadn't. However, if you think sacking Mesurier will make Tony marry him, I won't do it. Because if she marries him she'll expect me to call him Rudolph, and I don't mind telling you that I don't like the name. In fact, I think it's a damn' silly name. What's more, if I had to call him by it I should feel very self-conscious. Not that I really like Giles either, but that's merely a matter of taste. There's nothing against the name as a name, nothing at all."

He startled Kenneth, who looked up quickly and said: "Giles? Do you mean—— Rot! She hasn't been on speaking terms with him for months!"

"I don't know anything about that," answered Roger. "All I do know is that if this Rudolph excrescence can be shifted, Tony will marry Giles."

"Well, I hope you may be right," said Kenneth. "Giles is a

nice chap. I must keep an eye on them."

"If you take my advice you'll keep your eye on your own pictures," said Roger. "I don't say I wouldn't rather look at almost anything else myself, but probably you don't feel like that about them."

"I don't," said Kenneth, on whom such inexpert criticism of his work made no impression at all. "And don't go putting your foot into it by sacking Mesurier."

"Well, all right," agreed Roger. "Only I won't have him at my party."

Mention of the party made Kenneth at once point out to him that his home-coming was no occasion for rejoicing for anyone but himself. He said that he had no intention of being present, but in the end he was present, not as a result of any persuasion on Roger's part, but because Violet had coaxed him into it. She was unusually kind to him throughout the evening, and paid so little heed to Roger that he became quite good-humoured after a while, and even enlisted Roger's support in an argument with Violet on the question of whether or not it was indecent to attend a public dance within a fortnight of Arnold's death. As this discussion was started in the restaurant which was attached to the flats, and conducted with a total disregard for whoever might overhear it, a good many shocked glances were cast at the Verekers' table, and one stickler for the proprieties spent the rest of the evening composing a letter of complaint to the landlord.

As might have been expected, Violet was firm in refusing to countenance the bare notion of appearing at the ball, which was to take place three days later. She said that there was such a thing as respect to the dead, to which Kenneth replied that he had no more respect for Arnold dead than he had had for Arnold alive. "Besides, I paid thirty bob for the tickets, and I'm going to use them," he added.

"You could sell them," Violet pointed out. "Don't you agree with me that he ought to, Mr. Carrington?"

"Yes, on the whole I think I do," replied Giles. "You're not going, are you, Tony?"

"No," said Antonia. "Because Rudolph can't manage that night."

"If Violet won't come, I'll take you, Tony," said Kenneth, glancing provocatively at his betrothed. "And if you won't, I'll take Leslie!"

"I've already told you, darling, I'm not going with you," Violet said. "We should be bound to meet any number of people we know, and what they would think I daren't imagine! Tony can please herself, but I hope she has too much sense, let alone proper feeling, to go near the ball."

" 'After this short speech, they all cheered,' " said Kenneth instantly. "Will you come, Tony?"

"She's dining with me, and going to a show," interposed Giles.

"I see. Thus evincing a proper respect for the dead."

Giles laughed. "More or less. Will you come, Tony?"

"Yes, please," said Antonia. "Is it a party, or just us?"

"Of course it's not a party," said Kenneth. "Where's your sense of decency?"

"I've no doubt these little social *convenances* seem absurd to you, dear," remarked Violet, "but Mr. Carrington is perfectly right. Going to a public ball and dining quietly with someone at a restaurant are two entirely different things."

"What a discerning mind you have got, my pet!" said Kenneth admiringly.

"Now, don't start quarrelling," besought Roger. "Personally, I've no objection to Kenneth's going to the ball, none at all. If I wanted to go to it, which I don't, I shouldn't bother about whether it was decent or not for an instant."

"That we believe," said Giles. "Oh, I'm your guest! Sorry, Roger, but you asked for it."

"You needn't trouble about my feelings, because they're not easily hurt," replied Roger. "My theory is that everybody should do just what they like. There's a great deal too much interference in this world. If Kenneth wants to go to a dance, why shouldn't he? And if Violet doesn't want to, that's her affair. I'll tell you what; you come and have dinner here with me, Violet."

This casual invitation produced a noticeable tension in two at least of the party. Antonia, thinking it a trifle crude, scowled at Roger, and Kenneth fixed Violet with a smouldering gaze, awaiting her answer.

She excused herself gracefully, but failed to satisfy Kenneth, who harked back to the invitation on the way home, and informed her that in case she had any idea of spending the evening with Roger she could get rid of it immediately.

"Darling, how silly you are!" she sighed. "Of course, I'm not going to do any such thing! Did you hear me refuse?"

"I heard," Kenneth said rather grimly. "But it also transpired, my love, in the course of Roger's artless chatter, that you dined with him two nights ago—a circumstance hitherto unknown to me."

She coloured slightly. "Oh, you mean the night you were out!" she said. "Well, what if I did? Tony apparently went off with Rudolph, and poor Roger was left alone in the flat. I merely took pity on him."

"You have a lovely nature, my sweet. I suppose it slipped your memory, which was why you forgot to tell me about it."

"I knew you would make a ridiculous fuss if I did tell you," replied Violet, in her calm way. "You're so taken up with your own grievance, Kenneth, that you don't see that Roger's really rather a pathetic figure."

"No, I can't say that I do."

"Well, I find him so. If he did commit the murder, of course it's dreadful, but I can't help feeling sorry for him. The whole thing is very much on his mind. I know he pretends it isn't, but he has the idea that the police are watching him all the time."

"Form of D.T.," said Kenneth callously. "The police haven't any more reason to suspect Roger than they have to suspect me. It's time we gave up thinking about it. No one will ever be arrested; and, what's more, the police know it. Are you coming to the Albert Hall Ball, or are you not?"

"But, darling, I've told you already——"

"Look here, Violet!" he said forcibly. "Let's get things straight! I've no use for any of your conventions, and I never shall have. If you mean to marry me you'll have to accept that."

He sounded a little dangerous, and she at once stopped trying to argue with him, and set herself to coax him out of his bitter mood. When they parted he had softened towards her, and she had said that perhaps she would go to the ball with him if he was so set on it. A quarrel was thus happily averted, but when at half-past six on the day of the ball she arrived at the studio, and said gently that really she didn't think she could go after all, because she had a bad headache, Kenneth looked her up and down for one minute, and then strode over to the telephone and called Leslie Rivers' number.

Violet said nothing, but stood looking out of the window while Kenneth arranged to call for Leslie to take her out to dinner at a quarter to eight. Apparently Leslie had no scruples about attending the ball in his company, and it was with a glint of triumph in his eyes that Kenneth glanced towards his fiancée as he put down the receiver. "Go home and nurse your headache, darling," he said sweetly. "Or have you other plans? I'm sorry I can't spare the time to discuss them with you, but I'm going to have a bath and change."

Antonia, who had entered the room at the beginning of this scene, and had been a silent but critical audience of the whole, watched him go out, and then looked at Violet with a certain amount of contempt. "Well, you've mucked that pretty successfully," she observed. "I should have thought anyone with a grain of sense would have known better than to have tried to pull that trick on Kenneth."

"Would you?" said Violet smoothly.

"I should. If you'd stuck to your original No he probably wouldn't have gone—not that I can see that it matters whether he goes or doesn't. But if you wanted to make him utterly pig-headed about the whole thing, you've gone the right way to work. I never thought you were such an ass. Help me to do up this frock for the lord's sake! Giles will be here by seven, and I've got a couple of letters I must write before I go."

Giles arrived at seven o'clock to find her standing in the middle of the room with Violet kneeling on the floor at her feet, mending a tear in the hem of her chiffon frock.

Antonia said penitently: "Oh, Giles, I'm so sorry to be late, but I had to dash off two letters, and then I went and stuck my heel through this accursed skirt. I shan't be a minute."

"If you'd only stand still!" begged Violet. "You've got some ink on your finger, too."

"I'll wash it off. Thanks awfully, Violet. Could you also find a couple of stamps, and stick them on my letters? Top drawer of my bureau, I think.''

"Yes, I'll see to them," said Violet soothingly. "Hurry up and wash and get your cloak." She found the stamps, after a little search, fixed them to the letters, and said with her slow smile: "Rather a miracle to find a stamp in this house. Tell Tony I've taken the letters, and will post them on my way home, will you, Mr. Carrington?''

"You are not going to the ball?" Giles asked. "I thought——''

"No, I am not going," she replied. "I shall spend a quiet evening at home instead. I hope you enjoy your theatre. Good-night!''

He escorted her to the front door, and opened it for her. As he shut it again behind her Antonia came out of her bedroom, her evening-coat tumbled over her arm. He took it from her, and helped her to put it on. "Violet has gone," he remarked. "I thought you told me she was going to the Albert Hall show after all?''

"Yes, but she changed her mind, and came to tell Kenneth so just now. So the balloon went up good and proper. Have you got my letters?''

"Violet took them.''

"Oh, that's all right then. I've been writing a pretty thank-you letter to Roger.''

"A what?" demanded Giles.

She grinned. "Yes, I thought you'd be surprised. But it had to be done. According to Rudolph, he drifted into the Shan Hills office this morning, and sent for Rudolph, and told him it was all right about cooking the accounts, and said he wasn't going to do anything about it. Rudolph rang me up at lunch-time, and I must say I think it's extremely decent of Roger—particularly as he doesn't like Rudolph. And if only we can clear Rudolph of suspicion of having done Arnold in, I can break off the engagement with a clear conscience," she added happily.

CHAPTER 18

GILES CARRINGTON had just finished his breakfast next morning when the telephone rang, and his man came in after a short pause to say that Superintendent Hannasyde would like to speak to him.

Giles laid down his napkin, rose in a leisurely way to his feet, and strolled out into the hall of his flat, and picked up the telephone receiver. "Hullo!" he said. "Carrington speaking. What can I do for you? Very bright and early, aren't you?"

The Superintendent's voice sounded unwontedly sharp. "I'm speaking from Scotland Yard. Roger Vereker is dead."

The lazy smile was wiped from Giles Carrington's face. He said incredulously: *"What?* Say that again!"

"Roger—Vereker—is—dead," enunciated the Superintendent with great clarity.

"Good God! But how—where?"

"In his flat. I've only just had the news."

"But—you don't mean murdered, do you?"

"I don't know. The Divisional Inspector seems to think it's suicide. I'm going round immediately."

"I'll join you there," Giles said.

"Good; I hoped you would. We may want you," replied Hannasyde.

Roger Vereker's flat was in a new block erected between Queen's Gate and Exhibition Road. Giles Carrington arrived there shortly behind the Superintendent, and was admitted to Roger's flat on the second floor by the plain-clothes man stationed at the door. In the hall of the flat Sergeant Hemingway was interrogating a frightened housemaid, who explained, between sobs, that she had come up to "do" the flat at seven o'clock that morning, and had found the poor gentleman dead in his chair. She did not suppose that she would ever recover from the shock.

The Sergeant nodded to Giles. "Good-morning, sir. You'll find the Superintendent in there," he said, jerking his thumb in the direction of the sitting-room.

Nothing had been touched there as yet, and the first thing that met Giles's eyes as he entered the room was the figure of Roger Vereker, seated in a chair turned a little away from his desk. He had fallen forward; his head rested on the edge of the desk, and his right arm hung loosely down to the ground. An automatic pistol lay on the floor just under his hand, and there was an ugly wound in his right temple, from which the blood had run down his face and arm, to form a congealing pool on the pile carpet.

The Superintendent was listening to what a dapper Inspector had to say, but he looked round as Giles entered, and smiled. "Good man. I hope you don't mind; we'll have it taken away in a minute."

"I can put up with it," Giles said rather shortly, his frowning eyes on Roger's body.

The Superintendent said: "You're quick. I've only just arrived myself. I'm afraid he's been dead some hours." He turned back to the Inspector, and nodded to him to continue.

The Inspector had not much to tell. A maidservant, whose duty it was to sweep and dust the flat before breakfast, had entered at seven o'clock, using a pass key, and had been surprised to find the hall light still on. She had switched it off, concluding that it had been forgotten overnight, and had then noticed a streak of light under the sitting-room door. She had opened the door and had found the room lit by electricity, all the curtains drawn, the ashes of a dead fire in the grate, and

Roger Vereker dead in his chair. She had let fall her dustpan and brushes, and rushed screaming from the flat, downstairs, to sob out her discovery to the hall-porter.

The porter's first action had been to go upstairs and see for himself, but one glance had been enough to satisfy him that this was a case for the police, and before notifying the manager of the flats, who occupied a suite on the ground floor, he had rung up the police-station.

A Sergeant had come round at once, with the police-surgeon, and, upon discovering the name of the deceased, had instantly connected it with the Vereker case, which he had been following in the newspapers with a good deal of interest. He had taken care to touch nothing in the flat, but had notified the Station Sergeant, who, in his turn, had rung up the Divisional Inspector.

"And though it looks like an ordinary suicide, Superintendent, I thought proper to advise you before going any further," ended the Inspector.

"Quite right," Hannasyde answered. He glanced down at the pistol, and then at the dead man, his lips slightly pursed. "We'll have a photograph, I think," he decided, and opened the door to give a brief order.

Sergeant Hemingway came in with the photographer, and went to stand beside Giles Carrington while the flashlight-photograph was taken, and the dead man's body removed. "Looks like we know who murdered Arnold Vereker, sir," he said cheerfully.

"It does, doesn't it?" agreed Giles.

The Sergeant looked sharply up at him. "You don't think so, sir? Now, why?"

"I didn't say so," replied Giles, his gaze resting for a moment on a meerschaum pipe lying on the mantelpiece.

"It fits together all right," argued the Sergeant. "He knew we were on his track; guessed, maybe, we should break that alibi of his; lost his nerve; and put a bullet through his head. It fits; you can't say it doesn't, sir."

"No, it fits beautifully," said Giles.

"And still you don't like it. Would it be family feeling, sir, if I may make so bold as to ask?"

Giles shook his head. By this time the body had been taken out on a stretcher, and Superintendent Hannasyde, having got rid of the Inspector, was looking thoughtfully at the desk. He turned after a moment and said briskly: "Well, what about it —Mr. Holmes? I'm not going to waste any time commiserating with you on the death of your cousin, because I know enough of your family by now to be sure not one of you will feel the slightest regret. What do you make of this?"

"Obviously suicide," drawled Giles.

"H'm! I don't think much of you as a detective. Nothing strike you as being a little unusual?" He lifted an eyebrow. "Or does it, and are you hoping it doesn't strike me?"

Giles smiled. "Three things—at first glance."

"Three?" Hannasyde looked round the room. "Now, I only spotted two. This is interesting. There is first the glass of whisky-and-soda on the desk. I can readily imagine Roger Vereker drinking that prior to shooting himself. What I can't imagine is him pouring it out and leaving it untouched. Secondly—though I don't know that it signifies much—is his position. It struck me so forcibly that I had that photograph taken. He was turned away from his desk. Take a look at the angle of the chair. Why had he shifted it? If he sat at his desk, presumably he had been writing. But he could not have written at it seated almost sideways."

"That's right," agreed the Sergeant. "You mean he pulled the chair round a bit to talk to someone else in the room?"

"I think he might have done so." Hannasyde took out his handkerchief, and with it opened the leather blotter on the desk. A sheet of notepaper lay in it. He picked it up, read it, and handed it to Giles. "Well?" he said.

The letter, written in Roger's untidy scrawl, was dated the day before, and was unfinished.

"Dear Sirs," it began. *"Enclosed please find cheque for £15. 6s. 3d. in payment of your account herewith. I should be glad if you would send me—"*

There the brief note ended.

"Does that seem odd to you, or not?" inquired Hannasyde.

"It does," said Giles. "Roger in the act of paying a bill seems more than odd to me."

"In some ways you are very like your cousins," said Hannasyde tartly.

"Interrupted," said the Sergeant, in his turn reading the note. "Stands to reason he wouldn't want anything sent him if he meant to commit suicide. Something might have happened to make him do it after the interruption, of course. You can't tell. But certainly he was interrupted. Say there's a ring at the door-bell, Super. He slips the letter into his blotter—or no! he has the blotter open, writing in it. All he does is to close it while he goes to see who's at the door. Sort of instinctive movement, if you follow me."

"Yes, something like that," Hannasyde said. "But we haven't heard Mr. Carrington's third point yet."

Giles, whose good-humoured countenance had grown rather grim, said:

"Are you a pistol-shot, Hannasyde?"

"No, I can't say I am."

"So I should suppose. Your expert won't like *that.*" He pointed to the ground at his feet, where, half hidden in the shaggy hearth-rug, a cartridge-case gleamed.

Both men looked down. "Yes, I'd already seen it," Hannasyde said. "It's in the wrong place? Is that it?"

"That's it," nodded Giles. "If Roger Vereker, seated in that chair, put the pistol to his right temple and pulled the trigger, the empty cartridge-case ought to be somewhere between the desk and the window, not here by the fire." He lit a cigarette, and flicked the dead match behind him, into the grate. His eyes measured the distance between himself and the chair by the desk. "I think, when the autopsy takes place, you will find that the pistol was not held quite so close to the head," he remarked.

"Thanks," Hannasyde said, glancing curiously at him. "I seem to have been doing you a certain amount of injustice. I suspected you of being more anxious to impede than to assist —on this particular case."

"One murder I can stomach," replied Giles shortly. "I find my gorge turns a bit at two of them. Moreover—bad lot though he was—Roger was utterly inoffensive. There might be several pardonable reasons for killing Arnold: only one reason for killing Roger, and that one not pardonable. No, definitely *not* pardonable.''

"Quite," said Hannasyde. His eyes narrowed suddenly, looking at something beyond Giles. "Was your cousin a pipe-smoker?"

"I don't think so."

Hannasyde stepped forward and looked more closely at the pipe on the mantelpiece. "A meerschaum, coloured more on one side than the other," he said. "I fancy I have seen it before."

"Possibly," said Giles. "It belongs to Kenneth. But I shouldn't build on it as a clue. Kenneth was one of a party held at this flat three—four evenings ago."

"Wouldn't he miss his pipe?" inquired the Sergeant. "I'd miss a pipe of mine quick enough. The dottle's in it still, what's more. You'd expect Roger Vereker to have seen it and knocked it out, and sent the pipe back to his brother."

"On the contrary," said Giles, "I shouldn't expect Roger to do anything so energetic."

"You are probably right," said Hannasyde, "but a little of the ash has fallen out of the pipe, as you see. Would you not expect the housemaid who cleans this flat to have dusted that away?"

"It depends on the housemaid," answered Giles.

Hannasyde picked the pipe up, and slipped it into his pocket. "I'll see the hall-porter, Hemingway," he said. "Ask him to come up, will you?"

Giles smiled. "I take it you'd like me to stay?—to be sure that I don't get to Chelsea ahead of you?"

"Quite right, I would," answered Hannasyde. "Not that I think you'd do that, but at this stage I'm taking no risks. Would you have said that Roger Vereker was likely to commit suicide?"

"No, I shouldn't," said Giles. "He certainly complained that it got on his nerves to have detectives cropping up at every turn, but he didn't appear to me to be particularly alarmed. However, I didn't see very much of him, so I may be wrong."

"I don't think you are wrong," Hannasyde said slowly. "Do you remember the day he told me that preposterous story of how he went to Monte Carlo? I have a vivid recollection of him saying: *'Do I look the kind of man who'd shoot himself? Of course I don't!'* "

"Yes, I remember that," Giles replied. "But you never know with a man who drinks as much as he did. That cartridge-case is more to the point, and I think it argues an unaccustomed hand. Had I done this, for instance, I should have looked carefully for that case after firing the shot."

"People don't always keep their heads under such circumstances. If they did there would be more unsolved mysteries."

"True, but didn't we decide some time ago that the murderer in this case must have been a very cool customer?"

"Assuming the murderer of Arnold Vereker and the murderer of Roger Vereker to have been one and the same person?" said Hannasyde a little ruefully. "I haven't much doubt of that myself, but whether I shall ever prove it is another matter. Where, by the way, were you last night?"

"I thought that was coming," remarked Giles. "From seven o'clock, when I called for her at the studio, until about a quarter to twelve, when I took her back to the studio, I was with Miss Vereker. We dined at Favoli's, and went on afterwards to Wyndham's. After I left Miss Vereker I drove back to the Temple in a taxi—the same taxi that took us home from the theatre. That ought to be easy to trace. When I reached the Temple I went to bed. I'm afraid my man was asleep by that time, so I can't offer you any proof that I stayed in bed till this morning. How long did the police-surgeon think my cousin had been dead?"

"According to Inspector Davies, at least seven or eight hours, and possibly more. He saw the body at about seven-forty-five this morning, I understand."

"Well, I suppose I could just have done it," reflected Giles. "Only I rather doubt, from my knowledge of him, whether I should have found Roger still up, and writing letters, at one in the morning."

"You are not, at the moment, one of my suspects," replied Hannasyde, with a glimmer of a smile. He turned, as Sergeant

Hemingway came back into the room, escorting the hall-porter, and said in his pleasant way: "Good-morning. You are the porter here?"

"Yes, sir," said the man, looking rather fearfully round the room. "Leastways, the night-porter, more properly speaking."

"What is your name?"

"Fletcher, sir. Henry George Fletcher."

The Sergeant interpolated: "I've got the name and the address, Superintendent."

"All right. What time do you come on duty, Fletcher?"

"At eight p.m., sir, and go off the same a.m."

"Are you on the premises for the whole of that time?"

Fletcher gave a slight cough. "Well, sir—official—like—if you take my meaning. Sometimes I do stroll out for a breather. I wouldn't be gone more than a couple of minutes or so. Not often, that is."

"Did you go out last night?"

"No, sir."

"You're quite sure of that?"

"Yes, sir. It turned that chilly yesterday evening I wouldn't want to, me being what you might call susceptible to cold. I had a bit of a fire in my room downstairs, which the Sergeant here has seen."

"Small room, I thought," said the Sergeant. "Draughty, I daresay."

"It is that," agreed the porter.

"Sit with the door shut?"

"There isn't anything against it, not in my orders," said Fletcher defensively. "If I'm wanted I'm rung for, and I'd hear the lift working, door or no door. I can keep my eye on things with it shut, on account of the upper part being glass, like you saw."

"If you weren't having forty winks, you could," said the Sergeant shrewdly.

"I don't sleep when I'm on duty," muttered Fletcher.

Hannasyde said: "All right, Sergeant. I shouldn't imagine that anyone would blame you if you did doze a bit, Fletcher. It must be dull work. I take it you didn't hear anything that might have been a shot last night?"

"No, sir, else I would have up and said at once. But we're close to the Exhibition Road, and there was a lot of cars went down it last night on account of a big do they had at the Albert Hall. Charity ball, I believe it was. One way and another, there was a bit more noise than usual, though not in this building, that I'll swear."

"I see. Is your main front door open all night, or do you shut it?"

"Not till midnight, I don't."

"But you do shut it then?"

"Yes, sir. Them's my orders."

"So that anyone entering the building after twelve would be obliged to ring for you to let them in?"

"That's right, sir."

"Did anyone come in late last night?"

"Oh yes, sir! Mr. and Mrs. Cholmondley of No. 15, they did. Then there was Sir George and Lady Fairfax, and the two young ladies, what was all at this ball I was telling you about; and Mr. Humphries, of No. 6, he was out late, too; and Mrs. Muskett, of No. 9; and Miss——"

"These are all residents, I take it? You didn't admit any visitors after twelve?"

"No, sir. Well, I wouldn't hardly expect to, not at that hour."

"And before twelve do you remember whether you saw any stranger enter the building?"

The porter rubbed his chin. "Well, it's a bit hard to say, if you understand me," he confided. "Of course, if I was to see anyone hanging about suspicious-like I should be on to them quick enough; but there's twenty flats here, sir, and people coming in and out a good bit. If anyone passes my door, I take a look, naturally, but I wouldn't always like to swear who it was, not if they go straight past to the lift or the stairs. For instance, there was a couple of ladies went up last night, and three gentlemen to my certain knowledge. I fancy the first lady was Miss Matthews, but I only saw her hat, it being all on the side of her head, like they wear them now. She must have come in about eight-thirty or thereabouts. The other one come in soon after eleven, but I didn't get more than a glimpse of

her. I never saw her go out again, so I expect it was Miss
Turner, Mrs. Delaford's personal maid, come home a bit late.
Then there was a gentleman went up in the lift to the fourth or
fifth floor. He was a stranger all right, because he came down
again about eleven, and had me call him a taxi. Tall, military
gentleman, he was. The second gentleman wanted Admiral
Craven's flat, and I took him up. I didn't see the other, not
properly. He must have come in about half-past ten by my
reckoning, but he went up on his own, not using the lift. I
rather thought it was young Mr. Muskett, because he was
wearing one of those black felt hats, which Mr. Muskett does
with his evening-clothes, but now you put me in mind of it I
wouldn't wonder if it wasn't him at all, on account of Mr.
Muskett's flat being on the third floor, and him not being one
to walk up when there's a lift."

"Did you see him leave the building?" Hannasyde asked.

"Well, I can't rightly say as how I did," confessed the
porter.

"And are you sure that these were the only people who
might have been strangers who came in last night?"

"I wouldn't say that," replied Fletcher cautiously. "Not to
take my oath on it, that is."

It was quite evident that the porter had spent some part of
the evening at least nodding comfortably over his fire. Nothing would be gained by forcing him to admit it, so Hannasyde
wisely abandoned the subject. "Who occupies the flat beside
this one?" he asked.

"Mr. Humphries does, sir. Him as I told you about. He was
at the ball, and came home close on half-past four in the
morning, very happy."

"And on the other side of the landing?"

"Well, Mr. and Mrs. Tomlinson has No. 3, but they're
away, and No. 4 is empty."

"Is there anyone in the flat above this?"

"Yes, sir, Mrs. Muskett, what was out late too. Well, when
I say late, half-past twelve it would have been when she come
in. But if you was thinking she might have heard the shot, I
wouldn't like to say she would. These flats is built sound-
proof."

"I'll go up and see her, all the same," Hannasyde said.

"You needn't wait; I expect you want to get home."

"Well, it is past my time," agreed the porter. "Of course, if there's anything I can do——"

"No, nothing, thanks. But if I were you I wouldn't talk about this."

"Not me, sir. Mr. Jackson—he's the manager—will be in a rare taking over it when he gets to hear of it."

Hannasyde paused. "Yes, where *is* the manager?" he asked.

"Away for the night," answered the Sergeant. "Expected back this morning."

"I see. If Hollis turns up while I'm gone, tell him to take the pistol for fingerprints, and to go over the likely places in this room, and the hall, and the bathroom. I shan't be long, I hope."

He went out as he spoke, and the Sergeant and Giles Carrington were left to entertain one another until he returned. Sergeant Hollis arrived five minutes later, and Giles, watching him set to work, said: "Well, this is interesting, anyway. Do you think you could do the telephone first, Sergeant? It dawns on me that I had better ring up my office and tell them I'm frying other fish this morning."

"Wasting your time a bit, aren't we, sir?" said Hemingway sympathetically. "It's routine-work, this. I'd be willing to bet a fiver we don't get a single print, unless it might be on that cartridge-case."

Giles had just concluded a conversation with the elder Carrington (who said explosively that if Giles meant to spend all day and every day in his cousins' pockets the sooner they were all wiped out the better it would be) when Hannasyde came back into the room. He paused for a moment, watching Hollis, and then glanced towards Giles. "Sorry to keep you hanging about like this. I'm going to Chelsea now. There's no reason for you to come if you don't want to, you know."

"I'm coming, if only to see fair play," said Giles. "Any luck with the Musketts?"

"Rather dubious. One thing I have ascertained: the man the porter saw was not young Muskett. He came in at six-thirty last night and didn't go out again. Somewhere round about eleven he heard a noise which he thought was a car back-firing. The trouble is it may well have been." He turned to Hemingway. "I'm leaving you here, Sergeant; you know what to do. I'll see you at the Yard. If you're ready, Mr. Carrington, let's go."

CHAPTER 19

THE journey to Chelsea was accomplished in Giles Carrington's car. The Superintendent cast a quick look at his face as he settled down beside him, and said: "I'm afraid this is rather a nasty case for you, Mr. Carrington."

"It's a very nasty case indeed," said Giles calmly. "Not particularly for me." He changed into second gear, and then into top. "I see whither your thoughts are tending, of course; but you'll hardly expect me to believe that a cousin—or, to be strictly accurate, a connection of mine—would be capable of committing so cold-blooded a murder."

The Superintendent was silent. After a moment Giles added, with a faint smile: "Moreover, I hardly think he would have overlooked the cartridge-case."

"You think I'm prejudiced against young Vereker," said Hannasyde. "But I can honestly say that I hope very much you may be right. But it's no use blinking facts: Roger Vereker's death—assuming it to have been murder—narrows the field down considerably. I don't think there's much doubt that the man who killed Arnold also killed Roger. You yourself said that although there might have been several motives for the first murder there can only have been one for the second. That seems to dispose of Mesurier for one, and of

190

Arnold's chauffeur—never a very probable suspect, I admit
—for another. Neither stood to gain anything through Roger's
death. There is just one person who stands to gain a fortune:
you know it as well as I do, so we may as well be frank about
it. What is more, Mr. Carrington, you have never been sure
that Kenneth Vereker didn't commit that first murder. You
believed him to be capable of it: I've known that from the
start. What sticks in your gullet is this second murder. But if
you think it over you must see that it follows perfectly logi-
cally, almost inevitably, on the first. Admitted, it wasn't foreseen. It takes a pretty hardened criminal to plan to kill two
people. One murder only was planned, but when Roger Vereker turned up that murder was useless unless he also could be
got rid of. You know the French saying that it's only the first
step that counts: well, you can apply it here. If a man can
murder one half-brother for his money, and get away with it,
he won't find it so hard to murder a second half-brother. And
I don't in the least mind admitting that Arnold's murderer
looked like getting away with it completely—which Kenneth
Vereker was well aware of."

"It would have to be an abnormal mind!" Giles said
harshly.

"Yes, certainly."

"Rubbish! That boy's not abnormal at all. Nor, had he
planned to kill Roger, would he have been fool enough to
show his animosity so plainly."

"Wouldn't he?" Hannasyde's voice was very dry. "I think
that is just what Kenneth Vereker would do. But don't run
away with the idea that I've ruled out every other possible
suspect. I haven't—but I should be a fool if I didn't go into his
movements last night very carefully."

They had come to a crossing, and the traffic lights were
against them. Not until the car had moved forward again did
Giles Carrington answer. Then he said, with a smile: "Yes,
you'd be a fool—but I told you I was going to take a hand,
didn't I?"

"Well, if anything has occurred to you, let me have it," said
Hannasyde placably.

"Two possibilities have occurred to me, but both are so

wildly improbable that I think I won't bother you with them,''
replied Giles. "One is obvious enough for you to have thought
of for yourself——"

Hannasyde gave a chuckle. "Thank you!"

"Sorry, I didn't mean it quite like that. The other"—he
paused—"the other, as far as I know, has absolutely nothing
to support it. I'll see if I can find something."

"It doesn't sound very promising," said Hannasyde, rather
amused. "But by all means go ahead with it."

In another few minutes they had arrived at the studio. Giles
ran his car a little way down the mews, and followed Hannasyde up the stairs to the door of the flat.

It was opened to them by Murgatroyd, who exclaimed:
"What, again?" in tones of deep disgust. "Well, one thing's
certain—you can't go worrying my young lady and gentleman
now. They're having breakfast. Good-morning, Mr. Giles.''

"Having breakfast, Murgatroyd?" Giles said. "Do you
know it's nearly eleven?"

"Yes, and it was nearly five before Mr. Kenneth and Miss
Leslie came back from that dance," said Murgatroyd grimly.

"Well, I'm sorry, but Superintendent Hannasyde is a busy
man. Mr. Kenneth will have to be disturbed.''

"If you say so, sir," conceded Murgatroyd, disapprovingly,
and stood back. "Not but what I doubt whether Miss Leslie's
dressed to receive company, but I'll see."

"Miss Leslie? Is she here?"

"Oh yes, she's here, and has been all night—what there was
left of it by the time Mr. Kenneth brought her back," replied
Murgatroyd. "What must she do but leave her latchkey
behind, so sooner than knock up her landlady she wakes Miss
Tony, and gets into her bed." She opened the door into the
studio as she spoke, and looked in. "Here's Mr. Giles with the
Superintendent, Miss Tony. Will I let them in, or not?"

"Oh, my God, at this hour!" groaned Kenneth. "Say we're
out.''

"No, don't. Of course they can come in," said Antonia.
"You don't mind, do you, Leslie? Hullo, Giles! Good-morning, Superintendent. Have some coffee!"

The breakfast-table had been laid in the window. Antonia,

fully dressed, was seated at one end, behind the coffee-pot, with Leslie Rivers, in a kimono, on one side of her, and Kenneth, in pyjamas, a pair of flannel trousers, and an old blazer, on the other. Kenneth, who looked half asleep, blinked somewhat morosely at the visitors, and said: "Well, what's happened now? Don't spare us. For God's sake cover up those repulsive eggs, Tony! Murgatroyd must be mad. Where's the ham?"

"We finished it yesterday. Do sit down, Superintendent! This is Miss Rivers, by the way. You're looking rather grim, Giles. Is anything the matter?"

"I'm afraid something very serious, Tony. Roger is dead—shot."

There was a moment's frozen silence. Then Antonia gasped out: "Gosh!"

Kenneth, who had stayed his coffee-cup half-way to his mouth, blinked again and drank with a good deal of deliberation. Then he set the cup down in the saucer, wiped his lips with his napkin, and said coolly: "If true, slightly redundant. Is it true, by any chance?"

"Perfectly true, Mr. Vereker," said Hannasyde, watching him.

It struck Giles, also watching, that Kenneth's control over his features was almost too perfect. There was a suggestion of rigidity about his mouth, a curiously blank look in his eyes. They travelled from Giles's face to Hannasyde's. Then Kenneth picked up his cup and saucer, and handed it to Antonia. "More coffee, please," he said. "How my fortunes do fluctuate!"

"You don't seem to be greatly surprised, Mr. Vereker."

"I should hate you to know how very greatly surprised I am, my friend-the-Superintendent. You did say shot, didn't you? What does that mean? Suicide?"

"That or murder," said Hannasyde. The word, uttered so baldly, had an ugly sound, and made Leslie Rivers shiver involuntarily.

"Let's stick to suicide," suggested Kenneth. "It's more likely."

"Do you think so? Why?"

"Obvious inference. He killed Arnold, thought you were on to him, lost his nerve, and pulled the trigger. Violet said he had the wind up."

"Did she?" It was Giles who spoke. "What made her think that?"

"I didn't ask."

Leslie said in rather a strained voice: "He must have had the wind up. I thought so myself."

"Well, I never saw any signs of it," said Antonia flatly.

Leslie looked steadily at her. "Oh yes, Tony! He often had a sort of scared expression in his eyes."

"That was only because he thought you'd like to murder him," replied Antonia irrepressibly. "He said you—" She broke off, flushing scarlet. "Oh, lord, what on earth am I saying? It was only a joke, of course! He didn't really think so!"

"No, I should hardly suppose he did," said Leslie quietly. "I can't say I liked him much, but I hadn't any desire to murder him. However, perhaps it's just as well that I've got an alibi." She turned to Hannasyde and smiled. "I was with Mr. Kenneth Vereker last night, from a quarter to eight onwards. We had dinner together at the Carlton, and went on from there to the Albert Hall, where we danced till after four o'clock. Then we came back here."

"Were you together the entire evening, Miss Rivers?"

"Yes, of course," she answered.

Kenneth's eyes went swiftly to her face with a look in them hard to read.

"Did you go to the ball alone, or in a party?" asked Hannasyde.

It seemed to Giles that she hesitated for a moment. "We joined a party," she said.

"A large party, Miss Rivers?"

"No, not very."

"How many were in it?"

"About a dozen, all told," said Kenneth. "We shared a box."

"And you naturally danced with other members of the party besides Miss Rivers?"

"Naturally," concurred Kenneth.

"But we always met at the box again after each dance," Leslie struck in. "I don't think we lost sight of each other for more than five minutes at a time the whole night, did we, Kenneth?"

"No," said Kenneth slowly. "Probably not."

Giles thought, with a sinking heart: That's a lie. And Kenneth isn't doing it well.

"You didn't leave the Albert Hall during the course of the dance, Mr. Vereker?"

"No."

There was a pause. Hannasyde put his hand in his pocket, and drew out the meerschaum pipe. "Have you ever seen that before?" he asked.

Kenneth looked at it, then held out his hand. Hannasyde put the pipe into it. Kenneth inspected it more closely and gave it back. "Many times. It belongs to me."

"I found it upon the mantelpiece in your half-brother's flat, Mr. Vereker."

"Did you?" said Kenneth. "I must have left it there."

"When?"

"Two or three nights ago. I was dining there."

"You haven't missed it?"

"No," said Kenneth indifferently. "I don't always smoke the same pipe."

"A meerschaum is usually a somewhat cherished possession," Hannasyde said. "I too am a pipe-smoker, you know."

"You may be, but you're not a Vereker," returned Kenneth, the ghost of his impish look in his eyes. He pushed his plate aside, and set his elbows on the table. "And now may I ask a few questions?"

"In a moment, Mr. Vereker. I want you first to tell me the names of the other members in your party last night."

"You are going to have a busy day," remarked Kenneth. "Leslie, who was in our party?"

"Well, the Hernshaws, for one," began Leslie thoughtfully.

"Two, darling, Mr. and Mrs. Gerald Hernshaw, Haltings, Cranleigh, Superintendent. That'll be a nice little jaunt for you."

"And Tommy Drew," continued Leslie.

"Honourable Thomas Drew, Albany. That's an easy one for you, but he wasn't noticeably sober after eleven, so he may not be so useful."

"And some people called Westley. I don't know where they live."

"Were those the blights that came with Arthur and Paula?" inquired Kenneth, interested. "I danced with the female one. They live somewhere on Putney Hill, and breed Pomeranians."

"You made that bit up," said Antonia accusingly.

"I did not. The She-Westley said she got three firsts at Richmond with her bitch Pansy of Poltmore."

"Then Poltmore is probably the name of her house," said Antonia. "I call Pansy a perfectly rotten name for a dog."

At this point Giles intervened. "This would be done more expeditiously if Miss Rivers told Superintendent Hannasyde what he wants to know, and you two kept quiet," he said.

"Well, don't forget the copper-headed wench," said Kenneth, getting up and strolling over to the fireplace. "She came with Tommy, and appeared to regret it," he selected a pipe from the rack on the mantelpiece and began to fill it from an earthenware jar of tobacco. By the time it was alight Leslie had come to the end of her list, and the Superintendent was jotting down the last name in his notebook. Kenneth puffed for a moment, and then said: "And now, if you've no objection, when did my half-brother shoot himself?"

"Your half-brother, Mr. Vereker, was shot sometime last night—probably before midnight, but on that point I have as yet no certain information."

"And the weapon?"

"The weapon was a Colt .32 automatic pistol."

Kenneth's brows lifted. "It was, was it? Where's your gun, Tony?"

She looked startled, saw the hint of a frown in Giles Carrington's eyes, and said jerkily: "What are you driving at? I didn't shoot Roger!"

"Nobody said you did, my child. Where is it?"

"In the top left-hand drawer of my bureau."

He moved towards the bureau. "I'm willing to bet it isn't."

"Well, this time you'd lose," retorted Antonia. "I happened to know it's there, because I had it out and oiled it that day we spring-cleaned this room.''

Kenneth opened the drawer, and turned over the papers in it. ''I win,'' he said. ''Think again.''

''But I know I put it there!'' said Antonia, growing rather pale. ''Under the used cheques. Leslie, you were here: don't you remember?''

''I remember you oiling it, but I don't think I saw you put it away,'' said Leslie. ''Try the right-hand drawer, Kenneth.''

''Not there either,'' said Kenneth.

''I am utterly positive I put it in the left-hand drawer!'' stated Antonia. She got up, and went to the bureau, and turned the contents of the drawer upside down. Then she said in rather a frightened voice: ''No, it isn't there. Someone's taken it.''

''You're quite sure you didn't move it later, and forget about it?'' Giles asked.

''Yes. It always lives in my bureau. I'll look, but I know I never moved it.''

''I shouldn't bother,'' said Kenneth.

Hannasyde said quietly: ''Did anyone other than your brother and Miss Rivers know where you kept your pistol, Miss Vereker?''

''Oh yes, lots of people!''

''Can you be a little more precise?'' he asked.

''Anyone who knew the flat well. You did, for instance, didn't you, Giles?''

''Yes, I knew you kept it in your bureau, Tony. I think it was my suggestion. But didn't I also suggest a lock and key?''

''I daresay you did, but I lost the key ages ago, and anyway I never remembered to keep it locked up.''

''Do you think your half-brother knew, Miss Vereker?''

She reflected. ''Roger? I should think he must have found out, because he told me himself he'd been through my bureau to see if I kept any money there. Kenneth, is that what you're driving at? Do you think Roger took it?''

''Yes, of course I do,'' replied Kenneth. ''My friend-the-Superintendent, on the other hand, thinks I took it.''

Hannasyde paid no heed to this, but merely asked Antonia if she knew the number of the pistol.

"On your licence, Tony," prompted Giles. "Can you lay your hand on that?"

"It's sure to be somewhere in my desk," she said hopefully.

Exhaustive search, in which she was aided by Kenneth, Giles, and Leslie Rivers, at last brought the Arms Licence to light. She gave it triumphantly to Hannasyde, apologizing at the same time for its somewhat dilapidated appearance. She said that dogs got hold of it once when Juno was a puppy.

Hannasyde noted down the number of the pistol, gave her back the licence, and prepared to depart. Kenneth stopped him. "How serious are you in thinking that this may not have been suicide, friend Osric?" he demanded.

"You have reminded me yourself that I am not a Vereker," replied Hannasyde. "I don't joke on such matters."

"Some reason up your sleeve for thinking it murder?"

"Yes," said Hannasyde. "Several reasons. Is there anything else you would like to know?"

"Certainly there is," answered Kenneth, a trifle unexpectedly. "I want very much to know who, after me, is the next heir."

His words produced a surprised silence. Hannasyde broke it. "That is hardly my province," he said.

"I hate to contradict you," said Kenneth, "but it is very much your province. If this was murder, I look like being the next victim. And, frankly, I don't fancy myself in the part. I want police protection, please."

CHAPTER 20

THE Superintendent looked at him for a moment, under slightly frowning brows. It was Antonia who spoke. "But aren't I the next heir?" she asked. "Giles, aren't I?"

"I'm not sure, Tony. Your father didn't visualize the deaths of all three sons when he made his Will. You may be."

"What of it?" said Kenneth blandly.

Antonia said, with feeling: "You beast, Kenneth!"

"If you are serious in wanting police protection no doubt you will get it, upon application to the proper quarter," said Hannasyde. "Meanwhile, I should like to see your maid—Murgatroyd—please."

"That ought to be good value," observed Kenneth, and lounged out the door, and called Murgatroyd.

She came at once, and, upon being told that the Superintendent wanted to speak to her, confronted him with undisguised hostility in her eyes. "Well?" she said. "No need to tell me something's happened: I can see that."

"You'd never guess what, though," said Kenneth. "Roger's dead."

She looked quickly from one to the other of them. "Dead?" she repeated. "You're not making game of me, are you, Master Kenneth?"

"Ask my friend-the-Superintendent," he shrugged.

She drew in her breath in a hissing sound through her teeth. "Well, that's a surprise, I will say. Dead! And drunk at the time, I'll be bound. And no loss, either—though I'm sure I didn't wish him as much harm as that." She glanced at Hannasyde. "What is it you want to ask me? I don't know how it happened, if that's what you're after."

"Where were you last night?" he asked.

"What's that got to do with you?" she retorted. "You're not going to try and make out Mr. Roger was murdered, are you?"

"I am afraid I have a good deal of reason for thinking that he was," replied Hannasyde. "He was found in his flat, early this morning, shot through the head."

Murgatroyd's rosy cheeks turned quite pale. She took a step backwards, was stopped by a chair, and sat down in it with a plump. "Oh, my goodness gracious me!" she gasped. "Whatever next? Of all the unnatural—I never did in all my born days!"

"And needless to say," put in Kenneth, "the police think I did it."

This brought her up out of the chair with a bounce. "Oh, they do, do they? Well, let me tell you," she said, rounding upon Hannasyde, "that Mr. Kenneth was at a dance all last night, as Miss Rivers here can swear to!"

"That wasn't what I asked you," said Hannasyde quietly. "I want you to tell me where you were."

"At the Pictures," she replied.

"Alone?"

"Yes, I was."

"And afterwards?"

"Straight back here, where I was when Miss Tony came in."

"What time did you get back?"

"Twenty minutes past eleven. You can ask Mr. Peters, if you like—you'll find him farther down the mews. He owns the lock-up garages, and he saw me come in, and asked me what the picture was like. Which I told him."

There was nothing more to be got out of her. Hannasyde let

her go, and in a few minutes had left the flat himself.

For some moments after the front door had shut behind the Superintendent no one spoke. It was Murgatroyd, coming back into the room, who broke the silence. "I've got my vegetables to do," she said prosaically, "let alone all this washing up, so it stands to reason I can't waste time talking. You'd better come and give me a hand, Miss Tony. You won't do any good sitting there looking scared. It's a nasty set-out, and no mistake, but brooding won't mend matters."

Antonia looked at Giles. "Giles, it's all getting so beastly," she said. "I didn't mind about Arnold, but I hate this! Kenneth—you were at the Albert Hall the whole night, weren't you?"

"God bless the girl, now *she* thinks I did it!"

Giles said, watching Kenneth: "You lied badly. You were in Roger's flat last night, weren't you?"

"He wasn't! I tell you he never left the Hall!" Leslie struck in fiercely.

Giles paid no heed to her, but kept his eyes on Kenneth's face. Kenneth met that look challengingly. "Why should I have been in Roger's flat? Can you think of any reason?"

"Yes," said Giles. "I can."

Kenneth's lip curled. "I see. Murder. You're wrong."

"Not murder. Jealousy."

A flush crept into Kenneth's lean cheeks. "Again you're wrong."

"Very well, what was the reason?"

"You've already heard me say that I didn't leave the Albert Hall until past four."

"Is that statement likely to be corroborated by the other members of your party? Miss Rivers gave that alibi, not you. I was watching you; you weren't expecting it. I think you nearly denied it."

"Why don't you join the police-force?" inquired Kenneth. "You've missed your vocation."

Giles got up. "You young fool, can't you see what a tight corner you're in?" he said. "Lie to Hannasyde if you must, but if you lie to me you can look for another lawyer. I won't touch your case."

"As you wish," Kenneth said.

"Don't throw him over, Giles!" Antonia begged, a catch in her voice. "Please, please don't desert us!"

His face softened; he said more gently: "I shan't do that, Tony. But I can't handle a case where I'm kept in the dark."

"All very moving," remarked Kenneth. "So far I haven't asked you to handle my case. Supposing someone in my party did lose sight of me for half an hour? Have you ever danced at the Albert Hall? It's a largish sort of a place, you know."

"Yes, and we sat out a good bit," Leslie said.

Antonia looked anxiously at Giles. "You think he's in a mess, Giles?"

"I know he's in a mess."

"Any fool could see that," said Kenneth contemptuously. "First I kill Arnold, then Roger turns up, so naturally I kill him as well. All for filthy lucre too. Take that worried look off your face, Tony; there's no evidence."

"There's your pipe," she pointed out.

"They won't hang me on that," he answered.

They could get no more out of him than that. He walked up and down the studio, his hands in his pockets and his pipe clenched between his teeth. "It's possible they may arrest me," he said, frowning.

Giles, who had moved to the desk, and was flicking over the pages of the telephone directory, glanced up. "More than that."

"Very well, more than that. You ought to know. But it isn't enough if they prove I left the Albert Hall during the dance. They must prove I went to see Roger, and that they can't do."

Giles, having apparently found what he was looking for, shut the directory, and laid it down. "Think it over," he advised. "And don't overlook the fact that no one has so strong a motive as you for murdering Arnold and then Roger. I'm going now, but if you come to your senses, ring me up!"

"What, with a full confession?" jibed Kenneth.

Giles did not answer. Antonia went out with him, and at the front door detained him a few moments. "Giles, it's getting worse. I'm dead sure he was with Roger last night. You can always tell when Kenneth's lying. He does it so badly. What will happen if they find it out?''

"Tony, my dear, I don't know, because I've no idea when he went there, or what he did there. But things are going to look remarkably ugly if he's caught out in a lie. Everything points to him already.''

"Yes, I can see that, but I don't believe he did it all the same,'' she replied. "I wish Leslie hadn't nipped in with that alibi before he had time to speak. I think she's queered his pitch.'' She paused, and then said in a troubled way: "There's one rather horrid thing, Giles. I don't know whether you've thought of it. If Kenneth didn't do it—who could have? Nobody else had any reason to kill Roger.''

"Yes, I have thought of it,'' he said curtly.

"I expect a jury would too?'' she suggested, raising her eyes to his face.

"Undoubtedly.'' He took her hands, and held them comfortingly. "Don't worry, chicken. I don't believe Kenneth did it any more than you do.'' He smiled down at her. "Here's one cheering thought for you at least: Mesurier looks like being cleared of all suspicion.''

"Oh, him!'' said Antonia. "I'd forgotten about him. He's fed up with me, by the way. Not that I blame him. I don't think I'll get engaged any more. It doesn't seem to lead anywhere.''

"It will next time,'' said Giles. "That I promise you.'' He gave her hands a quick squeeze, released them, and ran down the stairs to his car.

Five minutes later he drew up outside a house in a street leading up from the Embankment. It had been converted into two maisonettes, the one on the ground and first floor having Violet Williams's name on a brass plate beside the door.

He rang the bell, and was presently admitted by a middle-aged woman in a dirty overall. Her method of announcing him was to call out: "Oh, Miss Williams, here's somebody to see you!''

Violet came out of a room at the front of the house. She gave an exclamation of surprise at seeing Giles. "Why, Mr. Carrington! I'd no idea! Do come in!''

He followed her into a sitting-room furnished in bleached

oak with jade-green curtains and cushions. A table in the bay window had a litter of sketches on it, and the chair, pushed back from it, seemed to indicate that Violet had been working there. Giles said: "I hope I'm not disturbing you. You look as though you were busy."

"Of course not. Won't you sit down? I apologize for the creature who let you in, by the way! I don't keep a proper maid. She's just a char who comes to clean in the mornings." She picked up a cigarette-box from a low table by the fireplace, and offered it to him. "Don't think me terribly rude," she said, smiling, "but what on earth do you want to see me about?"

He struck a match, and held it to the cigarette she had taken from the box. "I'm hoping you will be able to induce Kenneth to behave sensibly," he answered.

She laughed. "Oh, I'm afraid he's impossible! What has he been up to?"

"I wish I knew, Miss Williams. You see, something rather shocking has happened. Roger Vereker has been found shot in his flat."

She gave a start. "Mr. Carrington! Oh no!"

"I'm afraid it is quite true," he said gravely.

She put a hand over her eyes. "How *awful!* Poor, poor Roger! I never dreamed he was feeling it all as badly as that. I knew he was on edge, of course, but that he would actually—oh, it doesn't bear thinking about!"

"Was he in a very nervous state?" Giles asked. "I believe you saw more of him than anyone—you would probably know."

"Yes, he was," she answered. "He had it fixed in his mind that the police were hounding him down. I was saying so to Kenneth only the other day. He didn't see it—or wouldn't see it, but then Kenneth isn't always very observant." She let her hand fall. "But that he should actually have taken his own life! I can't get over it!"

"I don't think he did take his own life, Miss Williams."

She turned very pale. "You mean—oh, impossible!"

"It was meant to look like suicide," Giles said, "but there are one or two circumstances which point rather conclusively to murder."

She shuddered. "I can't believe that. Please tell me what reason you have for saying such a thing!"

"My chief reason is purely technical," he replied.

"But the police—do they think it was murder?"

"They think it very probable," said Giles.

She was silent for a moment, still very white, her eyes fixed on the glowing end of her cigarette. She raised them presently, and said: "You mentioned something about Kenneth. But whatever happened no one can suspect him of having had anything to do with it. He was at the Albert Hall last night with Leslie Rivers."

"He was at the Albert Hall, I know," agreed Giles. "But the Albert Hall is not five minutes' walk from Roger's flat, Miss Williams. Nor are the police at all satisfied that he didn't leave the dance for a time during the course of the evening. In fact, though he won't admit it, I am pretty sure that not only did he leave the dance, but he also called on Roger."

"I'm sure he didn't!" she said quickly. "Why should he? There could be no reason for doing such a stupid thing!"

He hesitated. "I think there was a reason," he answered. "May I speak quite frankly?"

"Oh, please do!"

"Well, Miss Williams, Kenneth has—as you probably know —a very jealous temperament. Do you remember that on the evening when we all dined with Roger he invited you to dine with him again on the night of the ball?"

She said rather coldly: "Yes, certainly I remember that, but it was merely a joke."

"It is just possible that Kenneth took it seriously," Giles said.

"Really, I think that is a little too ridiculous!" she said, half-laughing. "Why do you assume that he was at Roger's flat last night? Does he admit it?"

"No. But we found his pipe, with the ash in it, on the mantelpiece in Roger's sitting-room," he replied.

"His pipe——?" she stared at him. "How do you know it was his?"

"Both Hannasyde and I recognized it."

"Recognized a pipe!" she exclaimed. "How could you?"

He smiled. "To a pipe-smoker all pipes don't look the

same, Miss Williams. But that's beside the point. Kenneth admitted it was his as soon as he saw it.''

She looked at him with an expression of incredulous horror in her eyes. "But it's impossible! I don't believe it! What time was Kenneth in the flat? What was he doing there?''

"That is precisely what I, as his legal adviser, want to find out,'' said Giles. "According to Miss Rivers he was never out of her sight the entire evening. Kenneth corroborated that statement, but only after a moment's perceptible hesitation, Miss Williams. To put it baldly, he was quite obviously lying. His tale—or rather Miss Rivers's tale—is that the whole party met after each dance, in the box they were sharing. Superintendent Hannasyde has only to question the other members of the party to find out whether that is true or not. If—as I am very much afraid—it is not true, Kenneth will be in an extremely dangerous position. And since he has this bee in his bonnet, that he's capable of handling his own case without assistance, I can't do anything to help him.''

"But why do you come to me?'' she interrupted. "What has it got to do with me? What can I do about it?''

"I hope very much that you will exert your influence to make him see sense,'' replied Giles. "He doesn't realize how serious the situation is, nor how essential it is that I at least should know the truth about his movements last night.''

She struck her hands together, as though exasperated. "He's a fool!'' she said. "Why on earth should he elect to call on Roger last night? What took him there? It's utterly mad!''

"There is one all too obvious reason, Miss Williams,'' said Giles.

She looked at him uncomprehendingly for a moment. "I can't imagine——'' She stopped; her eyelids flickered. "I see what you mean,'' she said. "You will hardly be surprised at my not considering that. Nothing would induce me to believe that he had any hand in Roger's death! You can't think——''

"No, I don't think it,'' he said. "I am trying to discover what other reason he can have had for that visit. What I suspect is jealousy.''

"I don't understand you.''

Giles said deliberately: "He heard Roger invite you to dine

with him, Miss Williams. It was evident that he didn't like the idea. He is, as I said, an extremely jealous young man, and we know that he resented from the outset any friendliness on your part towards Roger. Last night—at the eleventh hour—you cried off that dance, didn't you?"

"I never definitely said I'd go with him," she answered. "I always disapproved of it, and hoped he'd give it up."

"Quite. But you did allow him to think that you might go with him after all, didn't you?"

"Oh, to avert a scene——! But I didn't promise."

"At any rate, your last-minute refusal made him very angry," said Giles. "Now, I know what Kenneth is like when he's roused. I think that he lashed himself into suspecting that you had cried off the dance so that you could spend the evening with Roger. That may have been why he called on Roger —just to assure himself that you were not at the flat."

"I never heard of anything so insulting!" she said, stiffening. "I in Roger's flat at that hour? It may interest him to know that so far from being with Roger I was at home the entire evening! And if he doesn't believe me, you may tell him to apply to Miss Summertown, who came to dinner with me and stayed till eleven, when I went to bed!"

"I don't suppose that in his cooler moments Kenneth would dream of suspecting you," said Giles in his calm way. "And if he went to Roger's flat he must know that you weren't there, mustn't he?"

"Perhaps he suspects I hid behind a screen," she said icily. "I think it is just as well that I can produce a witness to prove that I was in my own home the whole evening!"

"Well, please don't condemn him on the strength of what may prove to be my idle imagination," he said, smiling. "He may have had another reason for going to see Roger."

She was silent, her lovely mouth compressed into a thin red line. She sat very straight in her chair, one hand clenched on the arm. There was an air of implacability about her, and the unconscious hardening of her face made her beauty seem a brittle thing, surface-deep.

She turned her head presently, and looked directly at Giles. "You're thinking that I'm stupidly annoyed?" she said.

"Well, I am rather annoyed, but that doesn't matter. I mean, it's so much more important to get Kenneth out of this dreadful mess. Personally, I have an absolute conviction that it was suicide. I don't know what your reasons are for thinking it wasn't, but I keep remembering things Roger said. I didn't set any store by them at the time—at least not enough to foresee this—but now that I look back I can't help feeling I ought to have guessed. Only I don't know what I could have done, quite, if I had. I did speak to Kenneth about it, but he paid no heed."

"It wasn't suicide, Miss Williams."

She frowned. "I don't see how you can say that so positively. Why wasn't it?"

"I don't think you'd be much the wiser if I explained," he answered. "It is a question of where the empty cartridge-case should have been found. Moreover, I can't for the life of me see what could have induced Roger to shoot himself when he must have known that there was no evidence against him. He was no fool."

"Technicalities about pistols are beyond me, I'm afraid. Where ought the empty case to have been found?"

"In quite a different place," he replied. "There were other points too—minor ones, but significant."

"I see. But they can't prove Kenneth did it. He might have left his pipe there any time, and if Leslie sticks to her story——"

"If Arnold Vereker had not been murdered things might not look so black," he said. "But Arnold Vereker was murdered, and Kenneth had no alibi that he could prove. Everything he said was calculated to make the police look askance at him. He said he came here to see you. According to him you were out. He then said he went to a cinema. But he didn't know which one, and he slept through the greater part of the programme."

"Oh, I know, I know!" she said. "He was utterly impossible."

"Well," Giles said, getting up, "he's being just as impossible now, Miss Williams. It amused him to see how far he could fool Hannasyde over the first murder, and he was so successful that it has gone to his head. But he's in a far more precarious position now."

She, too, rose. "Yes, I quite see. I'll go round to the studio at once, and talk to him. Of course, he must take you into his confidence. I shall tell him so, and I expect he'll call on you at your office."

"Thank you," said Giles. "I hope he will."

CHAPTER 21

FROM Violet's maisonette Giles drove to Adam Street, where he found his father upon the point of going out to lunch. Mr. Charles Carrington looked him over, grunted at him, and said that he had better come to lunch too. "Heaven knows I don't want to hear anything about this disgusting affair," he said irascibly, "but of course I shall have to. What's more, your mother's anxious. Says Kenneth isn't capable of murder. Bunkum! Did he do it?"

"Good God, I hope not!"

"Oh! Feel like that about it, do you? Quite agree with you. Don't like scandals. What was that red-headed little minx, Tony, up to last night?"

"She was with me," replied Giles.

"The devil she was! So your mother was—— What were you doing, the pair of you?"

"Dinner and theatre," said Giles. "And mother was quite right. She usually is."

Charles Carrington coughed, and changed the subject rather hastily.

Giles did not spend much of the afternoon in Adam Street. At four o'clock he put a call through to Scotland Yard, and having ascertained that Superintendent Hannasyde was in the building, left his office and drove to Whitehall. The news of

Roger Vereker's death was in the evening papers, and several glaring posters announced a startling sequel to the Stocks Mystery.

At Scotland Yard Giles was conducted almost immediately to Hannasyde's office, where he found not only the Superintendent, but Sergeant Hemingway as well.

"I rather expected you to look in," Hannasyde said. "Sit down, won't you? I've just had the report on the P.M. You were quite right, Mr. Carrington: Dr. Stone considers that the pistol must have been fired from a distance of about two feet."

"When, in his opinion, did death occur?" Giles asked.

The Superintendent glanced down the typewritten report. "Always rather a difficult question," he said. "Approximately, between 10:00 p.m. and 2:00 a.m."

"Thanks. Was anything found in the flat?"

"Nothing useful. A slight trace of oil on the handle of the sitting-room door, and a fingerprint—Miss Vereker's—on the cartridge-case."

"It was her gun, then?"

"Yes. She was here only half an hour ago"—he smiled faintly—"displaying the greatest interest in the business of taking an impression of her own hand."

"That I can imagine. And the position of the cartridge-case?"

"You win over that too." He paused, looked squarely at Giles. "You may as well know it now as later, Mr. Carrington: the evidence of the other members of that party at the Albert Hall does not bear out the story told me by Miss Rivers and Mr. Vereker. As a matter of fact, I was on the point of going to the studio when you rang up."

Giles nodded. "I see. I'll come along, if you don't mind."

"No, I don't mind," said Hannasyde. "I've no power to stop you if I did. It'll probably save time if you come, as I imagine Mr. Vereker would be quite likely to refuse to talk until he's consulted you—if only to annoy."

Kenneth, however, when they found him a little while later at his studio, seemed to be in one of his more cheerful moods, and showed no desire to be obstructive.

His sister was present, and also Violet Williams and Leslie

Rivers. It was evident that they had foregathered to discuss the situation, and equally evident that Kenneth himself was paying very little heed to what they were saying. Giles and Hannasyde entered the studio to discover him sketching idly on his knee. He looked up as the door opened, and said: "I thought as much. *A la lanterne!*"

Antonia betrayed neither surprise nor dismay at the Superintendent's arrival, but the other two girls looked a trifle startled. Leslie threw a swift, anxious look at Kenneth, and seemed to stiffen herself.

Kenneth continued to sketch. "Come in and make yourselves at home," he invited. "I won't say I'm pleased to see you, because that wouldn't be true."

"You don't always stick so rigidly to the truth, I think, Mr. Vereker," said Hannasyde, closing the door behind him.

Kenneth smiled. "Nearly always. Sometimes I get led astray, I admit. Tell me the worst."

"Three of the other members of your party last night state that for about half an hour you were missing from the ballroom," said Hannasyde, without beating about the bush.

Kenneth looked up from his sketch. His eyes were narrowed and keen, but they were focused not on Hannasyde, but on Leslie Rivers.

"You've rather a nice-shaped head, Leslie," he remarked. "Don't move! Sorry, my friend-the-Superintendent. Anything else?"

"To be missing from the ballroom at a dance for half an hour is not unusual," said Leslie. "One sits out occasionally, Superintendent."

"In a box, Miss Rivers. There is not, I believe, very much accommodation for sitting out anywhere else at the Albert Hall."

"Except outside in one's car," she replied.

"Hush, misguided child!" said Kenneth. "The most elementary methods will discover that my car went to Hornet's Garage to be de-coked yesterday. Am I not right, Superintendent?"

"Quite," said Hannasyde. "And am *I* not right, Mr. Vereker, in saying that you left the Albert Hall by the main entrance at twenty minutes past ten, and returned just before eleven?"

"Pausing on both occasions to exchange a few words with the commissionaire," added Kenneth, still at work on his sketch. "Thus doing what I could to stamp myself on his memory. The question which is worrying you at the moment is, of course, Am I diabolically cunning, or incredibly stupid?"

"Don't pay any attention to him!" Leslie said quickly. "This is all nonsense—every word of it! He didn't leave the Albert Hall until we came away after four o'clock, together."

Kenneth tossed the sketch aside. "My dear girl, do, do dry up! I'm sick of this involved story, anyway, but don't you realize that at any moment now my friend-the-Superintendent is going to produce that commissionaire out of his hat to identify me?" He glanced at Hannasyde. "Well, my friend, produce him! Let it be admitted that I did leave the Albert Hall during the course of the evening. It does not follow that I went to my half-brother's flat, and you know it. You have—as they say in American films—nothing on me."

"Oh yes, I have, Mr. Vereker," replied Hannasyde quietly.

Kenneth looked contemptuous. "One pipe, which I may have left in Roger's flat four nights ago."

"Not only your pipe. An automatic pistol also."

"I shouldn't build on it," said Kenneth. "At a rough estimate, half a dozen other people could have laid their hands on that pistol."

"Had half a dozen other people any motives for killing your half-brother, Mr. Vereker?"

"Not having been in Roger's confidence, I can give you no information on that point," replied Kenneth.

The Superintendent looked at him under his brows. "What sort of a hat were you wearing last night, Mr. Vereker?"

Kenneth smiled. "Unworthy of you, my friend. Didn't your commissionaire tell you?"

"I asked you."

"Don't answer!" Leslie said, gripping her fingers together in her lap.

Violet's cool, well-modulated voice interrupted: "Really,

Leslie, you are making yourself positively ridiculous. You had much better keep quiet, if you don't mind my saying so. You seem to me to have done quite enough harm already."

Leslie flushed, and answered rather unsteadily: "It's easy for you to be superior. *You* weren't at the ball, *you* aren't involved! What do you care?"

"You forget, I think, that I am engaged to be married to Kenneth."

Leslie was silent. Kenneth said: "Leave the kid alone, Violet. If she's misguided, at least it's with the best intentions."

"Oh, certainly, my dear!" Violet said silkily. "But her anxiety to make us believe that you were with her all the evening would almost lead one to suppose that she would like to prove an alibi for herself."

Antonia removed the cigarette from her mouth. "Cat," she remarked.

Hannasyde interposed. "I am still waiting to know what sort of a hat you wore last night, Mr. Vereker."

"A black felt," said Kenneth.

"Thank you. When you left the Albert Hall shortly before ten-thirty, where did you go?"

"That question," said Kenneth, "I must regretfully decline to answer."

There was a short pause. Violet looked towards Giles, who had strolled to the other end of the studio, and was standing by the window, one hand in his pocket, his shoulders propped against the wall.

"You realize, do you not, Mr. Vereker, that your refusal to answer me may have extremely serious consequences?"

"Produce your handcuffs," recommended Kenneth flippantly.

Giles's eyes rested thoughtfully on Hannasyde's face. It was quite impassive, nor was there much expression in Hannasyde's voice as he said: "Very well, Mr. Vereker. If you are determined not to answer, I have no option but to detain you."

Giles carefully tipped the ash off the end of his cigarette. He still said nothing.

Kenneth's brows rose. "Now, I thought you'd arrest me,"

he remarked. "Why don't you?"

The Superintendent made no reply. Antonia got up rather suddenly, and said with a curtness which informed all those who knew her how much alarmed she was: "Giles! For God's sake, why don't you *do* something?"

He said in his calm way: "There is nothing I can do at the moment, Tony. Don't panic."

"But it's impossible! You're making an absurd mistake, Superintendent!" Leslie cried. "He didn't do it! I *know* he didn't do it!"

Violet, who had turned very pale, fixed her eyes on Hannasyde's face and said slowly: "One sees, naturally, that the evidence is very strong, but surely you are being a little hasty? I mean, Kenneth isn't the only person who could have done it. And I must say—though I know perfectly well that it won't be appreciated—that I should like very much to know what Tony was doing last night."

"Thanks, we'll cut out that bit," said Kenneth. "Tony was out with Giles, as you very well know."

"You needn't look at me like that," Violet said. "I know she says she was with Mr. Carrington until twelve, but personally I feel——"

"No one is interested in your feelings, personal or otherwise. Dry up!"

She rose, a spot of colour on each cheek. "It's no use talking to me in that rude way! I've a right to say what I think—more right than Leslie Rivers, let me tell you! Of course, I'm getting used to being snubbed in this household whenever I open my mouth, but I'll thank you to remember that I'm your fiancée, Kenneth!"

He looked at her in a detached way, as though he found her a curious but not uninteresting specimen. "Funny," he remarked. "Tony always said you had a streak of vulgarity. I see what she means now."

"How dare you insult me?" she flashed, her lips thin with anger.

"If you don't want me to insult you, lay off my sister!" he said, a hard light in his eyes.

"I shall do no such thing. You've behaved like a fool over the whole of this affair, but if you won't help yourself you needn't think I shall keep my mouth shut! If you weren't utterly selfish you'd try and understand my point of view. You don't suppose I'm going to enjoy seeing you arrested for murder, do you? You haven't even thought of what will happen to me if they convict you!''

"No," said Kenneth, with a crooked smile. "I haven't."

"Well, I *have* thought! And I want to know whether Tony really was with Mr. Carrington till midnight. You needn't tell me that Murgatroyd saw him bring her back here: Murgatroyd would say anything. In fact, it wouldn't surprise me at all to discover that she had a great deal more to do with both these murders than we've any idea of!''

"One moment, Miss Williams," said Giles. "You are forgetting my evidence, aren't you?''

"No, Mr. Carrington, I'm not. But it's quite obvious that you'd say or do anything to shield Tony. I'm sorry if you're offended, but I can't and I won't stand by and see Kenneth taken to prison for want of a little plain speaking!''

At this point Hannasyde interposed by asking Kenneth if he was ready to go with him.

"No," said Kenneth, "I'm not. I want a word in private with my cousin.''

"Certainly," Hannasyde replied.

"Come to my room, will you?" Kenneth said to Giles. "I've no intention of running away, Superintendent, so you needn't worry.''

Giles followed him out of the studio and across the little hall to his bedroom. He shut the door and watched Kenneth sit down on the end of his bed. Kenneth had a taut look about him, and when he spoke it was a little jerkily.

"Go on! You're my solicitor. What do I do now?''

"Keep your mouth shut," answered Giles without hesitation. "Were you at Roger's flat last night, or were you not?''

A faint smile flickered in Kenneth's eyes. "Wouldn't you like to know?''

"If I don't know, I tell you in all seriousness, Kenneth, I won't touch your case.''

Kenneth shrugged. "I haven't needed you so far, but it looks as though I may. I was in Roger's flat.''

"At what hour?''

"Precisely the hour specified by our clever detective."

"What did you go there for, Kenneth?"

"Private affairs."

"Luckily I can interpret that," said Giles. "You went to see if Violet Williams was there, didn't you?"

Kenneth flushed. "What a lively imagination you have!"

"Was she there?" Giles demanded.

"She was not."

"Quite sure of that?"

"Quite."

"Your error, in fact."

Kenneth burst out laughing. "Yes, blast you! My error."

"Why did you think she was, Kenneth?"

"My unfortunate temperament," said Kenneth lightly. "I thought that might have been the reason she turned me down at the last minute over that ball. So I went to see for myself. She wasn't there, and hadn't been."

"Did you part with Roger on good terms?"

"No, not at all."

Giles sighed. "Why not? What was there to quarrel over if Violet hadn't been there?"

"I could always find something to quarrel over with Roger," replied Kenneth. "In this case it was his Advice to a Young Man about to marry. But I didn't kill him."

"All right, leave it at that. Does Violet know?"

"What, that I went to the flat in search of her? You bet she knows! Haven't you noticed the air of outraged virtue? If I have the least regard for her feelings or my own dignity, I shall keep my disgraceful conduct to myself. How long am I likely to be in jug?"

"I hope not more than a day or two. Don't annoy the police more than you can help."

"The temptation," said Kenneth, getting up and opening the door, "is pretty well irresistible!"

Hannasyde was waiting for him in the hall, and at sight of him Kenneth's eyes gleamed. "Hush! Not a word!" he said. "This is where I fade out, skipping the leave-takings. On your way, my friend-the-Superintendent!"

Hannasyde, propelled towards the front door by an insistent hand on his elbow, looked back to say: "I'll send a man

round to fetch what Mr. Vereker needs. Would you ask Miss
Vereker to pack a suit-case, Mr. Carrington?''

"Tell her to shove my sketching-block in, and the usual ap-
purtenances,'' ordered Kenneth. ''I'm going to do a series of
black-and-white policemen. After you—Macduff!''

Giles went back into the studio. Violet was standing by the
fireplace, her lips still tightly compressed and a look in her
face more of exasperation than concern. Leslie had put on her
hat, and seemed to be on the point of departure. Antonia was
lighting a cigarette from the stub of her old one. They all three
looked towards the door as Giles entered, but it was Violet
who spoke. "Well?'' she said. "Where's Kenneth?''

"Gone,'' replied Giles unemotionally.

"Gone!'' exclaimed Antonia. "I quite thought you'd be
able to think of something, Giles. Couldn't you get him out of
it?''

"Not yet, Tony. Don't worry; he'll be all right.''

"I think,'' said Violet, in a voice of still anger, "that that is
the last straw!''

"Oh, damn you, shut up!'' snapped Antonia. "How could
he help going?''

Violet spoke with meticulous politeness. "Will you please
not swear at me? I am quite aware that he had to go, but I
don't in the least understand why he could not take the trouble
to say good-bye. It is a piece of rudeness which——''

"If you don't hold your tongue there will be a third
murder,'' said Leslie, with deadly calm. "You've said more
than enough already. In fact, there's only one thing you
forgot; why didn't you advise the Superintendent to inquire
into my movements last night?''

"I am quite sure that he had done so, dear,'' replied Violet
sweetly. "Not that I think you did the murder, for, after all,
what motive could you have?''

"If it comes to that, what motive could Tony have had? *She*
doesn't inherit.''

"Not while Kenneth is alive,'' agreed Violet, with meaning.

Antonia, not in the least indignant at this remark, frowned
thoughtfully. "Well, I don't know,'' she said. "I should have
to be pretty hard-boiled to commit three murders. It would be
dam' silly too, because I'd be bound to get caught out.''

"It seems to me that anyone of normal intelligence can get away with murder," said Violet scornfully. "What have the police done over this case? Absolutely nothing! They've no idea who murdered Arnold Vereker, and the best they can think of to do now is to arrest Kenneth. Utterly obvious, and utterly brainless." She bent and picked up her gloves and handbag from the chair where she had left them, and began to draw on her gloves, working her fingers into them. "There's no point in my staying," she said. "If Mr. Carrington can't help Kenneth, I am sure I can't."

Giles made no reply to this, but when the gloves were at last on, he moved in his leisurely way towards the door, and opened it for Violet to pass out.

"Well, Tony," she said, tucking her bag under her arm, "if I've said anything I shouldn't, I'm sorry, but this thing is getting absolutely on my nerves. You had better come along, too, Leslie; Tony wants to talk to her cousin."

Leslie said stiffly: "Of course. But please don't wait for me. I'm not going your way."

"Oh, just as you like, my dear," Violet replied, shrugging. She walked to the door, but paused there as a thought occurred to her. "I don't know if you've any of you realized it, but there's one person we've left out of our calculations. Where was Mr. Mesurier last night?"

"Old Boys' Dinner," said Antonia briefly.

"Really? But it wouldn't have been impossible for him to have left early, I suppose."

"I do wish you'd stop making fatuous suggestions," Antonia sighed. "What on earth should induce Rudolph to murder Roger?"

"You needn't be so high-and-mighty, my dear. I can think of one very good reason. We all know that he said he meant to murder Arnold because of his—well, really, I must call it *pilfering*. Now, if Roger knew about that, and meant to prosecute——"

"You're missing on all your cylinders," interrupted Antonia. "Roger knew, and he told Rudolph he wouldn't do anything about it. And if you don't believe me, I wrote a letter to Roger, thanking him. Can't you think of somebody else to suspect?"

Violet gave a little laugh. "Oh, nothing I say will meet with approval in this house! I'm well aware of that! Good-bye, Mr. Carrington. No, please don't bother to see me out. I know my way."

"Of course, she just had to say, 'I know my way,' " commented Antonia gloomily, as Giles, disregarding her request, went with Violet to the front door. "I used to collect her *clichés* at first, but it got so boring I gave it up. This is a most sanguinary affair, Leslie."

"I know," Leslie said. "Only don't worry, old thing. I'm absolutely sure Kenneth didn't do it, and they practically *never* convict the wrong person. If there's the least doubt——"

"They give them penal servitude," said Antonia in a hollow voice. "You needn't tell me. And he'd rather be hanged than that."

Leslie patted her shoulder, and said with a gulp: "They won't. I—I'm certain they won't." Then, as Giles came back into the room, she said: "If that sickening female has gone I'll push off too. Mr. Carrington, you'll look after Tony, won't you, and try and cheer her up? Good-bye, Tony darling. I'll come round first thing in the morning. Good-bye, Mr. Carrington."

The door closed firmly behind her. Antonia was left alone with her cousin. She said forlornly: "You needn't be afraid I'm going to cry, because I'm not."

He sat down beside her. "There's nothing to cry about, chicken," he said.

She turned a rather wan face towards him. "Giles, I have such a ghastly fear that he may have done it after all!"

"Have you, Tony? Would you like to bet on it?" he asked, smiling.

Her eyes questioned him. "You don't think he did?"

"I'm very nearly certain he didn't," replied Giles Carrington.

CHAPTER 22

THIS pronouncement did not have quite the desired effect, for after staring at Giles blankly for a moment or two Antonia tried to smile, failed, and felt a choking lump rise in her throat. Giles saw her face begin to pucker, and promptly took her in his arms. "Don't cry, Tony darling!" he said gently. "It's going to be all right."

Antonia hid her face in his shoulder, and gave way to her overwrought feelings. However, she was not one to indulge in an orgy of tears, and she soon stopped crying, and after one or two damp sniffs, sat up, and said shamefacedly: "Sorry. I'm all right now. Thanks for being nice about it."

Giles drew his handkerchief out of his pocket, and compelled Antonia to turn her face towards him. He looked down at her lovingly, and said: "I won't kiss a wet face. Keep still, my lamb."

Antonia submitted to having her tears wiped away, but stammered, rather red in the face: "D—don't talk rot, Giles!"

"I'm not talking rot," he replied, and took her in his arms again, this time not gently at all, and kissed her hard and long.

Antonia, unable to utter any protest, made one feeble attempt to push him away, and then, finding it impossible, grasped his coat with both hands and clung to him. When she was able to speak she first said, foolishly: "Oh, Giles!" and then: "I can't! I mean, you don't really—I mean, we couldn't possibly—I mean——"

"You don't seem to know what *you* mean," said Giles, smiling into her eyes. "*Luckily*, I do know what I mean." He possessed himself of her left hand, and drew the ring from her third finger, and put it into her palm, closing her fingers over it. "You'll send that back to Mesurier tonight, Tony. Is that quite clearly understood?"

"I was going to, anyhow," said Antonia. "But—but if you actually mean you want to m-marry me instead, I can't see how you can possibly want to."

"I do actually mean that," said Giles. "Just as soon as I've finished with this affair of Kenneth's."

"But I can't think Uncle Charles would like it if you did," objected Antonia.

"You'll find that he's bearing up quite well," replied Giles. "Will you marry me, Tony?"

She looked anxiously at him. "Are you utterly sure, Giles?" He nodded. "Because you know what a beast I can be, and it would be so awful if—if you were only proposing to me in a weak moment, and—and I accepted you, and then you regretted it."

"I'll tell you a secret," he said. "I love you."

Antonia suddenly dragged one of his hands to her cheek. "Oh, darling Giles, I've only just realized it, but I've been in love with you for years and years and years!" she blurted out.

It was at this somewhat inopportune moment that Rudolph Mesurier burst hurriedly into the studio. "I came as soon as I possibly could!" he began, and then checked, and exclaimed in an outraged voice: "Well, really! I *must* say!"

Antonia, quite unabashed, went, as usual, straight to the point. She got up, and held out the ring. "You're just the person I wanted to see," she said naïvely. "Giles says I must give this back to you. I'm terribly sorry, Rudolph, but—but Giles wants me to marry him. And he knows me awfully well and we get on together, so—so I think I'd better, if you don't mind *very* much."

Mesurier's expression was more of astonishment than of chagrin, but he said in a dramatic voice: "I might have known. I might have known I was living in a fool's paradise."

"Well, it's jolly nice of you to put it like that," said Antonia, "but did you really think it was paradise? I rather got the idea that most of the time you thought it pretty hellish. I don't blame you a bit if you did, because as a matter of fact I thought it was fairly hellish myself."

This frank admission threw Rudolph momentarily out of his stride, but after a few seconds' pained discomfiture, he said with a good deal of bitterness: "I can't grasp it yet. I expect I shall presently. Just now I feel merely numb. I don't seem able to realize that everything is over."

"You can't really think that everything's over merely because we're not going to be married," said Antonia reasonably. "I expect you only feel numb because I took you by surprise. You'll be quite thankful when you do realize it. For one thing you won't have to have bull-terriers in your house, and you know you never really liked them."

"Is that all you can say?" he demanded. "Is that the only crumb of comfort you can find?"

It was apparent to Giles that Mesurier was enjoying himself considerably. He rose, feeling that the jilted lover did at least deserve to hold the stage alone for the last time. "I'm sorry about it, Mesurier," he said pleasantly. "But Tony made a mistake. I expect you'd like to have a little talk with her. I'll go and get Murgatroyd to help me pack Kenneth's suit-case, Tony."

Mesurier was so much interested in this that he forgot his rôle for a minute. "Why, what's happened? Is Kenneth going away?"

"He's gone," said Antonia, recalled to present trials with a jolt. "He's being detained, whatever that means."

"My God!" said Mesurier deeply.

Giles went out of the studio, and shut the door behind him.

Twenty minutes later Antonia joined him in Kenneth's bedroom, remarking with a sigh of relief that Rudolph had gone at last.

"And a good job too!" said Murgatroyd, fitting a bulging sponge-bag into the suit-case that lay, half-full, on the end of the bed. "If it weren't for this dreadful thing that's happened I should be congratulating you out of the bottom of my heart, Miss Tony. But when I think of my poor Master Kenneth, locked up in a horrid cell with ten to one no proper bed or anything—well, it's just too much for me! I can't seem to take much notice of anything else. Not that shirt, if you please, Mr. Giles; it's only just back from the laundry.''

"Giles says he doesn't think Kenneth did it," said Antonia.

"Thank you for nothing!" retorted Murgatroyd. "He'd better not let me hear him say anything else, that's all. Him or anyone. There's a case for those brushes, Mr. Giles. You leave them to me."

Antonia picked up a folding leather photograph frame from the bed, and grimaced at Violet's classic features. "What on earth do you want to put this in for, Giles?" she inquired. "Just when he seems to be going off her, too. He won't want it."

"You never know," Giles answered. "Put it in."

The rest of the packing was soon done, and in a few minutes Giles had locked the suit-case, and set it on the ground. "I shall have to go, Tony," he said. "Promise me you won't worry!"

"I'll try not to," said Antonia dubiously. "What are you going to do?"

"Save some constable or other the trouble of having to fetch Kenneth's things," he replied.

She raised her eyes to his face. "Shall I see you tomorrow?"

He hesitated. "I'm not sure. I think probably not until late, if at all," he answered. "I'm going to be pretty busy."

"Busy for Kenneth?" she asked quickly.

"Yes, busy for Kenneth." He took her hands, and held them clasped together against his chest. "Keep smiling, chicken. Things aren't desperate."

"You've found out something!" she said. "Oh, what is it, Giles?"

"No, I haven't," he said. "That's what I hope to do! At present I've only got one suspicion. I'm not going to tell you any more in case I'm wrong. But I do tell you not to worry."

"All right," she said. "If you say I needn't I won't."

It was past six o'clock when Giles Carrington left the studio. He delivered the suit-case first, and then, after a glance at his wrist-watch, drove to the Temple, and changed into evening dress. His subsequent proceedings might not have seemed to

Antonia to be the actions of a man trying to aid her brother. He visited three cocktail-bars, four hotels, one night-club, and two dance-halls. He partook of refreshment in all of these resorts, and engaged various headwaiters, assistant-waiters, hall-porters, and page-boys in conversations which they at least found profitable. He reached his flat again in the small hours, swallowed a couple of aspirin tablets in the hope of defeating the inevitable headache, and got thankfully into bed.

In the morning, when his man brought in the early tea-tray, he awoke with a good deal of reluctance, and said: "Oh, God! Not tea. One of your pick-me-ups. And turn on my bath."

"Yes, sir," said his man, thinking that it was funny of Mr. Carrington to go out on the binge when his family was in such a packet of trouble.

A bath, followed by an excellent pick-me-up, more or less restored Giles. He was able to face the task of shaving, and even, when that was over, to partake of a very modest breakfast. While he sipped a cup of strong coffee, he told his man to put through a call to Scotland Yard, and to ask for Superintendent Hannasyde.

Superintendent Hannasyde, however, was not in the building, and an inquiry for Sergeant Hemingway was equally fruitless. The voice at the other end of the telephone was polite but unhelpful, and after a moment's reflection Giles thanked the unknown, said that it didn't matter, and rang off. His next call was to his own office, and his man, hovering discreetly in the background, had his curiosity whetted by hearing that Mr. Carrington was to be told that Mr. Giles Carrington had important business out of town, and would not be at the office that day. It was certainly a queer set-out, and what Mr. Giles Carrington thought he was playing at heaven alone knew.

At half-past five in the afternoon Giles walked into Scotland Yard and once more asked for Superintendent Hannasyde. This time he was more fortunate; the Superintendent had come in not half an hour earlier. He was with the Assistant Commissioner at the moment, but if Mr. Carrington would care to wait? Mr. Carrington nodded, and sat down to wait for twenty minutes. At the end of that time he was escorted to Hannasyde's office, and found Hannasyde standing by his desk, a sheaf of papers in his hand.

Hannasyde looked up. "Good-afternoon, Mr. Carrington.
I'm sorry I was out when you rang up this morning. I've had
rather a busy day." He looked more narrowly at Giles, and
said: "Sit down. You look as though you'd been having a busy
day too."

"I have," said Giles, sinking into a chair. "And a still
busier night. What I want to know is, did your men find
anything that had any possible bearing on the case when they
searched Roger Vereker's flat yesterday?"

Hannasyde shook his head. "No, nothing. Was that what
you wanted me for this morning?"

"Partly that, and partly to let you know what I'd been
doing." He moved rather restlessly in his chair, frowning. "I
want to see that night-porter, by the way. I wish I'd been
present when the flat was searched."

Hannasyde regarded him with some slight show of amusement. "My dear Mr. Carrington, there was nothing there
other than what we saw."

"Kenneth's pipe? Oh, that's not it! Kenneth had nothing to
do with either murder. I wanted you to come and piece out the
first murder with me to-day, but when I couldn't get hold of
you I thought I'd better do it myself rather than hang about
perhaps for hours."

Hannasyde stared at him in astonishment for a moment,
and then drew out his chair from behind the desk, and sat
down on it. "Forgive me, Mr. Carrington, but have you been
drinking, or are you just having a little joke with me?" he inquired.

A rather weary smile touched Giles's lips. "To be frank
with you, I've been drinking," he answered. "Not quite lately,
but last night, from seven o'clock onwards. I had to be so tact-
ful, you see—pursuing what might have turned out to be a
wild and scandalous goose-chase."

"Mr. Carrington, what have you got hold of," demanded
Hannasyde.

"Arnold Vereker's murderer, I hope."

"*Arnold* Vereker's murderer?" exclaimed Hannasyde.

"Roger's too. But if there was no clue of any kind in the
flat——"

Hannasyde drew in his breath. "What there was you saw, Mr. Carrington," he said patiently. "You saw the pipe, the pistol, the half-finished letter in the blotter, the glass of whisky-and-soda, and the note from—no, you didn't see that, now I come to think of it. Hemingway found it after you'd left. But it hasn't any bearing on the case that I can see. It was only a note from Miss Vereker, thanking her half-brother for——" He broke off, for Giles Carrington's sleepy eyes had opened suddenly.

"A note from Miss Vereker . . ." Giles repeated. "A note—where was that found?"

"Screwed up in a ball behind the coal-shuttle. I should say that Roger Vereker meant to throw it into the fire, but missed his aim. Do you mean to tell me——"

"Where was the envelope?" Giles interrupted.

"We didn't find it. I suppose Vereker had a luckier shot with that. I wish you would stop being mysterious and tell me just what you're driving at."

"I will," said Giles. "But when I think that if I'd only been present when that flat was searched you and not I would have spent an entirely hellish twenty-four hours trying to induce half-wits to identify a face—— However, I'm glad I've found the link between the two cases. It annoyed me not to be able to present you with all the facts." He saw the smouldering light in Hannasyde's eyes, and smiled. "All right, all right," he said pacifically. "Violet Williams."

Hannasyde blinked at him. "Violet Williams?" he said. "Are you seriously telling me that she murdered Roger Vereker?"

"Also Arnold Vereker," said Giles.

"She had never met Arnold Vereker!"

"Oh yes, she had," replied Giles. "She was the dark girl you couldn't trace."

Hannasyde had been twirling a pencil between his fingers, but he put it down at this, and sat a little straighter in his chair. "Are you sure of that?" he asked, watching Giles keenly.

"I've found two waiters, one commissionaire, and the leader of a dance-band to identify her photograph," answered Giles. "One of the waiters volunteered the information that he had several times seen her with Arnold Vereker, who was an habitué of that particular restaurant. The commissionaire also said that he had seen her with Arnold. The leader of the dance-band did not know Arnold by name, but he recognized his photograph. In fact, he said instantly that he was the man who was with the most striking woman in the room that night. He is an intelligent fellow, that musician—I've got his name and address for you. He not only recognized both photographs, but he was able to state on what date he saw the originals. The locality—my dear Watson—was Ringly Halt, which, as you probably know, is a very popular road-house about twenty miles to the east of Hanborough. And the date (which was imprinted on my observant friend's memory by the coincidence of its having been the date on which his pianist sprained his wrist and had to be replaced by a substitute) was June 17th."

"Good—God!" said Hannasyde very slowly. "But—she never came into the case at all!"

"No," agreed Giles. "And if she hadn't committed the second murder she never would have come into the case. She said she had never set eyes on Arnold; both my cousins said it; and not a soul came forward to explode that fallacy. Moreover, no one ever would have come forward. None of my witnesses have any idea of her name, you see."

"But"—Hannasyde was trying to puzzle it out—"how did she meet him? And having met him, why did she keep it so dark? Do you suggest that she set out to become acquainted with him with the idea of murder in mind? It's almost incredible!"

"No, I don't think she did. From what I've seen of her I imagine she started with the intention of getting Arnold to marry her. But when it came to marriage Arnold was very wary. He would never be caught by a girl of her type. I've no doubt it didn't take her long to realize that. She's acute, though not clever. And then she planned to get rid of him."

"What made you suspect her in the first place?"

Giles reflected. "I don't think I know. It first occurred to me when Roger was killed, but it seemed wildly improbable. Then I made an excuse to call on her, and it struck me—perhaps because I was already suspicious—that she was a little too anxious to convince me that she had an alibi for that evening. That might have been my imagination, of course, but it

was enough to make me go back over everything I knew about
her, and add it up, and find what the total was. To start with, I
knew she was a gold-digger. My cousins were continually
pointing that out to her. Also, I saw her setting her cap at
Roger in a highly determined manner. She thinks more of
money than anything else; that was always evident. To go on
with, I learned from Kenneth (I think you were present too)
that she was a close student of every kind of detective fiction.
In itself that didn't mean anything, but added to the rest it
seemed to me to mean quite a lot. Thirdly, Kenneth went to
call on her on the night of Arnold's murder—and she was
out." He paused. "Little things like that—not much in themselves. Also the fact that she was obviously not in love with
Kenneth. I could never imagine why she got engaged to him. I
remembered, too, that Miss Vereker had told me, quite light-
heartedly, that Violet had always been in the habit of picking
up well-to-do men in hotel lounges, and that sort of thing.
Then came Roger's death. You didn't know it, of course
—how should you?—but she did a thing that evening that
seemed to me stupid, and curiously unlike her. At the last moment she told Kenneth Vereker that she wouldn't go with him
to that ball. She put his back up so badly that he at once rang
up Miss Rivers, and invited her to go in Violet's stead. At the
time I was merely surprised that Violet had handled him so
clumsily—for the attitude she had adopted was that it would
be indecent for either of them to appear at such a function.
Now I think that she did it on purpose to ensure Kenneth's
going to the ball, and thus providing himself with an alibi. She
meant Roger's death to look like a suicide, and it was she who
launched the theory that he was in a state of nerves on account
of the police. That was one of the most suspicious things she
did, I thought. The first murder had been so perfectly planned,
and was so successful, that it went to her head. She's a con-
ceited young woman, you know, and she ran away with the
idea that if you could fool people once you could fool them
any number of times."

Hannasyde nodded. "Very often the way."

"So I believe. Well, she was perfectly confident she could
stage a convincing suicide, but in case of accidents she took
care to provide herself with some sort of an alibi. Actually, it

wasn't an alibi at all, but it might have worked if she hadn't made her fatal mistake.''

"Something to do with that mysterious letter,'' Hannasyde said instantly.

"Yes, everything. You see, I was present when Miss Vereker gave Violet Williams that letter to post. She gave it to her on the night of Roger's death—*after seven o'clock.*'' He paused, and looked at Hannasyde. "Which meant, of course, that having missed the six-thirty collection it would catch the next —I don't know the exact time, but I suppose not earlier than eight-thirty, and probably later. I have a great respect for the Post Office, but I can't bring myself to believe that a letter posted at that hour can possibly be delivered at its destination the same evening. Violet Williams must have used the letter as an excuse to call on Roger at that unconventional hour.''

"What hour?'' Hannasyde asked. "Have you any idea?''

"Sometime after eleven—when the girl she had invited to spend the evening with her left—and certainly before twelve, when she knew the main door would be shut.''

"Yes, I see. Coinciding with the entrance of the woman who might have been Mrs. Delaford's personal maid, and the noise which was thought to be a tyre burst, heard by Mr. Muskett. Is there a possibility of her having delivered the letter by hand prior to the arrival of her visitor?''

"No, I think not. She told me that her visitor came to dinner with her, and I expect you'll find that she was speaking the truth. She wouldn't have had time.''

There was a long silence. Then Hannasyde said ruefully: "If all this turns out to be true, you'll have made me look rather silly—Mr. Holmes.''

"Not at all,'' replied Giles. "I only got on to it because I'm on very intimate terms with my cousins, and have been in a position to watch every move in the game at close quarters, as you never could.''

"I ought to have thought of it,'' Hannasyde said. "If it hadn't seemed so certain that she'd never met Arnold Vereker, I *must* have thought of it. She was the only other person who had a motive.''

Giles laughed. "I really don't think you can blame yourself! My young cousin has been building up far too damning a case against himself to admit of your looking beyond him for some really unlikely suspect. All the same, you've never felt sure that Kenneth did it, have you?"

"No," confessed Hannasyde, "I haven't. It always seemed to me that he was enjoying himself at my expense, for one thing, and for another—if he killed Arnold Vereker, why the stocks?"

"You gave up your first idea of a practical joke? Yes, that was what made me sure it wasn't Kenneth, and must have been a woman. The more I thought about it the more certain I felt that the stocks had an important bearing on the case. Whoever stabbed Arnold wanted to get him in a helpless position—in case, I suppose, the first blow didn't kill him. That pointed to a woman. Whether the stocks were a premeditated feature I suppose we shall never know. I'm inclined to think not. Perhaps Arnold's tyre burst occurred in the village, and Violet got the idea of using the stocks while she was waiting for him to change the wheel. Or perhaps—since it was a moonlight night—she caught sight of them when they were driving through Ashleigh Green, and got him to stop then, on the spur of the moment. It must have occurred to her that it would be safer to kill him in the open than to wait until they reached the cottage."

Hannasyde did not speak for a moment or two. Then he said: "What a case! I apologize for not taking your amateur efforts seriously, Mr. Carrington. You ought to be in the C.I.D. That pistol, by the way, had been recently oiled. There should be traces of the oil on the gloves Violet Williams wore, or in her hand-bag, where I suppose she carried it. Probably not noticeable to her. What a fool she was to use Miss Vereker's gun! Suspicion was bound to fall on young Vereker."

"Yes, but she thought he was provided with a safe alibi," Giles reminded him. "I don't suppose, either, that she could lay her hands on any other pistol. Nor is she a clever woman by any means. I grant you that she planned the first murder neatly, but it was quite easy to kill Arnold and leave no trace. When it came to staging a suicide it was far more difficult. There were no clues to destroy in the first place, several in the second."

"A thoroughly diabolical young woman!" Hannasyde said roundly. "Now, Mr. Carrington, if you'll let me have the names and addresses of your witnesses——?"

"Yes, certainly," Giles said, smothering a yawn. "And then perhaps you'll release my client."

Hannasyde said seriously: "I'm sorry for that boy. This'll be a bad business for him."

"I expect he'll get over it," Giles answered. "It wouldn't surprise me if, when he's had time to recover from the shock of it all, he and Leslie Rivers made a match of it."

"I hope they will," said Hannasyde, glancing sideways at Giles. "And does Miss Vereker mean to marry Mesurier —er—soon?"

Giles smiled. "No, that's off. Miss Vereker has become engaged for the third and last time."

Hannasyde stretched his hand out across the table, and gripped Giles Carrington's. "Splendid!" he said. "Many congratulations! Yes, come in, Sergeant; while we've been chasing red herrings, Mr. Carrington has solved our case for us. We shall have to let Mr. Vereker go after all."

"Let him go?" said Hemingway. "You'll have a job to make him go. The last I saw of him he was asking what they'd charge for board-residence till he's finished a set of the most shocking pictures you ever laid eyes on. *Portraits of the Police*, he calls them. Libels, *I* call them. Are we going to make an arrest, Super?"

"Yes, thanks to Mr. Carrington. Just take down the addresses he's got for us, will you?"

The Sergeant drew out his notebook and opened it, and moistening the tip of his pencil, looked at Giles, waiting for him to begin.

ABOUT THE AUTHOR

The news of GEORGETTE HEYER'S death in July 1974 came as a great shock to her hundreds of thousands of devoted readers. During a career that spanned more than fifty years she produced over fifty books, most of them historical novels set in Regency England. Her vast readership maintains a fierce loyalty.

Miss Heyer, born in Wimbledon, Surrey, England, on August 16, 1902, was educated in various day schools. After her marriage to George Ronald Rougier in 1925, she lived for six years in Tanganyika and Macedonia. Afterward the Rougiers established themselves in London, settling in the Albany, Piccadilly's celebrated address. Here, seated before her beloved antique typewriter, she worked tirelessly. Georgette Heyer's enduring fame springs equally from her Regency romances and her sparkling, wicked mysteries. Though Miss Heyer shunned public attention, intimates will remember her vigor, wit and charm.

A BRAND NEW MYSTERY SERIES!

By Lilian Jackson Braun

"The new detective of the year!"
—**The New York Times**

Certain to thrill mystery lovers everywhere,
this exciting series stars Qwilleran—
a prize winning reporter with a nose for crime.
Together with his two very unusual sidekicks—
Siamese cats—he's always eager to tackle
peculiar crimes the police can't solve.

___ THE CAT WHO SAW RED
08491-3/$2.95

___ THE CAT WHO COULD READ BACKWARDS
08604-5/$2.95

___ THE CAT WHO ATE DANISH MODERN
08712-2/$2.95

Available at your local bookstore or return this form to:

 JOVE
THE BERKLEY PUBLISHING GROUP, Dept. B
390 Murray Hill Parkway, East Rutherford, NJ 07073

Please send me the titles checked above. I enclose _____. Include $1.00 for postage
and handling if one book is ordered; add 25¢ per book for two or more not to exceed
$1.75. CA, IL, NJ, NY, PA, and TN residents please add sales tax. Prices subject to change
without notice and may be higher in Canada.

NAME_____

ADDRESS_____

CITY_____ STATE/ZIP_____

(Allow six weeks for delivery.)   J448

NGAIO MARSH

"She writes better than Christie"
—The New York Times

____ 08775-0	CLUTCH OF CONSTABLES	$2.95
____ 08718-1	SPINSTERS IN JEOPARDY	$2.95
____ 07627-9	BLACK AS HE'S PAINTED	$2.95
____ 07507-8	NIGHT AT THE VULCAN	$2.95
____ 07606-6	OVERTURE TO DEATH	$2.95
____ 07505-1	PHOTO FINISH	$2.95
____ 07440-3	DEAD WATER	$2.95
____ 07851-4	THE NURSING HOME MURDER	$2.95
____ 07501-9	A WREATH FOR RIVERA	$2.95
____ 07700-3	DEATH AT THE BAR	$2.95

Available at your local bookstore or return this form to:

 JOVE
THE BERKLEY PUBLISHING GROUP, Dept. B
390 Murray Hill Parkway, East Rutherford, NJ 07073

Please send me the titles checked above. I enclose _____ Include $1.00 for postage and handling if one book is ordered; add 25¢ per book for two or more not to exceed $1.75. CA, IL, NJ, NY, PA, and TN residents please add sales tax. Prices subject to change without notice and may be higher in Canada.

NAME_____

ADDRESS_____

CITY_____ STATE/ZIP_____

(Allow six weeks for delivery.)   **SK-7/b**